VISIBLE THREAT

VISIBLE THREAT

from veteran police officer Janice Cantore

TYNDALE HOUSE PUBLISHERS, INC.
CAROL STREAM, ILLINOIS

Visit Tyndale online at www.tyndale.com.

Visit Janice Cantore's website at www.janicecantore.com.

TYNDALE and Tyndale's quill logo are registered trademarks of Tyndale House Publishers, Inc.

Visible Threat

Copyright © 2010, 2014 by Janice Cantore. All rights reserved.

Previously published in 2010 as *A Heart of Justice* by OakTara under ISBN 978-1-60290-155-1. First printing by Tyndale House Publishers, Inc., in 2014.

Cover photograph of woman copyright © pkripper503/iStockphoto. All rights reserved.

Cover photograph of road at night copyright © Visage/MediaBakery. All rights reserved.

Designed by Mark Anthony Lane II

Published in association with the literary agency of D.C. Jacobson & Associates LLC, an Author Management Company. www.dcjacobson.com.

Scripture taken from the Holy Bible, *New International Version,*® *NIV.*® Copyright © 1973, 1978, 1984, 2011 by Biblica, Inc.™ Used by permission of Zondervan. All rights reserved worldwide. www.zondervan.com.

Visible Threat is a work of fiction. Where real people, events, establishments, organizations, or locales appear, they are used fictitiously. All other elements of the novel are drawn from the author's imagination.

Library of Congress Cataloging-in-Publication Data

Cantore, Janice.
 [Heart of justice]
 "Previously published in 2010 as A Heart of Justice by OakTara"—Title page verso.
 ISBN 978-1-4143-7554-0 (pbk.)
1. Policewomen—Fiction. 2. Bulgarians—United States—Fiction. 3. Human trafficking victims—Fiction. I. Title.
 PS3603.A588H43 2014
 813'.6—dc23   2013036929

Printed in the United States of America

20	19	18	17	16	15	14
7	6	5	4	3	2	1

Dedication and thanks to
Cheri Fresonke, for your help, prayers, and support.

Also, thanks to
the Reunioners, for their friendship, guidance, patience,
and prayers.

HOPE

IVANA AND VILLIE SAT CLOSE, heads together as they pored over the magazines—*Glamour*, *Vogue*, *Self*—oohing and aahing at the clothes and the stick-thin models. The sisters had been up for almost sixteen hours, unable to sleep as they anticipated their new adventure. Ivana could hardly believe their good fortune.

They were about to dock in America.

After growing up in a small, poor village in Bulgaria, this trip was a dream, often imagined but rarely realized. But because of Demitri, Ivana and her older sister, Villie, were on the journey of their lives to the Promised Land. They'd lost their parents ten years ago when Villie was twelve and Ivana eight. A bleak orphanage had been their home since then, each being asked to leave when she turned eighteen. Now they had the hope of making a home together, just the two of them, in a magnificent new country.

While they giggled and imagined the wonderland where they would live and work, Demitri was behind them talking on the phone, making plans. Ivana noticed he'd been agitated lately but had no idea why. She and her sister tried hard to keep out of his way.

"Just a lot of business on his mind," Villie had whispered one night, and Ivana agreed.

Demitri had gotten them away from their drab village and arranged work for them in America, so their debt to him was huge. They would work for a rich American. There was a Bulgarian shop in California—a wonderful place that paid clerks more money than Ivana and Villie could imagine. Or maybe they could even work for a movie star, taking care of her babies. For Ivana, the possibilities were endless and wonderful.

Currently they were on a huge ship. There were no windows to tell them if it was night or day, but they had not minded at all. Demitri had said they would be arriving soon, and the anticipation had kept their spirits up.

Demitri finished his phone call and stood. He walked to where Ivana and Villie had stored their belongings and began to pull things out.

"What are you doing?" Villie asked.

"I want your passports and visas—now. Hurry; give them to me."

"Have we arrived?" Villie asked, excitement in her voice as she rose from her chair in tandem with Ivana.

Suddenly dread hit Ivana's stomach like a fist. Something was wrong.

Demitri's face scrunched in a scowl. "Soon. Get me the paperwork now!" He reached out and grabbed Villie, and she screamed.

"Ow! What is the matter?"

Demitri gripped her by the shoulders and picked her up, pulling her close. "You move when I tell you to move," he growled. "You are mine now; do you understand? Mine." He shook Villie as if she were a rag doll, and fear cemented Ivana to the floor.

They had trusted Demitri; he had been their gracious benefactor. But now as he squeezed Villie until she cried out, he was the very devil.

1

OFFICER BRINNA CARUSO rounded the corner just as the vehicle she'd come looking for pulled away from the curb. She'd know the car anywhere; the battered black Buick belonged to a registered sex offender named Henry Corliss. He'd been on her radar since his parole to the city of Long Beach three months ago with the designation of "high-risk offender." Her intuition had screamed that he would not be a model parolee, and today her suspicions were confirmed.

Corliss was wanted for abducting a young girl.

Brinna followed the Buick slowly, not wanting to spook her prey, wanting instead to stop him when her backup caught up with her. Three more units would be with her in minutes. Questions swirled through her mind: Had Corliss seen her? Did he know the police were onto him, or was his departure a coincidence? Where was the girl?

Even as she asked the last question, she knew the girl

was most likely in the Buick. This sick puppy's MO was to transport victims to secluded areas. With that thought, just following the creep at a residential speed caused a jolt of adrenaline to slam through her, and she tightened her grip on the wheel.

"Where are you off to, Henry?" she said out loud to no one. Today she didn't even have her K-9 partner, Hero, with her to talk to. Rain had been falling steadily for two days, so even if there was a need for a K-9 search today, this weather would hinder a dog, and she'd left him home. The vehicle's wipers beat a high-speed rhythm on the windshield, yet Brinna's view was still clouded by water.

She reached for her radio mike to inform dispatch and her backup that the suspect was on the move. The Buick slowed at a T intersection, and Brinna relaxed, thinking maybe Corliss's leaving when she showed up had been coincidental.

Her relaxation was short-lived. With a puff of smoke from the muffler, the battered vehicle accelerated rapidly to the left, rear wheels throwing up a cloud of water and steam, fishtailing on the wet streets. For a second Brinna anticipated the driver would lose control and crash. But the rear wheels caught and the car leaped away.

Brinna dropped the mike on the passenger seat and gave her black-and-white Ford Explorer as much gas as she dared, trying in vain to close the distance between her and the fleeing car. The rain seemed to fall harder, and the Buick flew through the next intersection against a red light. She knew it was Corliss behind the wheel, and he was not going to stop.

"No," Brinna yelled as she was forced to slow for the light, nearly stopping before it changed to green and she could accelerate through the intersection. As she reached out to pick up the dropped mike, she clicked on her lights and siren. The Buick widened the gap between them.

"King-44, the suspect vehicle left the location just as I arrived. He's westbound on Wardlow, approaching Orange." She spoke a little too loud, her voice ramped up because of the noise from the siren. "I'm in pursuit."

The vehicle extended its lead, making a wild, out-of-control left onto Orange. Brinna followed, frustrated as she was forced once again to slow. Her high-center-of-gravity SUV was no match for the more stable sedan on the wet roadway. The mixture of another siren caused her gaze to flicker across the rearview mirror. There was at least one assisting unit behind her.

"King-44, did you see the victim with the suspect?" Sergeant Rodriguez's voice crackled through the speaker.

Brinna smacked the wheel before responding. *No, I didn't see her, but I know he's got her in the car* was what her mind screamed. What she answered the sergeant with was a simple "Negative, just the suspect."

She again tossed the mike on the passenger seat as the Buick ran another red light and turned right onto Willow.

Corliss was the one and only suspect in the abduction of a local twelve-year-old girl, Nikki Conner. Two hours ago a 911 call had alerted police to the abduction and kicked off an intense search involving all of Long Beach and neighboring agencies in mutual aid. Corliss had been conversing with Nikki on the Internet, posing as a fourteen-year-old boy, complete with a fake Facebook page. They'd arranged to meet at a park. Fortunately Nikki had a friend who followed and watched the meeting from a distance. Her description of the abduction that transpired in the park—complete with photos snapped with a cell phone—was what led police to Corliss. And Brinna wasn't about to let him slip away.

The radio speaker exploded with unintelligible gibberish as several units tried to get on the air at the same time. Brinna tuned it out to concentrate on her driving, struggling to keep the suspect vehicle in sight while preventing her SUV from hydroplaning.

When the dispatcher deftly regained control of the air, Brinna heard Sergeant Rodriguez assign a unit to check the suspect's house. She started to ask Brinna for an update on her location but was cut off.

Brinna swerved around a slow vehicle as a high-pitched, nasal male voice came through loud and clear. *Lieutenant Harvey.* Brinna groaned. He was new to the watch; he'd just been promoted last week and he was by the book.

"King-44, this pursuit is not authorized. Weather conditions are too severe. Terminate immediately!"

Brinna kept after the Buick with a white-knuckled grip on the wheel. She'd feared this response from Harvey. A pursuit with the rain falling in buckets would never be approved except in the direst of circumstances. And someone like Harvey, a bean counter in a blue suit, would never agree with Brinna that this was the direst of circumstances. Henry Corliss had kidnapped a young girl.

Harvey would say: "We know who he is and where he lives; we'll get him."

Brinna would respond: "The girl is in danger now."

Harvey: "If she is in the car, you're endangering her by your pursuit. What if he crashes?"

Brinna: "I know him. You don't understand what he'll do to her if he's not stopped now."

All of this played in Brinna's mind as she raced over city streets on the suspect's tail. She heard Harvey continue to try to raise her on the radio, but she ignored him.

"The victim is not at the suspect's house," the unit assigned to check the residence announced on air when the lieutenant took a breath.

"Brinna." Sergeant Rodriguez's voice came over clear and calm, using her first name and not her call sign. Brinna flinched as she heard the pleading in her sergeant's voice, asking for her location. "What is your 10-20?"

They were downtown now, and the path of the Buick was more erratic, with the driver crossing to the wrong side of the street, moving perilously close to the Blue Line train tracks, not slowing for stop signs or red lights and nearly crashing every few seconds.

Brinna blew out a frustrated breath and pounded the wheel. She couldn't shut out Sergeant Rodriguez like she shut out Harvey. She clicked off her siren and picked up the mike.

"He's still heading south, now on Atlantic, crossing PCH." She kept following without the benefit of her light bar and noted that one assisting black-and-white stayed with her as well. It had to be Maggie and Rick.

"King-44, I want that pursuit terminated and you to return to the station. Meet me in the squad room. Now!" Harvey was practically hysterical.

Just then the Buick slowed to make a tight right turn onto Tenth Street. Brinna finally had a chance to close some distance between them, and she took it, accelerating. Copying the next wild left he made on Magnolia, she pulled even closer. As a testament to her good fortune, even the rain seemed to be letting up, pounding drops giving way to a light shower. Lieutenant or no lieutenant, Brinna knew she couldn't quit yet.

She also knew Harvey had issued his order over the radio so it was clear and easily documented. But for Brinna, a young girl in danger mattered more than anything Lieutenant Harvey could say.

Brake lights flashed as the fleeing driver attempted to turn right onto the Seventh Street freeway on-ramp but couldn't; the ramp was closed for repairs. For the first time since the Buick had sped away from her, Brinna smiled. The vehicle fishtailed back onto Magnolia and continued south. Brinna knew that if he tried the Third Street ramp, he would be out of luck there as well. God bless Caltrans. The puke had finally made a mistake.

Sure enough, he made the same aborted turn attempt at the Third Street ramp, almost coming to a complete stop. For a moment Brinna thought she'd won. Off came the seat belt, and her hand gripped the door handle. But once more the driver of the Buick punched it, continuing south on Magnolia toward the harbor, with Brinna gaining ground.

They passed the police station and the main fire station before the driver made a final, crucial mistake. Standing water in a low spot on the street disguised the depth of the puddle. The vehicle never slowed as it approached the dip. The Buick hit the water hard, and the driver lost all control.

Brinna slammed her brakes as the black car spun out in front of her. The driver couldn't pull out of it, and with a sickening bang, the vehicle's back end hit a parked car, sending the driver's side careening around into another parked car, where it came to rest in a splash of water, steam, and amber and red plastic from the taillights.

Brinna flung her door open and hit the pavement at a full run, dodging the falling rain and the deep puddles. She saw movement as the driver slid to the passenger side and pushed the door open. He jumped out, cut between two parked cars, but Brinna was on him as he reached the sidewalk. She grabbed his shoulders and threw her weight into him, knocking him off his feet and into a planter. She managed to keep her balance and a hold of one of his arms.

"You're under arrest, Corliss. Stop resisting." Brinna almost lost her grip because both she and the suspect were drenched and muddy within seconds.

"Police brutality!" Corliss wailed.

"No audience here," Maggie yelled at the man as she appeared on Brinna's right and grabbed his other arm. Between them, they had Corliss handcuffed and sitting on the planter ledge in short order.

"Where's the girl?" Brinna demanded, hands on hips, glaring at the suspect through the rain, blood pumping, heart racing. A slight man with thinning hair and a sallow complexion, Corliss looked like a muddy, drowned rat and wouldn't meet her gaze.

"I want my lawyer."

Brinna caught Maggie's eye and shook her head. It was times like these she wished she could shake information out of uncooperative suspects. But she couldn't. She couldn't touch him or talk to him now that he'd cried for a lawyer, and he knew it.

"Rick's checking the car as we speak," Maggie said, and Brinna followed her gaze back to the Buick. "He also told dispatch where we are." She caught Brinna's eye and looked down her nose, lifting an eyebrow, an unspoken reprimand for Brinna's radio silence during the chase and a reminder that Brinna was in trouble. Harvey would not just drop the matter of her ignoring him. It would make no difference that the suspect was in custody.

"Hey." Rick stuck his head out of the suspect's car. "She's here, and she's okay!"

Brinna looked at Maggie and then at Corliss, whose head was down, rain dripping from his forehead.

"Go." Maggie waved toward the car. She pulled Corliss to his feet. "I'll put him in my car because he is most certainly going to jail."

Brinna hurried to the Buick and peered into the backseat. Nikki Conner had been tied up and wrapped in a blanket. As Rick loosened the rope and pulled the blanket from her face, she sobbed but appeared otherwise unharmed.

Brinna felt every negative emotion drain away. This was

what mattered. The girl was safe, and the creep was in custody. Her throat clogged with emotion.

She looked up to see the lieutenant's car turn the corner, coming her way. Brinna folded her arms, ignoring the rain and her drenched uniform. Whatever the consequences for her now, it just didn't matter.

2

MAGDA BOTEVA heard the sound of sirens slicing through the air, coming closer, and for a moment her heart stopped. Were they on the way to stop Demitri? Would they put an end to the madness she could do nothing about?

Without realizing it, she held her breath. But the sirens, and maybe her salvation, faded away. Letting out a ragged breath, Magda felt her shoulders sag. She brought her hand to her mouth and closed her eyes. Now, nothing competed with the sound of the beating. Magda heard the young girl beg Demitri to stop hitting her and then cry out for forgiveness, but the beating continued, and Magda could not stop it.

To say or do anything while Demitri was this angry would shift his focus to her, her husband, Anton, or—God forbid—her own young children. As sorry as she felt for the unfortunate girl enduring Demitri's cruelty, Magda could not and would not change places with anyone on the receiving end of his vicious rage.

Standing at the far end of the warehouse, as far away from Demitri as possible, staring through a dirty window at rain falling on a choppy ocean, Magda flinched with every slap. Sucking in a shuddering breath, she crossed her arms tightly over her chest. Her inability to help the girl caused guilt to rise up like bile from a sour stomach. The guilt soon morphed to a feeling of utter helplessness.

I may not be the one being beaten, she thought, *but Demitri holds me just as captive as he holds that girl.* A decision she'd made years ago, to borrow money from Demitri to start a business, had turned into a heavy chain entangling her life, sometimes threatening to suck the very breath from her body.

Finally the slapping stopped. The crying and the whimpers didn't. Magda heard Demitri shout orders and then a struggling and a scraping as he dragged the girl across the rough floor because she didn't move fast enough. Magda could picture in her mind's eye Demitri's hulking form lifting the bleeding girl and throwing her into the small room where he would keep her locked up until it suited him to release her.

The door slammed.

The lock clicked shut.

Demitri was out of patience, and Magda told herself to be careful.

"Magda, Magda, where in the devil are you?" he growled.

"Here. I'm here." Quickly Magda turned and moved across the floor to Demitri as fast as her spike-heeled boots would allow. Fury creased his brow, and she prayed it had nothing to do with her.

He wiped his hands with a rag, then tossed it into the corner. "Hurry. That brat has made me late; don't you make me later."

Magda grabbed her purse. "I'm ready to go." She followed him outside, holding the purse over her head because of the rain. She climbed into the car while Demitri shut the heavy metal outer door of the warehouse. Magda could hear him cursing the rain.

He slammed the huge padlock closed and jogged to the car. Magda worked to keep an expression of neutral indifference on her face as Demitri climbed into the driver's seat, angrier now because he was wet. If he thought she had any opinion at all about what he'd done to the girl, the car ride into the city would be unbearable. Demitri made her part of these power plays to ensure she understood her place in his world. She couldn't let him see the pity she felt for the girl, the disgust she felt for herself, or most of all, the hatred she felt for him.

Anton's face floated into her thoughts, and she bit her lip to keep from sobbing. Her dear Anton was a Christian, a religion Magda flirted with only because it pleased her husband, not because she felt the same way he did about it. Her father's atheism was too deeply ingrained in her, and life had convinced her she could never give in to the hope that a Supreme Being existed who really cared for her. The fact that no God intervened to help the people Demitri victimized seemed to prove her opinion.

Regardless, she didn't mind Anton taking their children to church or reading the Bible to them. Sometimes she listened, enjoying the family time and watching the rapt attention her children gave their father. For some reason the last story she'd heard him discussing with them came to mind.

It was about the first murder, when Cain slew his brother, Abel. Magda remembered wondering why Anton would tell their children such a story, but as he continued, she realized what he sought to teach them. Anton's pleasant voice explained a deep meaning of the story: God knew that Cain had murdered Abel, but he asked Cain, "Where is your brother?" He was giving Cain the chance to come clean, to be redeemed, Anton told the twins.

Alas, the murderer would not confess. Instead he answered with a dodge: "Am I my brother's keeper?" Anton said that Cain was without excuse. He should have been his brother's keeper, should have been more connected, more careful for the life he took. The essence of humanity, her husband explained, is that we are all God's children, brothers and sisters, and we need to take care of one another.

Magda bit her lip to keep from crying, knowing Anton would be repulsed if he knew what had transpired in the warehouse today . . . and many times before this. And if his God did exist, Magda would be like Cain, guilty and without defense. Even though none of the girls had been her blood sister, there was an ethnic bond, a human bond. If Anton's God did exist, and he asked Magda about the girls, would she answer with a question like Cain: "Am I my sister's keeper?"

Even as she considered the question, a deeper horror rose to grab her in the throat. Worse than the fact that she hadn't acted to save the girl today was the knowledge that this was not the end. The poor girl crying in the warehouse now would not be the last one Demitri victimized. How many more could Magda let suffer?

She knew that as long as her family was in danger, there was no answer to that question.

3

Brinna couldn't get out of the wet cotton K-9 jumpsuit fast enough. Lieutenant Harvey had ordered her to take the rest of the night off. He'd wanted to make it an emergency suspension, but Sergeant Rodriguez had talked him out of it. Harvey was adamant about filing an internal affairs complaint on Brinna, but he would go through normal channels without making it an emergency situation. Brinna had time to think about a response or obtain union representation before she faced a formal complaint.

Doesn't matter, she thought, pulling on some dry sweatpants. *I'd do it again. The girl is safe and sound, and the creep is in jail.*

"Hey, John Wayne." Her friend Maggie, damp but no longer dripping, entered the locker room. As she squished across the floor, it was obvious the water had settled into her shoes. "I swear, just when I think you can't surprise me, you do. Ignoring Lieutenant Harvey?" She faced Brinna with her hands on her hips. "Are you crazy?"

Brinna rubbed her hair with a towel and sighed, letting the towel rest on her shoulders. "You of all people know why I kept going. Corliss needed to be stopped before he hurt the girl. How could I have backed off?"

"But the way the rain was falling and he was driving . . . Gee, Brin, what if he'd crashed and Nikki was hurt or killed in the crash? What then?" Maggie shook her head and took off her wet gun belt.

"It didn't happen that way," Brinna answered, even though her gut clenched at the thought. There'd been a dozen places during the pursuit where a tragic crash scenario could have played out.

"But it could have. Don't you ever consider the risk?"

Brinna shrugged with a nonchalance she really didn't feel. "Why second-guess? The girl is safe; that's all that matters." *Why didn't I stop when I knew that I should? I never would have forgiven myself if anything had happened to Nikki because of me.*

The end result is all that is important, she told herself as Maggie continued dressing. Mentally she erased the thought of an alternative ending, denial calming her stomach and easing her mind.

4

Jack took the call from dispatch as soon as he sat down at his desk, before he even got his first sip of coffee. It was five minutes after 8 a.m.

"Detective O'Reilly, we've got a DB in the water at the end of the San Gabriel River. Jogger found her—no ID."

"Foul play?"

"NFD." The dispatcher paused while Jack considered the "no further details." There must be something, he thought, or this wouldn't be a homicide.

"Sorry, Detective, my computer hiccuped. The patrol unit on scene says there appears to be signs of a beating. I'll send the entire call to your computer."

"Let them know we'll be en route." Jack noted the location and looked at the clock. His partner, Ben Carney, was not yet in the office, and that gave Jack an opportunity to review the call. He punched up the message from dispatch and saw that the dead body was a young girl. His stomach tightened, but not as badly as it would have three months ago.

Jack had been back in homicide that long after taking a break from the detail. He'd had a rough time getting over the loss of his wife and found it impossible for a while to deal with the violent deaths homicide assignments sent him to. A short stint in patrol helped him refocus and heal, and he felt stronger with every case. He and Ben had handled and successfully closed three murder cases in two months. But this was the first female victim to cross their desk.

I'll be okay, he thought as he finished the last page of the call and his stomach relaxed. *And we'll catch the guy who put her in the flood control, and that will make me feel even better.*

Strengthened by fresh resolve, Jack got up and went to the duty board to sign out and grab a set of car keys. He and Ben were David-Henry-6, and he'd just finished marking them out in the field when Ben jogged in.

"Hey, sorry I'm late. There was a crash on the freeway." Ben stopped at the board and frowned. "Already?"

"Yep, body in the San Gabriel River. Already got us a ride." Jack held up the keys.

Ben sighed and turned around the way he'd just come, Jack beside him.

The San Gabriel River wasn't really a river, but a flood control channel. During the brief Southern California winters, it could swell to river strength when there was rain and runoff, but the rest of the year it was basically a concrete basin. With the rain they'd experienced the last few days, the river had been raging.

There were two ways to reach the spot they were dispatched to. They could take a water company access road, unlock a gate, and drive over a dirt lot. The second way was a bit faster and the one they chose: drive along the bike path on the riverbank. Uniform patrol units had unlocked the bike gate and blocked the area off to any other bike or foot traffic, so Jack and Ben quickly reached the area where the body had been found.

As he surveyed the surrounding area first, Jack could tell by the debris and dirt mark made along the concrete bank when the water was rushing down the channel that it had been much higher during the night than they were seeing now.

He felt anger bubble up as his perusal reached the pale body caught in trash and debris about halfway up the bank. Jack studied the young girl's body—she lay facedown about five feet below him—and the area adjacent, looking for any evidence that might lead them to her identity and to the killer. Even from this distance, he could see the girl had endured a tremendous amount of abuse before her death, and what he saw was heart-wrenching. Bruises and what looked like the lines of a belt crisscrossed her back. Old bruises, visible even after the insult of death. The patrol unit was right to call them. This was no accidental fall into the river; it was definitely a murder, and he became angrier by the moment.

What will we see when the coroner turns her over?

A TV program came to mind, one of the many that dealt with crime scene investigations. No stupid TV show could ever capture the full heartbreak and tragedy of a homicide.

No dramatic reenactment could adequately re-create the reality of a brutal killing. Up close, no makeup could turn your stomach, no fake odor could duplicate the stench of decay, and no model could rip your heart out when you thought of the pain, waste, and tragedy you were witness to.

And nothing ever hit Jack quite as hard as when the victim was so young and vulnerable. His fists clenched and unclenched, and he wished there were something or someone he could squeeze to find out the identity of the animal responsible.

The coroner arrived just after the LBPD lab technician, who began photographing the scene before anything was touched or moved. Once the entire scene had been recorded, Jack and Ben slipped on gloves and stepped down with the coroner to the body, moving carefully on the steeply angled concrete. While Ben assisted the coroner with a cursory exam, Jack dug around in the debris for anything that might be clothing or possessions, but all he found were plastic grocery bags, cans, bottles, bits and pieces of trees and shrubbery, and mud. Below them, the San Gabriel River flowed a dirty-brown color.

When it was time to lift the girl from the channel, Jack and Ben helped position the body carefully on the sheet the coroner unfolded. As they lifted, Jack doubted she weighed a hundred pounds. The threesome carried the girl up and out, placing her carefully in the body bag waiting for her. Once on level ground and before the bag was closed, they did a more thorough overview of the girl's battered body.

"Most of these marks are old," the coroner said. "I don't

see bullet holes or knife wounds. It's possible, from the bruising on her neck, she was strangled, but I can't make a complete assessment here."

Jack nodded. Aside from the abuse, there was nothing present on or near the girl to tell him who she was or what exactly killed her. She was nude, probably in her teens, or maybe a petite adult. Only one distinct mark tagged the girl's body that wasn't a bruise. It was a tattoo on her right hip, very detailed, of a rose wrapped up in a chain. Jack had seen his share of tattoos, from prison art to trendy designs, and this was certainly unique. The lab tech stepped up to take photos of the artwork to be shown around to different tattoo shops if the girl couldn't be identified any other way.

"Want me to see if Brinna and her dog are available to search the area?" Ben asked. "Of course, she might not find anything," he continued. "This body could have been dumped way upriver. It rained hard last night."

Jack bit his lower lip and considered his partner's words before answering. "Look carefully," he said finally. "I don't think she's been in the water that long. I think a trip downriver with all the debris present in the water right now would have cut her up a lot more. The autopsy will give us a more definitive answer about the injuries, but I think she was dumped nearby, and the only reason she isn't in the ocean right now is the stuff she snagged on." Jack pointed back to the tangle of trash, branches, and one beat-up shopping cart they had just climbed past. The current from the river had not yet dislodged the entire mess.

"Maybe you're right," Ben conceded, bending down next

to the girl. "The water would have been much higher last night. If she'd been caught up in the tangle then, there would be more scrapes where the concrete bank rubbed against her."

Jack nodded and folded his arms. This November had been a wet one—record-breaking in fact. The dirt line he'd noticed before proved that the water had raged very close to the top at some point during the early morning hours.

Yes, Jack thought, *she went in after the rain ended, around dawn. I'm sure of it.* He scanned the area, squinting in the early sunlight, the first bright, sunny day in a while. The body's location and the crime scene were just past the second-to-last bridge before the river emptied into the Pacific Ocean, on a bare section of land across from the Department of Water and Power.

The body could have been dumped from the bridge or from the access road. It would have been a hike if the killer used the access road, but it was secluded, well hidden from prying eyes, she was light, and that was the route Jack's instincts told him the killer took.

"Yeah, see if Brinna's available," he said to Ben. "Tell her we want her to check out the access road and the surrounding area in case any evidence was dropped or disposed of."

"Will do." Ben pulled out his handheld radio and requested the K-9 unit.

5

Brinna sat on her porch sipping coffee. She hadn't slept very well, dogged by guilt about the reprimand she'd received as a result of her conduct on the Henry Corliss pursuit the day before.

"Reckless! Insubordinate! You disobeyed a direct order!" Harvey's face had been purple with rage.

She knew Harvey was right. After a case a couple of months ago when she and her then-partner, Jack O'Reilly, had raced against orders to save kidnapped twins, she realized she needed to be more of a team player. While she loved the appellation "Kid Crusader," she knew she couldn't do it all on her own—she needed partners and coworkers, and with everyone working together, more kids would be saved.

She opened the Bible in her lap and wondered where she should turn. It was new to her, like going to church with her mother was new, but it was something her mom would do. Looking at the Bible, a gift from Jack, she could hear her mother's voice say that if she realized her wrong and confessed it, she'd be forgiven, no strings attached. Forgiveness from God was a free gift.

Maybe from God, she thought, but Harvey and internal affairs might not have the same policy. It would still be a couple of days before she heard from internal affairs. The only positive was the picture in her mind of the grateful faces of Nikki Conner's parents. And Corliss was going to prison for good—this was his third strike; he'd never have the chance to abduct another girl. She could live with her actions because of that, but she knew she'd have to work hard to regain Harvey's trust. When he'd dressed her down, Brinna had listened, not trusting herself to speak. It wouldn't have done any good for her to try to justify what she'd done; Harvey was just too angry. He'd taken it personally, and for that she was sorry. It really had nothing to do with him.

She'd fallen back into the habit of taking the world onto her own shoulders to save a young girl. And while it had turned out okay in the end, Brinna didn't want that same thing to happen again. She had to find a way to stand down and take a breath.

Her mom, her brother, Brian, and Jack said the answer was in the book she held in her hand. Accept what God freely gives and find peace. Was it really that easy?

Her phone rang and she saw a PD extension.

"Caruso."

Surprise and anxiety hit at once. She recognized her sergeant's voice, but it was too early for Janet to be at work. Bracing herself for bad news from IA, she answered, "Yeah, Sarge, what's up?"

"I'm afraid something has come up—something you need to be aware of." Rodriguez paused. "The PD just received notification from Homeland Security that they're not going to renew the grant that funds Hero."

"What?" Brinna felt her face flush. The call was about Hero? This was like walking around a blind corner into a sucker punch.

"There have been cutbacks everywhere," Janet continued. "You knew the position with Hero was likely temporary." Her tone was meant to be soothing, but Brinna could not be soothed.

"But he's done a good job; we've accomplished so much." Words fled, and Brinna could only stare into space. She knew it was a numbers game, but she didn't want to accept it. The budget for police officers paid for a specific number of bodies. The federal grant had basically added extra money for a position that was not in the budget. She knew the PD approved the position only because of the salary savings. While Brinna, as an officer, would still be in the budget, the search-and-rescue dog unit position, which required extra funding for the take-home K-9 car and K-9 training, would disappear.

"This is not a reflection of performance," Janet was saying. "Federal funding is capricious; you know that. It floats on political winds, and unfortunately the winds have changed. There is a slight chance the city will pick up the tab for Hero, but I can't get your hopes up." Janet sighed. "I don't have to tell you how many old-timers thought Hero was a waste for a city PD. And frankly, pulling stunts like you did last night does not endear you to the brass. They have to *want* to do you a favor to pitch a case to the city council to keep funding the dog position."

Brinna started to protest, but her sergeant kept talking.

"The department has a shortage of patrol officers," Rodriguez continued. "The most likely scenario is that you'll be plugged in somewhere in patrol. I'm sorry."

It was a moment before Brinna felt able to speak. "How long do I have?"

"Six weeks at most. That's when the fiscal quarter ends," Janet said. "Look at the bright side: the Feds will likely let you buy Hero; maybe the two of you can still take part in search and rescues on your off time."

After the call ended, Brinna closed the Bible and held her head in her hands. The last two and a half years with Hero as her partner replayed in her mind. Yes, she had known it might not last forever, but that didn't make the inevitable any easier to accept. Of course she'd buy Hero, even if she had to drain her savings to pay for him. But not work with him every night? The thought caused a knot to form in her stomach.

How can I go back to patrol? How can I leave Hero home every night and work with a two-legged partner? For that matter, who would put up with me? She remembered how hard it had been to leave him when she'd been temporarily assigned to work with Jack O'Reilly. As much as she liked Jack, she'd missed Hero, and that was only temporary. How would it be to be permanently without Hero?

Her phone rang again; this time she saw a dispatch extension. There were no patrol dogs assigned to days, so Brinna immediately hoped this was a callout for her K-9. *I want to work with him as much as possible while we still have time.*

"Officer Caruso, we have a homicide unit requesting you on the flood control for a search."

Brinna didn't even ask what for. "I'll be en route in ten minutes. Please send the call to my computer."

* * *

The sound of a vehicle approaching caused both detectives to turn toward the bike path. Brinna Caruso had arrived with her K-9. Jack felt a strange tingling in his gut, not quite butterflies but close, as he watched Brinna climb out of her K-9 vehicle. It was good to see her again. A few months previous she'd been instrumental in helping him over a hurdle—accepting his wife's death and getting on with his life. Because of their shifts, hers afternoons and his days, their paths did not cross often. Though there wasn't anything romantic between them, then or now, he had to admit that as he put the grief further behind him, Brinna was definitely someone he wanted to see more and spend time with.

"Hey, guys," Brinna hailed as she walked down the path toward them, her dog, Hero, on a short leash. "What have you got?"

"Let me show you." Jack directed her to where the body had been placed, pointed out where it had been, and told her the observations he and Ben had already made. The coroner was ready to zip the body bag and head to the morgue.

"So what we need from you," Ben explained after Jack had

finished, "is a search of the immediate area. See if you turn up anything. Maybe there's clothing or a purse nearby. Even though it has rained a lot, it's all concrete, asphalt, and hard-packed dirt out here. No footprints or tire tracks anywhere."

Brinna did a slow 360 and surveyed the area. "Sure thing." She walked Hero to the edge of the flood control and then to the body bag to let him sniff. She frowned when she saw the girl, noting the tattoo.

"She looks young. But she's not from any of my flyers. And that tattoo is certainly different." She peered closer. "My, that is detailed work. You two didn't find any missing reports even close?"

Jack shook his head. "No. Although we'll double-check once we get back to the station. We don't think she's been here long, so one may yet come in."

Brinna sighed, frowning. "I hope we turn up something out here." She walked a few feet upriver, then unclipped the dog's leash. "Find, Hero, find."

Jack watched the dog take off at a trot, nose to the ground. For the young girl at his feet—and her family, whoever they were—he prayed that Hero would turn up something . . . anything that would lead them to a killer.

6

As Brinna watched Hero, she knew he had a scent. Based on the direction he traveled, she bet someone had carried the young girl up the access road to toss her into the channel.

Like so much garbage.

She twisted Hero's leash in her hands as anger at what one evil person could do to an innocent overshadowed the anxiety she felt about losing Hero.

The dog reached a gate that was locked to restrict access to the channel. The access road was part of a water company easement. It allowed the water company to drive up to a pump station on a ribbon of concrete that jutted into the riverbed. Police and fire could also access the area with keys to the city lock, but public vehicular traffic was kept out.

Hero sat and barked. Something.

Brinna jogged to her dog. She had to look carefully and pull some brush back, but she saw it. Snagged on a bush near the access road gate where it had been out of sight was a blanket or throw.

"Got something!" she called out, and Jack and Ben joined her immediately.

Brinna donned gloves and carefully retrieved the blanket. It was damp but not dripping, adding credence, she thought, to Jack's theory that the girl had been dumped after the rain stopped. All three of them studied the blanket carefully. There were rust-colored spots that appeared as though they could be blood.

"What do you think?" Ben asked. "It's too small to have covered her—"

"But it could have been in the car with her." Jack pointed to the likely place a car would have been parked. "I bet," he said, "the killer drove up to the gate but had to carry the body to the bank." Nodding to where the blanket was found. "It's a tight fit through the opening holding the girl, and even though she's light, she's deadweight. The rain stopped a little before dawn. Most likely when he was here, it was still dark. He didn't see this blanket snag. It's dark, multicolored, mostly green; it blended in."

"Then as he leaves," Brinna added, "he's in a hurry, doesn't want to get caught, doesn't see the blanket."

"Bingo," Jack agreed. "The dog keyed on it, so let's pray it's related and it leads us somewhere." He held an evidence bag open, and Brinna placed the blanket inside.

Brinna nodded, surveying the area. There was an opening next to the gate, a gap left for bike riders and walkers.

"The suspect would have walked through the opening—" Jack feigned having something over his shoulder—"and been forced to carry the body a good distance. I'm guessing it's two hundred yards to the river's edge, where he most likely tossed the poor girl into the channel. If this occurred after the rain let up but before full dawn, the river would have been very close to the top of the bank."

"I agree," Ben said. "The body snagged on debris not fifty feet from where she probably went in."

The two men conferred while Brinna gave Hero a treat and reattached the leash. It was good to see Jack. Brinna realized she'd love to sit down at coffee and talk to him about losing Hero. Once Jack had worked through the grief over his wife's death, he'd been a good patrol partner. A pang reverberated in her chest as she acknowledged that she couldn't be Jack's partner in patrol again. He was back in homicide where he belonged and obviously doing a good job.

"Thanks, Brinna." Jack flashed a warm smile and handed her the evidence bag. "You want to file this for chain of evidence?"

"Yeah, thanks." She took the bag.

"And good job catching Henry Corliss. I glanced at the bulletin before we came out here. What happened?"

"Uh, long story, but I caught him leaving his house. Turns out the girl he'd just kidnapped was tied up in the back of his car."

"I can tell from your face there's more to it than that. We need to have lunch, catch up." His gaze was so warm, so concerned, Brinna had to glance away.

"Sounds good. Give me a call?"

"Will do." He smiled again before turning back to the

investigation, leaving Brinna feeling suddenly better and very much looking forward to having lunch with him.

*   *   *

Aside from the blanket, Brinna and Hero didn't find any other physical evidence. She knew that Jack and Ben's hypothesis about how the body was dumped followed simple logic and basic gut instinct. Too bad logic and instinct alone couldn't put a face and a name on the suspect who did the dumping.

After she filled out the evidence tag, Brinna studied the multicolored bit of blanket. The cloth was filthy, but it wasn't hard to see that at one time it had been very pretty. It looked European to Brinna because of the pattern of color. It also looked like something that belonged to a child.

Makes sense, she thought. *The dead girl was young.* Anger swelled at the thought of a pretty young girl being murdered and tossed into the river like garbage. Brinna was glad she was part of the case now. Nothing would please her more than putting this killer behind bars.

When she left the flood control, she realized that by the time she filed the evidence, she would have about an hour before she had to report to the squad room for her shift. She had the choice to flex her time and leave early instead of filing for overtime and working her entire shift, but she hadn't made up her mind what she wanted to do. She was hungry and was hoping to meet up with Maggie and Rick for a meal to tell them about Hero.

"King-44."

Brinna grabbed the radio mike. "King-44, I copy."

"King-44, Sergeant Rodriguez requests you respond to community relations ASAP."

"10-4. I have to drop off some evidence. My ETA to community relations is probably twenty minutes." She replaced the mike and shrugged, wondering what in the world community relations would want with her.

A short drive later, the station loomed up on the right, and she parked in front, grabbing the evidence bag and heading to the property office.

"What have you got?" Tran, the evidence clerk, stepped up to the window to take Brinna's evidence.

"Something for the fridge and for DNA testing." Brinna held up the plastic bag. "We think there's blood on this. It's possibly from a homicide."

"The floater? I heard that call on the scanner. Was it a kid? Is that why the Kid Crusader is involved?" Tran smiled as he used Brinna's nickname. She knew it was a compliment, and she returned the smile.

Though, if I lose Hero, will the name still apply?

"Won't know her age for certain until after the autopsy, but you can bet I'll be on it. The lowest of the low are those who prey on kids."

"Unfortunately you've got eternal job security," Tran said as he took the evidence. "There never seems to be a short supply of those kinds of creeps and perverts out there picking on kids."

"They are like roaches. It's my mission to shine light on them and then squish."

* * *

Brinna walked across the street to the community relations office. Sergeant Rodriguez waited for her out front.

"What am I walking into, Sarge?" Brinna asked.

"I'm trying to help you out here, so put on your best public relations face." Janet folded her arms.

"Sure." Brinna brushed dog hair from her jumpsuit and straightened her gun belt. "I look okay?"

"Yep. Now, do you remember Gracie Kaplan?"

"Of course—the smart little girl who had the presence of mind to photograph that creep Corliss when he snatched Nikki? How could I forget her? She was very brave."

"Well, she's in the office with reporter Tracy Michaels. Tracy wants to do a human-interest piece for Friday's paper. It seems that Gracie has a severe case of hero worship, and I don't mean your dog."

"Huh?" Brinna frowned.

Rodriguez chuckled. "When Tracy went to interview the girl about the photos she took, all she could talk about was you. She wants to be and do everything just like you. She snapped the pictures that day because she thought it was something you would do. She's your biggest fan."

"I, uh . . . I don't know what to say."

Rodriguez grabbed her arm and pulled her toward the door. "Just answer the questions and talk up Hero. I'm letting this happen over Harvey's objections. Maybe some positive press like this will influence the city's decision when it comes to keeping the dog position."

A bright light of hope went off in Brinna's mind like a Fourth of July firework. "I get it. Thanks, thanks. I'll be charming, no matter how irritating I think Tracy's questions are." She grinned and rubbed her hands together.

Once inside the office, Brinna was met by Tracy Michaels, a reporter who had interviewed her before, along with Meg and Howard Kaplan and their twelve-year-old daughter, a girl with eyes so blue they reminded Brinna of a mountain sky. Gracie Kaplan was small for twelve, slightly built, with a mop of unruly red hair. Brinna thought perhaps the girl had tried to have her hair cut in the same manner she did. But Brinna's hair was stick straight while Gracie's was all curls, so the emulation didn't quite work.

"Officer Caruso." Gracie stood at attention and addressed Brinna in a solemn tone. "It's an honor to meet you." When she held her hand out, Brinna swallowed a chuckle, smiled, and shook it.

"I second that," Meg Kaplan said, extending her hand as well. "Thank you that you took Gracie seriously and that you saved Nikki."

Brinna felt the heat rise in her face. She was never comfortable with praise.

Mr. Kaplan stepped forward and his face was set in seriousness. "Nikki is still a bit traumatized or she and her parents would be here as well. We hope you can impress on Gracie how serious this is, how both girls were in danger because they tried to meet someone on the Internet without letting their parents know what they were up to."

Brinna shook his hand. "Yes, I agree with you." She turned

to Gracie. "Your dad is right. What people say online can't always be trusted, and this is a classic example. Henry Corliss pretended to be someone your age, and anyone can do that—they can say anything. People like Corliss take advantage of the anonymity of the Internet. I know it sounds lame, but girls your age should always let your parents check things out before you leap into something."

"I know." Gracie heaved a sigh. "I tried to stop Nikki, but she was just certain that guy was for real. Thank you for saving her."

"It's my job. I'm just gratified that everything turned out well."

As the interview progressed, it was obvious to Brinna that Gracie indeed idolized her. *How old were you when you decided to be a police officer? Was the training hard? How did you get Hero? Is it hard to train him? Does he mind when you fire your gun? Have you ever shot anyone? Do you like being called the Kid Crusader? How many kids have you saved?*

The questions took her thoughts back over the years to her own experience with idol worship. At six years old, she herself had been the victim of abduction. Sheriff's Deputy Gregor Milovich had rescued her, and from that point on, Brinna had idolized him until the day he died. Every year her family and Milo would meet to celebrate Brinna's rescue. As Brinna grew older and developed an interest in law enforcement, Milo nurtured and encouraged it. Brinna remembered how proud she'd felt the day of her academy graduation when Milo, in his dress uniform, had shaken her hand.

As she listened to Gracie, the tone of reverence in her

voice, and heard the girl tell Tracy, "I want to be just like Officer Caruso when I grow up," she was overcome by an uncomfortable feeling that made her hands clammy. A burden of responsibility settled on her soul like a heavy weight.

Is this how Milo felt when I looked at him like this little girl is looking at me? she wondered. *Did he feel totally inadequate to live up to my expectations, as I do to live up to Gracie's? For so long, he never failed me. I can only hope that Gracie can say the same thing about me many years from now.*

The effusive thanks she got from Gracie's parents was easier to accept than the naked hero worship. They posed together for pictures and Gracie beamed. She asked Brinna if she would sign one picture before it was framed.

Brinna left the meeting feeling somber and serious—and hoping that any and all decisions she made from this time forward would never crush or disappoint the girl who idolized her.

7

By the time Brinna finished at community relations, her shift had started and been in service for an hour. A message from dispatch asked her status. She couldn't enter *starving* as a status, so she simply punched the 10-8 in-service button. By now the last remaining clouds had burned away and the sky was a brilliant blue. A message on her computer told her Maggie and Rick had gotten a radio call right out of the gate but that they would meet her for dinner. She reached behind her and scratched Hero's head, fighting the lump in her throat and the tears that threatened to spill out when she thought of him not being there. There had to be a way to save this partnership. Had to be.

* * *

"No more Hero?" Maggie and Rick were as surprised as Brinna had been.

"Yep, no more federal dollars, so no more search-and-rescue

dog." Brinna sat back in the restaurant booth feeling bone-tired and a little numb.

The waitress came and took their order. Brinna gazed out the window at a world drying out in fresh sunshine. It did nothing to lift her mood.

"You knew this might happen," Rick said with a shrug. "And you're still a cop. I can think of several guys who'd make good partners."

"Yeah, but then Brinna wouldn't be in control," Maggie said with a twinkle in her eye. "There aren't many guys working afternoons who will let her lead them around on a leash or who wouldn't mind sitting in the back of the Explorer for the whole shift."

"Ha-ha." Brinna glared at Maggie. "It's more than working with Hero. If I have a regular partner, I'll be assigned a beat. No more keeping an eye on sex offenders or searching for kids." She sprinkled a pink pack of sweetener into her iced tea.

"Rodriguez did say you could do that on your own time." Maggie held her hands out, palms up. "Time for the glass-is-half-full person."

"You're right," Brinna conceded. "I did decide a while ago to look on the bright side more often. And six weeks is a long time. Anything can happen." She took a deep breath. "I'll be the optimist. I'll hope the city decides to pick up the tab for Hero." She waved at the window to navigate away from the painful subject. "It's nice to finally have a dry day. If we get much more rain, all of us will be working the city in kayaks and rowboats."

"It sure came down last night," Maggie said. "And it was

windy. My street lost two trees. Roots were so saturated they just fell over."

Brinna nodded. "The public service channel on my scanner was going crazy early this morning. I think trees fell all over the city. There's a lot of cleanup and clearing to do."

"I like the rain," Rick said. "It's a nice change."

"I like it too," Brinna said, "just not in buckets."

"Well, I got up early this morning and went to watch the swift-water rescue team practice," Rick continued. "The water in the flood control was raging. What a rush the way those guys work. Sometimes I think I stood in the wrong line. Those fire guys have all the fun."

"I don't know about all the fun—" Maggie arched her eyebrows suggestively—"but they sure have all the cute. I don't think they make bad-looking firemen."

Rick groaned.

Brinna forced a grin, determined to think positive thoughts about the Hero situation and lighten up about other things. "For once I agree with you, Mags: firemen, paramedics—they have the corner on the cute market. There's a new guy at station four who looks like Paul Walker." They slapped a high five in the booth while Rick rolled his eyes in annoyance.

He cut into their celebration, tapping Brinna's arm. "So tell us about the callout. Where'd you go this morning? he asks, desperate to change the subject."

"Homicide. They found a dead girl in the flood control."

"One of yours?"

Brinna shook her head. "No ID so far. Not sure how old she is." It was common knowledge that Brinna kept track of any and all missing-kid cases from Long Beach and the surrounding areas. A wall in her home office was dubbed the Innocent Wall, where she kept several missing flyers pinned up.

K-9 Officer Caruso was always ready to pick up a trail and search for missing kids with her search-and-rescue dog, Hero. She worked to ignore the stabbing in her chest.

"She's somebody's kid," Rick said.

Releasing a breath, Brinna stared out the window. "True enough. What I wouldn't give for a world where no one's baby ended up on our side of a homicide callout."

* * *

Ivana paced the small room that had become her jail cell. Though the windows were kept so dark she and the girls sharing the room with her could not tell night from day, she knew that Villie should have been back hours ago. Her sister had disobeyed their captor's order and been hauled out of the room almost two days ago. Demitri said it was for punishment. He'd done it once before, and she'd been back the next morning.

Arms folded across her chest, Ivana patted her elbows and studied the other two captives in the room. Ana and Galina sat together on a mattress, heads close, speaking in low tones. Ivana was hesitant to interrupt and ask them what they thought about Villie's absence.

"Do what you're told and nothing bad will happen to you," Ana, the oldest, had scolded Villie the day she and Ivana had arrived. She'd stood over them shaking an index finger and glowering as if she were their captor and not Demitri.

Demitri. Ivana could barely think the name without rage

boiling inside her. Demitri, all sweetness and light at home in Sofia. The same man who had promised her and Villie a bright future in America . . . but had turned out to be a liar once he'd gotten them to their new home.

Ivana thought of the beating he'd given Villie the day their ship had arrived and he'd asked for their passports and visas.

"You're mine now!" he'd yelled, showing a face they'd never seen before. He'd shoved them into a dark warehouse and ripped the clothes off Villie's back. There was a leather strap on the wall and he'd grabbed it, screaming about how ungrateful Villie was and how she'd better learn to do as she was told. The strap fell again and again on Villie and then on Ivana when she'd tried to intervene. Her back still bore the marks from the whipping she'd received that day.

It was then they learned what "job" Demitri had brought them to. Ana, while she lectured about obedience, told them their duties and warned them again that disobedience would be dealt with quickly and harshly. Here in this dark room, with four dirty mattresses on the floor and one bathroom for the four of them to share, Villie and Ivana lost their innocence. They were ordered to give themselves to any man who entered. They'd face Demitri and his whip if they refused.

Ivana felt bile rise in her throat and tears start in her eyes. She'd said yes to Demitri in Sofia because he'd promised she would work for a rich American. Dreams of working in a beautiful shop or perhaps for rich and generous celebrities had vanished in a painful haze of beatings and harsh, strange men.

Her heart had soared at the thought of leaving the squalid orphanage in Sofia where she'd been raised and coming to the fantasyland of America. When he'd offered to take Villie as well, that was too good to be true. Villie had already been out of the orphanage for four years, making a meager living sweeping city streets. They believed Demitri would take them to a bright future, where they might earn more money than would ever be possible in Sofia.

"Perhaps we'll even rent a two-bedroom apartment," Villie had gushed, eyes happier than Ivana had ever seen them. The lies Demitri told had given them hope . . . and the hope had been dashed here in this room on a dirty mattress.

Ivana choked back a sob, knowing there would be no sympathy from Ana or Galina. She couldn't understand how the two girls could give themselves so willingly to the men Demitri sent them. Ana was only a few months older than Villie, and Galina was Ivana's age. They smiled and fixed their hair, drenching the men with compliments. It was all Ivana could do to lie quietly and not scratch their eyes out.

Now Villie was gone. Demitri had taken her, told her he had a customer waiting at another location. It was a punishment, he said, because Villie had been disobedient. The man would be quite brutal.

"Let this be a lesson to you, Ivana," Demitri had said. "The men I bring here treat you nice, but the men I take you to will not be so nice." He'd then dragged Villie out of the room.

That was yesterday morning as far as Ivana could figure, but it seemed an eternity ago. For the first time since she'd been brought to this prison of hopelessness, she prayed for the door to open.

Open, and bring Villie back to me.

8

Magda busied herself with an inventory report. Next to her children and Anton, the store was her pride and joy and the biggest part of her life. As if returning her devotion, Black Sea Folk Art and Collectibles was thriving. Located in Long Beach, in a shopping area along the marina called Shoreline Village, the shop had been a success from the day Magda opened it six years previous. People in Long Beach and surrounding areas couldn't get enough of the ethnic art and knickknacks Magda imported from her native Bulgaria and other parts of Eastern Europe.

It was a blessing and a curse, she often thought. The success had made her a wealthy woman, allowed her family to move to California, but it had also brought her to Demitri's attention. She glanced at her salesclerk Anka, the only Bulgarian girl Magda had working for her. Demitri's daughter—and a spy, Magda was certain. Just twenty-five, Anka was blissfully ignorant of many things, but not of how to protect her father's best interests. And Magda fervently hoped Anka would never come to know how much she hated the girl's father and hoped to be free of him. Magda had made her unknowing alliance with the man long ago when she was just Anka's age.

Communism had fallen, and her father, a Bulgarian ambassador, and her mother were flying home from an assignment in France. Their plane went down in a snowstorm, and everyone on board was killed. At twenty, Magda had to make a life for herself alone in a country that was in flux. She'd turned to Demitri, knowing only that he was her wealthy cousin, and asked him for a loan to start a tourist business on the Black Sea. She had no idea then that his money had come from a thriving black market during Communist rule.

She could run a successful business, she'd told him. After all, as the daughter of an ambassador, she'd lived all over the world, spoke several languages, and could cater to the wealthy European tourists on the Black Sea. Demitri had kissed her forehead, told her he believed in his young cousin, and loaned her the money.

And she had been a success. That first shop in Varna had opened at the right time. Things were freeing up all over Eastern Europe. In two years it was obvious Magda had a profitable business on her hands. She had plenty of money to pay Demitri back, and she'd tried. He wouldn't take her money, saying only that he was proud of her success and for her to consider the money a gift.

It was only after she'd moved to the US and found success there as well that she discovered who and what Demitri really was, and that there was no such thing as a gift from his business. When he told her he wanted to piggyback on her business and move some of his operation to California, she'd said no. But *no* wasn't a word he'd wanted to hear. So much for his "gift" of start-up money. Magda was his, he said. Bought and paid for. To refuse Demitri would be dangerous. And to prove his point, the long arm of his organization reached across the ocean. She came home one day to find her husband beaten senseless and her children tied up in a closet.

The case was still open with the local American police. A home invasion robbery, they'd called it, with unknown suspects. Magda knew who was responsible, and she knew the American authorities could never keep her family safe from Demitri. The only thing she could do was cooperate with a monster. Eventually he'd installed his daughter, Anka, in the shop.

A shudder rippled through Magda. She looked up from her work and out the window at the parking lot. In the distance, boats bobbed in their slips. The rain had stopped, but looming clouds bore a dark promise of more to come. Magda bit her lip. Demitri was due any minute. She had a sick feeling in her stomach, having guessed what he wanted. He didn't visit her shop often, thankfully, but when he did, it was usually because he needed more girls. When he needed more girls, he took Anka back to Sofia for a week or two.

Anka was a simple girl whose head was filled with Kim Kardashian and the next great fashion fad. She would go home and gush to other young girls about life in America, which for her was wonderful after her backwoods life in a small village near Sozopol. Her tales helped convince girls to say yes to Demitri when he told them he wanted to bring them to America. Either Anka didn't know or she did not want to know what happened to the girls after they arrived.

Magda slammed her laptop shut, causing Anka and the customer she was helping to look her way. She smiled apologetically, and the pair went back to what they were doing. Anka would probably never believe that Demitri was the worst sort of man; she adored him. But he exploited all the women and girls he brought to America in the most evil ways.

And Magda's business had given him a foothold. Choking back a sob, she hurried to the restroom. She had to look presentable for Demitri or risk his wrath. But there was something else she needed to do. She had to break free of him or the guilt she felt would eat her alive. Splashing water on her face, she took in her reflection in the mirror. Worry lines creased her forehead, and dark circles marred her otherwise-flawless skin.

How do I break free? she asked herself. *How do I break the grip of a very evil man without becoming his next victim?*

A short time later Demitri roared into the shop like a whirlwind. After he kissed Anka and gave her a present, he attempted small talk with Magda, bragging about his cousin Christopher. The young man was a very talented tattoo artist. Demitri wanted to bring him to America, confident that if Christopher could do some work for one or two American movie stars, he'd become famous. He prattled on about what it would be like to hobnob with America's royalty.

"Will you open a tattoo shop?" Magda asked, feigning

interest but caring neither for the answer nor for what became of Christopher.

Demitri told her he had no need to open a shop since one of his men, Simon, had a cousin who owned a shop in San Pedro. He just needed the man to see the need to move his business to Hollywood. Whatever else he said to Magda went in one ear and out the other as she counted the minutes until he was ready to leave.

Finally he and his right-hand man, Emil, swept Anka away, leaving Magda breathless and seething in his wake. Magda cursed under her breath and shuffled through her schedule, struggling to get other clerks in to cover for Anka during the two weeks she would be gone. At least Demitri was on his best behavior whenever he made an appearance in the shop. He wouldn't want Anka to believe that he was anything but a happy-go-lucky businessman. She was always enthralled by the gifts he gave her and the trips he took her on. He pampered her and thus kept her cooperation.

They would land in Sofia, Bulgaria's capital city. Emil would round up young girls, mostly from the local orphanages because Demitri didn't want to deal with the probing questions of caring relatives. Anka would show them her wardrobe, her pay stubs, and pictures of her apartment, and the girls would fall over themselves to come back to America with Demitri. After a week, and commitments from several girls, Demitri would take Anka to Varna, on the Black Sea, where he'd put her up at an expensive hotel while he ironed out the details for the new girls.

Demitri's organization was based in Varna; in fact, it

mostly owned the city. A tourist community that catered to rich Europeans, Varna was actually a beautiful place—on the surface. But Magda knew all too well about the city's dark underbelly that tourists would never see.

Wistfully she thought back over the years, to that first store in Varna and her innocence. While never as flighty as Anka, there was once a time when she really didn't know that true evil existed. She'd believed that the decisions she made affected only her and that she made good choices. But one decision to accept money from Demitri, though it brought her success, had shattered her innocence . . . and damaged so many others, including her own family. It was something she'd regret to her dying day.

Now, years later, knowing what Demitri was, and unable to break free, Magda sometimes dreamed of the early days when she was innocent, and lamented the blissful ignorance of youth.

9

"SHE IDOLIZES YOU, HUH?" Maggie asked as she undid the tie that held her long blonde hair up off her collar.

"Yeah, it was kind of scary." Brinna sat on one of the benches in the locker room, leaning against a locker. Their shift was over, and this was the first time since dinner that they'd had time to talk. Brinna was tired since she'd worked the whole shift and filed for overtime. "To have someone look up to you like that . . . well, what a responsibility."

"Can't go ignoring any more lieutenants, can you?" Maggie teased.

"Ha-ha." Brinna waved her hand dismissively. "It's more than that, and you know it. When I think of how I used to look up to Milo, it makes me wonder if he felt this same sense of responsibility and how he dealt with it."

Maggie yawned and dragged a brush through her hair. "He dealt with it fine. Wasn't he a great mentor?"

"Yeah. Until the end, I never felt he let me down in any way." Brinna frowned with the memory of Milo's suicide.

Every time she thought she'd dealt with the deep feeling of betrayal she'd experienced when Milo died, wounded feelings would resurface and stab at her like the fangs of a snake.

"He was dying; cut him some slack." Maggie fixed her hair up again and shoved the brush into her purse. Casting a glance at Brinna, she waved her hand. "Oh, relax; you're a good cop. Just keep being a good cop, and everything will be fine."

"I hope you're right." Brinna shook her head as if to shake away doubts and fears. "If that interview with Tracy does anything, I want it to convince the powers that be that I'm worth as much as Gracie thinks I am so that they let me keep Hero."

* * *

Tracy's article came out on Friday, the day Henry Corliss was arraigned. Brinna was off that day but went to the arraignment anyway. She wondered if Corliss would fight—try to muddy the water with legal maneuvering. She hoped not. Nikki Conner didn't need to be put through a long, painful trial. Brinna was pleasantly surprised.

Corliss was held to answer on all charges, and he waived his right to a preliminary hearing. Wondering if his move was some slick legal trick, Brinna took a few minutes to speak to the prosecutor.

"Hey, if it isn't the hero cop," Assistant District Attorney Swift said with a grin. "Can I have your autograph?" She held up the article on the front page of the local section of the paper. "Local Hero Garners a Little Hero Worship" was the headline.

"What can I say? Positive press is always welcome, right?"

"I don't know about the press," Swift said, lifting an eyebrow, "but I do know it's a great thing when a witness photographs a crime in progress. Sure makes my job so much easier." She laid out the photos Gracie had snapped on her phone when Corliss forced Nikki into his car. Brinna had already seen them and knew they were clear. It was doubly fortunate that not only was Gracie brave enough to take the pictures, but she had one of the best phones on the market for photographs.

"So does this have something to do with Corliss waiving the preliminary hearing?"

"Yep." Swift grinned. "We're hammering out a deal with Mr. Corliss. The point being to avoid traumatizing the Conner girl any further. And to save this city from what is sure to be a media circus."

"It won't be a cake deal, will it?"

"Not on your life. Not with the type of evidence we have."

It was Brinna's turn to grin. "You just made my day."

"Inspire more hero worship, and we'll celebrate like this more often."

10

DAYS HAD PASSED, but Ivana had no idea how many. She could hear rain falling outside, but no longer was her time divided by sunlight and darkness. It was divided by quiet and cruel. During the quiet, she and Ana and Galina could wash, sleep, eat, and be alone with their thoughts. During the cruel periods . . . Ivana worked hard to black them out—those times when the men invaded the small room. She bit a cuticle so hard it bled. She wondered if she could stand one more section of time where the small space in which she was imprisoned was filled with men.

Rolling over in bed, she hugged a pillow to her chest. The only thing she was sure of right now was that Demitri was gone, and he had been for a few days. Lately there'd only been Simon. If it were possible to like anything about this situation, Ivana liked Simon. He was kind. At least, he was as kind as a jailer could be. He never raised his hand or a belt or his voice. But he still brought in the men.

Moving to her back, Ivana stared at the dingy ceiling. Her

chest burned with a hopeless certainty that she would never see Villie again. Demitri would be back—curse him—but Villie was gone forever. She fought hard to suppress the despair that engulfed her when she thought of her sister, but she couldn't stop the tears. They rolled down her cheeks freely and silently. On the other side of the room, Ana and Galina slept.

Instinct told Ivana it was late afternoon. The tears intensified as a smothering thought hit her: *I can't stand another night or another man.* Leaping up from the bed, she choked back a sob, not wanting to wake the other girls, who undoubtedly would scold her for the tears.

Dragging her palms down her cheeks, she made her way quietly to the bathroom. She rinsed her face off, dried it with a damp, dirty brown towel, and was about to throw it into the hamper when an idea formed. Her eyes traveled from the hamper to the toilet and back again. She remembered an accident at the orphanage when the toilets on the second floor backed up. It was chaos for a bit: water flooded the floor of one of the younger girls' dorms, and little girls screamed and jumped onto the furniture to keep dry.

Was American plumbing the same? she wondered. She recalled a matron grumbling because someone had flushed a towel down the toilet and this caused the overflow. Standing very still, Ivana forced herself to consider all the consequences. What was the worst that could happen? Demitri would kill her; would that be so bad? No more men.

Ivana stepped to the door of the bathroom, peered around the doorjamb, and considered the locked bedroom door. What she planned would get it unlocked. She just prayed it would be unlocked long enough. Decision made, she turned back to the toilet and threw the hand towel into the bowl and flushed. Two more towels did the trick. When water covered the floor, Ivana stepped to the bedroom door and screamed.

Her roommates, of course, heard her first and were out of bed in an instant. When they saw the flooded bathroom floor, their curses joined Ivana's screams. Sooner than Ivana would've expected, Simon knocked at the door.

"What is the matter?" he yelled in their native tongue.

As Ivana hoped, Ana took the lead. Ivana knew Ana considered herself in charge of the other girls, so this was natural.

"The toilet is backed up; there's water everywhere!"

Simon swore, and Ivana heard the key working in the lock. "It must be this blasted rain. Every day in this country it rains!"

The door came open, and Simon stepped in. He went directly to Ana, who now stood on the bed with Galina to avoid the encroaching flood.

"Why didn't you turn the water off?" he demanded.

Ivana didn't wait for Ana's answer. While Ana and Simon argued and surveyed the bathroom, she ran out the door and down the hall. Unfamiliar with the layout of the house, she ran blind at first, then came skidding to a stop when she heard voices.

The TV—that's the TV.

Heart pounding, fear gripping her like a vise, Ivana headed for the light. She burst into what she assumed was a living room once she saw a window and cloudy daylight. Just then Simon screamed her name.

Ivana didn't look back. Biting her lip, she worked the lock on the front door, pulled it open, and ran.

Ignoring the pain in her bare feet and the cold, driving rain, Ivana knew it would take death or absolute freedom to stop her.

11

"WHAT DO YOU MEAN you have to go again?" Brinna glared over her shoulder at her four-legged partner. From the back of the Explorer, Hero regarded her with soft brown eyes, panting, his sign to Brinna that he needed a pit stop. It was their first shift after a dry weekend. She faced the front and peered out the windshield. The respite from the rain had not lasted long. Right now the raindrops weren't big, but they were steady. The traffic light turned green, and with a sigh, Brinna directed the patrol vehicle to a local park.

In spite of the rain, she'd brought Hero to work for two reasons. The first was a hope the rain would stop, and the second was a premonition that he wouldn't be her partner much longer and she needed to make the most of every night.

"I guess it's my fault for giving you those table scraps," Brinna grumbled as she parked the car and climbed out. Hero jumped out after her and trotted to a tree to take care of business. She watched the dog, painfully aware that her act of annoyance was just that—an act. She would truly miss these moments, rain and all, if she were no longer able to work with Hero.

Besides, on a boring shift like this, it was nice to get out and stretch a little. She glanced at her watch, tapped it, and yawned. Two hours into the shift and not a single radio call. She looked around the soggy park. It felt as if Long Beach were becoming a bog. The rain no doubt contributed to the lack of business for the police force. Sometimes even crooks didn't want to get wet.

While Hero sniffed around and Brinna got wetter, her thoughts drifted back to the case she, Jack, and Ben were working on. It had been a week since the girl's body had been pulled out of the San Gabriel River, and they still had no ID for her. They knew a lot about her: that she'd gone into the water dead—there was no water in her lungs—and that she'd suffered many beatings and possibly rape in the weeks before her death. Her age was closer to twenty than twenty-five, and dental work verified she had been born and raised in Eastern Europe. But as yet, she had no name. Jack had taken to calling her Alice because she'd fallen through the looking glass in the worst way. Brinna liked Alice better than Jane Doe, but the absence of anyone stepping forward to identify the body nagged like a toothache.

Who was she?

Hero finished up and splashed toward her.

"You ready to get in the car and make it smell like wet dog?" Brinna asked. For an answer she got a tail wag. The pair navigated a path back to the patrol SUV, dodging puddles. They were halfway there when her call sign came up on the radio. Maggie wanted her on a clear radio channel, so Brinna switched over.

"Hey, Brin, Rick has been monitoring the fire channel. The swift-water rescue team has been called out. Seems someone fell into the river. We're heading down to watch them work and help if we can."

"Count me in. Where are they now?" Brinna opened the door and Hero jumped in. She grabbed a towel she kept in the unit and wiped her face as Maggie answered.

"They started up near Hawaiian Gardens, but they're sending a team south to the bridge at Seventh Street. River's moving fast. If there is someone in the water, they'll be flowing in a swift current."

"Not a false alarm?" Brinna asked even as she directed her unit toward the channel. Every wet year there were false sightings of people in the water. People mistook debris for bodies all the time.

"Doesn't look false right now. My partner sure thinks it's the real thing. You'd think he just mainlined caffeine."

"10-4. I'll miss everything to the north. I'll head down to Seventh Street in case they make a try there." Brinna belted herself in and drove as fast as was safe in the prevailing conditions. She felt energized. Rick was right: there was a rush involved with any type of dangerous work. The professionals who put on wet suits and stretched themselves to the limit to save someone from a rushing, dirty river had to be adrenaline junkies. Their lives were definitely on the line.

By the time she reached the flood control channel, the rain had stopped, but the sky was still dark. She parked on the bike path that paralleled the riverbed, got out, and quickly walked toward the channel. The rescue diver team hadn't yet arrived. She'd switched her radio to the fire channel and monitored the progress of the team farther north. It was definitely no false alarm. Even with the rain and the cloudy late-afternoon weather, someone had gotten too close to the water and was now in the current being pulled toward the ocean.

"I see the victim, current moving fast . . ." The exact location cut out, but the urgency in the voice infected Brinna. She cranked up the volume to hear how things were going even though she knew there would be no back-and-forth on the air. The men involved with swift-water rescue did not pause in the action to carry on a radio conversation.

"Rope in the water . . ." This time she heard the location. They were about a mile from her, and they'd thrown a rope with a life preserver across the channel in the hope the victim could catch it and hang on while they pulled the person out.

"Regroup! Caught the rope but lost it!"

Brinna clapped her hands in frustration. The victim must have been too weak to hang on.

Runoff roared down the channel, and Brinna felt more adrenaline surge through her. The power in the water was awesome. Could a rescue team snatch the unfortunate person from such a force?

Bright lights cut through the gloom as Rick and Maggie parked their unit behind Brinna's. A second unit pulled in behind them, and Brinna recognized Matt and Jeff, another pair of shiftmates. It was a slow night. This rescue, if it did happen at this bridge, was likely to be the only action.

"The rescue team should be here any minute." Rick's voice vibrated with excitement as he trotted Brinna's way. "They're not sure they'll be able to stop her farther up. The current is wild."

"It's a her?" Brinna asked.

"That's what the original call said. This started way upriver, probably in Hawaiian Gardens. Someone walking their dog called to say they saw a girl in the river. Apparently she caught a center bridge support and was stuck up there for a while but lost her grip just as a rescue diver went into the water to grab her." Rick was as animated as Brinna had ever seen him.

He and Maggie joined Brinna at the bank when the fire channel exploded with the news that they had missed the girl again. Sirens were audible, and Brinna knew the second team was close to their location.

"I can't believe anyone could last all that distance in this stuff." Brinna yelled to be heard over the roar of the water and shone her flashlight upriver. A dark, angry mass of dirty water, like fast-flowing brown lava, spewed down the riverbed.

The radio erupted with emergency traffic. "Rescue 7, rescue 7, we'll be delayed. There's a traffic collision at Studebaker and Willow, you copy? We need medics at our 10-20."

"Whoa!" Brinna and Maggie exclaimed simultaneously.

"Nothing happens all night, and now the rescue team runs across a crash." Brinna knew the dilemma: the firefighters were on their way to one emergency when they ran across another one they couldn't ignore. She wondered if their delay would cost the girl in the river her life.

She realized she couldn't passively sit by to wait and see. "Come on, we have to do something!"

Brinna started for the water's edge, grabbing her leash from her belt without any clear idea of what she would do with it.

"What can we do?" Maggie asked, hanging back on the bike path.

"The girl will be here any minute, so we need to think of something," Rick called as he jogged after Brinna. Matt and Jeff, also caught up in the adrenaline rush, hurried to the water's ragged edge.

Brinna slipped and narrowly regained her balance. She stopped and shone the light upriver again. "The only chance we'll have is if she's near this bank. We'll have to hope she's in reach." She hollered to the guys as she switched the focus of her light down to the slippery, rocky banks. Farther upriver the banks were concrete, angled down at forty-five degrees. Here rocks formed the steep banks, every bit as slippery as the concrete walls.

"Chance? In reach?" Maggie exclaimed. "We have no chance no matter how close to the edge she is. If she's even above the surface, she'll be going so fast we'll be lucky to see her go by!"

"Where is the glass-is-half-full person I used to know?" Brinna called over her shoulder. Yet even as the words were out of her mouth, she knew Maggie was right. The swift-water rescue teams were set up with ropes, pulleys—all manner of safety devices. The odds were that she would be forced to watch as the girl was dragged down the river to her death.

What transpired next happened so fast Brinna would

never remember it clearly. She and Rick stepped as close to the water's edge as possible. Frigid spray soaked the bottoms of their trousers.

"Here, Rick, hang on to this end." She tossed him the clip end of the leash. "I'll loop the handle around my wrist. That way if I slip, you'll have a hold on me."

"You're not going in the water, are you?" Rick asked as he took the clip. Matt and Jeff stepped up to either side of him, also ready to help.

"No, I just want to be as close to the edge as possible. This is just a precaution," Brinna answered as she took off her gun belt and threw it in Maggie's direction. "Let's see what happens."

She shone her light upriver and almost didn't believe what it illuminated. A blob of white bobbed toward her in the middle of a swarm of debris. An arm snaked up out of the dark water; it was the girl.

"There!" Brinna yelled.

She stepped forward, intending to kneel and steady her position. Instead her feet jerked out from under her; the flashlight flew from her grasp. Into the cold, dark water she fell, even as debris smacked into her. The frigid chill of the water took her breath away.

She was only vaguely conscious that mixed in with the debris that hit her was the girl, but Brinna held on to her with one arm. Her last thoughts were of the pain in her wrist and shoulder as the leash pulled taut and of the determination to hold on to what had hit her.

Then everything went black.

12

Brinna came to, coughing and sputtering. She was aware of two realities: her body was freezing, yet it also seemed to burn with pain. Her wrist and hand felt like they were on fire, and her throat felt as if it had been scraped with sandpaper.

"Take it easy, Officer Caruso," a calm voice soothed her.

She blinked and struggled to focus. "Where—?" she rasped, breaking into another coughing fit.

"You're in the back of my paramedic van. It's David—Dave Burton, from station four. We met last month."

Slowly Brinna focused on his face and remembered. *The river. The fall.* "The girl?" she asked.

Dave smiled. "She's on the way to the hospital. You actually caught her and held her until divers could get to her." His smile turned to a frown. "I have to admit, a dog leash is a novel rescue device. I'll run that by the swift-water rescue team, see if they want to add it to their equipment list."

Brinna ignored his sarcasm. "I never intended to go in the

water." Just then the rumble of the ambulance diesel motor cut through the fog in her brain. "Where are we going?"

"Memorial Medical Center. You need to be checked out."

"My dog!"

"Relax. Your sergeant was here. She said she'd take care of it."

Brinna grimaced and tried to relax on the gurney as the ambulance started moving. Shoving the pain she felt to the back burner, she told herself that the girl was safe—that at least she and Rick had accomplished that feat.

*   *   *

The frozen feeling didn't drown out every other sensation until they reached the hospital. Once there, Brinna's teeth chattered, and she felt completely wet and freezing. A nurse helped her out of the sodden cotton jumpsuit and Kevlar vest and into a dry gown. She draped Brinna in blankets straight from a warming drawer. Everything ached, but mostly Brinna's wrist and head felt like burning irons poked them through and through. She could already discern a knot forming on the back of her head and knew that was a big part of the problem. As for her wrist, it was swollen and difficult to bend, and there was an angry red welt where the leash had tightened when Rick tried to keep her from falling into the water. The nurse told her that she'd be getting X-rays as soon as a technician was free.

"Hey, hot dog, how do you feel?"

Brinna poked her head out from under the warm blankets at the sound of Maggie's voice. "I hurt. Can you tell me what happened?"

Maggie snorted and folded her arms. She looked as wet and bedraggled as Brinna felt.

"Well, first you went into the water, then Rick. Matt and Jeff were heroic, but it was the fire department that came to the rescue. Luckily the rescue team arrived at the bridge almost the same time you fell in." The tone of her voice changed from informing to scolding, and Maggie wagged an index finger. "You know, I'm traumatized. I just about lost my best friend and one very good partner. You guys better not ever do that to me again."

Maggie looked comical, but Brinna knew there was no levity in the lecture. She swallowed a chuckle. "Sorry, Mags. I realize it was a foolhardy thing to do. I didn't go down there intending to go into the water. How's Rick?"

Maggie sighed, and Brinna saw the worry cut across her face in deep creases. "I don't know. He's in the next exam room. They kicked everyone but medical personnel out. The rocks ripped a gash in the back of his head. There was a lot of blood."

Sitting up, Brinna frowned. "I can't believe it—that's horrible. I don't know what to say. Everything happened so fast."

"Yeah, well, I know you'd throw yourself in front of a train if you thought it would save a kid. And Rick—we all know he's an adrenaline junkie." She rubbed her brow and closed her eyes. "I just hope he's okay. I had to call Molly, his wife, and tell her. She's on her way." She clasped her hands together, interlacing her fingers and tapping her chin with her knuckles. "Do you want me to call your mom?"

"No." Brinna shook her head and grimaced at the pain. "I'm fine. No reason to get her all upset. Besides, I don't want to hear her lecture me."

"You deserve a lecture. Didn't we go through this a few days ago with that crazy chase in the driving rain? I really wish you'd think before you jump feetfirst into something. Literally and figuratively."

"Mags, I—"

A tech interrupted another apology when he came in to take Brinna to have her wrist x-rayed. As they went past the exam room where Brinna supposed Rick was, the door opened and a technician rushed out with a rack of vials. Brinna couldn't help but notice all the activity. The doctors' faces were grim, and cold fear gripped her midsection.

She thought about what Maggie had said, and guilt rushed over her. All she could do was hope Rick was okay.

13

JANET RODRIGUEZ was waiting for Brinna when she was brought back to her exam room. The sergeant had her clipboard in hand, and Brinna knew it was time for the injured-on-duty paperwork. The door to Rick's exam room was now closed, and Maggie was nowhere in sight.

"How do you feel?" Janet asked.

"Okay, I guess. Just a little sore. How's Rick?"

"That I don't know. Sergeant Klein is with him. You're my problem child. I took care of your dog, and I brought you some dry clothes." Janet pointed to a bag on the chair by the bed.

Brinna recognized her own athletic bag. Every rainy season she kept a change of clothes in her black-and-white just in case she got wet and needed them.

"I had someone drive your Explorer here. It's parked outside. I also made sure Hero got some food and water. Do you want me to call your mother?"

"No thanks. Maggie just asked me that." Brinna relaxed a

bit, happy Janet was her sergeant. Not many others would be as thoughtful. "I don't see any reason to worry my mother. As for Hero, he'll be fine for a few hours." She shifted in the bed, already antsy. "I guess I can't leave until the doc checks me out."

"You're sure you're going home?" Janet gave Brinna a look that said if it were up to her, Brinna would be staying the night.

"No way am I staying in the hospital unless I'm dying."

Janet gave a mirthless chuckle. "Guess we're lucky in that respect this time. What were you two thinking anyway? I'm told it's a miracle you weren't lost in the current and dumped in the Pacific Ocean."

"I guess I got caught up in the moment. I didn't think."

Janet tapped the clipboard with her pen. "Engage your brain next time before you engage your motor neurons and jump into trouble."

Brinna managed a rueful smile and nodded.

Clicking the pen, Rodriguez pulled up a chair and sat. "Now it's time for you to help me get started on the mountain of paperwork you just caused for me." Her tone was teasing.

Maybe a way to break the tension, Brinna thought, but still guilt washed through her anew. She started to speak.

Janet waved her quiet. "I'm glad everyone is still with us, but please don't do that again."

"Maggie also beat you to that lecture. But before we start the paperwork, can you tell me how the girl is doing?"

"She'll be okay, though she was almost drowned by the time you reached her. Any more time in the water and she'd be dead. But other than that and a lot of bumps, bruises, and scrapes, she'll be fine."

"Do we know how and why she was in the water?"

"No, she hasn't spoken, and the doctors don't want to rush it. I've got someone pulling files to see if she's a missing. We think she went in the water in Lakewood or Hawaiian Gardens somewhere. The Lakewood sheriff may have a report filed on her." Janet tapped the clipboard again and transitioned to the questions on the IOD form—a page and a half on how the injury occurred and what could be done to prevent such an injury in the future. At least Brinna hadn't violated policy. There was no written LBPD policy that addressed jumping or falling into the river.

They'd just finished the paperwork when Sergeant Klein, the patrol sergeant and Rick and Maggie's direct supervisor, appeared at the door, his expression grim.

"Rick?" Janet asked, beating Brinna to the question.

Klein didn't answer right away. Instead he stepped into the room and ran a hand across the stubble on his chin. Brinna felt her stomach knot. Finally he looked from Janet to Brinna. "Not good, I'm afraid. Along with a nasty gash in his head, he's got a fractured shoulder and a broken back. He hit the rocks hard."

"His back is broken?" Brinna asked, shock smacking her between the eyes.

"Several vertebrae." Klein sighed. "They don't know for sure, but it looks like he'll be paralyzed."

14

KLEIN AND RODRIGUEZ left Brinna to wait for the doctor after promising to get any news about Rick to her as soon as it was available. For Brinna, the minutes ticked by painfully. Several of her fellow officers stopped by to check on her condition, and the ribbing about being a swimmer began immediately. When the doctor eventually strode into her room, she felt sorry for him. He looked as tired as she felt. He had an envelope of X-rays with him.

"Hello, I'm Dr. Monroe. Sorry to keep you waiting. 'When it rains, it pours' seems to be an adage that applies to the ER tonight."

"I understand," Brinna said as she shifted in her bed. "Can you tell me anything about the condition of the other officer and the girl who came in with us?"

"No specifics without violating patient confidentiality." Turning his back to her, he shoved the X-ray film up on the light board and studied it for a minute. Brinna could see the bones of her hand from over his shoulder.

Dr. Monroe swiveled around to face her. "All I can say is that the girl is stable and will be admitted. We're waiting for a room to become available to send her upstairs. Now, about your condition." He proceeded to complete a brief exam and explain to her that she had a hairline fracture in her left wrist and a mild concussion.

The news was sobering for someone as active as Brinna. She'd be off work for a while.

As the doctor applied a cast, he told her he wanted to admit her for the night, just for observation because of the concussion. Brinna adamantly refused to stay and was eventually released with a note: *Against medical advice.*

Slowly and painfully she dressed in the warm, dry clothes Janet had left for her, not wanting to think about how she was going to get home.

I'll have to get into the car and put my hands on the wheel before I decide whether or not I can drive, she thought.

A knock on the door got her attention as she was gathering up her still-wet uniform.

"Hey, Brin, are they going to let you go?" It was Maggie, dressed in street clothes and looking tired but a lot better than she had seemed a few hours previous.

"Yep, it took some whining, but I have signed release papers." She grimaced with the effort it took to wave the papers.

"I figured as much." Hands on hips, Maggie rolled her eyes. "I knew you'd have to be dead before you stayed overnight."

"I hate hospitals." After her rescue as a child, she had to

spend the night in a hospital when all she wanted was to go home to her own bed. Back then, it was a scary place that was cold and smelled funny. Over the years, that feeling had morphed into being creeped out by hospitals. Her dad died in one, and even though they had reconciled in his room, Brinna could not shake the uncomfortable feeling that hospitals gave her.

"Which is why I had Rodriguez drop me off. I'll drive you home."

"I thought for sure you'd want to stay here for Rick."

"I was going to, but everything is immediate family only. Even though Molly would sneak me in, I don't want to take up space a family member could use. Besides, I'm sure you won't mind bringing me back tomorrow." She glanced at her watch. "Or later this morning, I should say."

Brinna smiled. "I won't mind at all. Thanks, Maggie. What would I do without you?"

Maggie snorted and took the bag of clothes from Brinna. "Just remember that the next time you want to dive into a raging river. By the way, I've walked Hero and given him some dog treats. He's asleep in the Explorer."

The pair left the exam room and walked toward the ER exit. Brinna's mood lifted as soon as they were outside the confines of the hospital and away from the smell of sickness and death.

She turned toward Maggie. "Thanks again. Janet said she fed him, but I'm sure he appreciated the walk. By the way, what is the latest on Rick's condition?"

"They don't know." The muscles in Maggie's jaw tensed.

"His vitals are good, but he can't feel anything below the waist. They're talking surgery when the swelling goes down." Her voice cracked.

Brinna stopped and took her arm. "I am so sorry." She looked into Maggie's moist eyes.

"I just wish you'd think first the next time—both of you." Maggie sniffled. "Rick would've dived in even if you hadn't been there. Leave it to me to pick crazy hero-types for friends." She started walking again, and Brinna fell into step with her.

"Let's just hope that whatever is wrong, they can fix it." Brinna took a deep breath and blew it out, feeling weighed down with guilt and fatigue. *Why did Rick have to get hurt following my lead?*

Her black-and-white was parked close, in one of the emergency room police slots. A glance at her watch told her it was about 2 a.m. The night sky was still cloudy, but here and there were patches of open spaces and stars.

"Officer Caruso."

Brinna turned at the sound of her name to see Paramedic Burton at the back of his rig wiping down a gurney. *He must've had another run,* she thought.

"Paramedic Burton." She returned his wave, acutely conscious of her sloppy appearance. She'd tried to brush her hair down, but after being dunked in dirty rain runoff, she really needed a shower.

Burton stopped his cleaning and walked toward her and Maggie. "Glad to see you're up and around. What's the prognosis?"

Brinna glanced at Maggie, then held up her cast. "Broken wrist, along with assorted lumps. I'll live." She nodded toward Maggie. "Did you meet Officer Maggie Sloan? She was out there too."

Burton shook his head and held out his hand to Maggie. "No, I think she was on her way to the hospital with the other officer. How's he doing?"

"Not sure," Maggie said as she gripped the firefighter's hand.

"This is the best place for him to be if his injuries are serious," Burton said. "The best doctors in the city work here. You take care of yourself, Officer Caruso."

"Thanks. And call me Brinna. I'll see you around." She nodded good-bye as she and Maggie reached the Explorer. It was an effort to climb into the car, and Brinna doubted the wisdom of wanting to go home. She would really be sore in a few hours.

"Was that the cute firefighter/paramedic you were talking about? From station four?" Maggie asked as she started the car.

"Yeah, his name is David."

"Hmm . . ."

"What's that supposed to mean?"

"Nothing, just hmm."

"Maggie, you are always thinking with your hormones."

"No, just thinking that if you had a partner off the job, one you really cared about, maybe you'd look before you leaped while at work."

15

Jack was already in the homicide office when Ben arrived.

"You're here early." Ben slapped Jack's shoulder on the way to his desk.

"Yep, been here about an hour. Coffee's fresh, though. Just brewed it." Jack nodded in the direction of the coffeepot.

Ben grunted and poured himself a cup. He doctored it with cream and sugar before he sat down. "So what are you working on?"

Sighing, Jack tossed a crime report to Ben. "There was a message on my desk, left by Sergeant Rodriguez about an incident last night. Another young girl was plucked out of the San Gabriel River. I would've called you earlier, but since I know you and Amy were away for the weekend celebrating the big ten-year wedding anniversary and all . . ."

Ben snorted. "Yeah, right, blame it on Amy. You're just a hard charger. Another dead body in our jurisdiction?" he asked as he glanced at the report.

Jack shook his head. "Nope, this one is alive. And a couple

of cops were injured on the call. Anyway, Sergeant Rodriguez noticed a rose tattoo on the girl, identical to the one on Alice." Jack didn't say he knew who the injured officers were, but he did, and the knowledge weighed heavily on his mind. It was all he could do not to rush to the hospital to check on Brinna. As it was, he'd checked the watch commander's logs of the incident about ten times in the hour he'd been in the office, looking for updates.

"Alive?" Ben looked up from the report and held Jack's gaze. "Is the girl talking? Is there a connection?"

Jack shrugged and rolled his pen between his palms. "She's foreign, just like Alice, but not talking. She almost drowned, so we're not sure how much is trauma and how much is language barrier. We're working on bringing in a translator. The medical people believe the girl is of Eastern European descent."

Ben whistled. "Like Alice. The dentist who looked over Alice's teeth said she'd likely had work done in Bulgaria. Was this girl beat up like Alice?"

"That's up in the air. She rode the San Gabriel River rapids for over a mile. That was bound to beat her up a bit. I figured I'd wait for you before going to the hospital to see what there is to see."

"Has to be related. What are the odds of two unrelated women of Eastern European descent, with the same tattoo, ending up hurt in Long Beach?"

Jack nodded and steepled his fingers. "I'd bet a paycheck they are related. And I thank God this girl is alive. This is the lead—the break—we've been waiting for."

* * *

While Ben went to admitting and checked with the doctors about the injured girl, Jack visited the ER and tried to find out any information he could about Brinna and Rick. Relief flooded through him when he discovered that at least Brinna had gone home. Another officer saw Jack and filled him in on Rick's condition and the circumstances of the rescue. Jack's anxiety ramped up anew. He was shocked by the seriousness of Rick's injuries and knew Brinna well enough to believe that she probably felt responsible for him.

"She's on the fifth floor." Ben rapped Jack on the shoulder as he relayed information about the girl from the river.

"Can we talk to her?"

"Well, they say she's doing better, but there's no translator yet. They have pinpointed her country of origin as Bulgaria."

Jack raised an eyebrow as the connection to Alice solidified.

Ben continued. "What'd you find out about Brinna?"

"She's been released. But Rick is still here and not doing very well. They think he may be paralyzed." Jack told his partner all he'd learned about Rick.

Ben shook his head. "That's tough. Rick's only been on the job about four years. I pray he pulls through 100 percent."

"Definitely," Jack agreed. "Did they have an idea when the translator would get here?"

"No. How about we go to the cafeteria and get some coffee? They said they'd let me know when someone gets here."

"Sure. Might as well be prepared to hurry up and wait."

16

When Brinna arrived home, tired as she was, she needed a shower to wash away the flood-control odor. And it felt like heaven. She wrapped her casted hand in plastic and stood under the hot spray, wishing the water could also rinse away the guilt she felt about Rick and all of the bad that had happened in the muddy runoff. The hot water worked to remove the odor, ease the physical aches and pains, but little else.

Maggie says I leap before I look, and I do. But am I responsible for Rick's injuries?

She couldn't answer the question and finished the shower in favor of bed. Fatigue brought her a blissfully dreamless sleep. When she arose around 8:30 a.m., stiff and sore, she tried to figure out how to scratch her wrist, which was driving her crazy. It didn't hurt; it just itched. Contemplating six weeks of that itch, Brinna feared she'd be cutting the cast off long before she was supposed to. The smell of the flood control lingered in her hair, so she took another shower, a quick one, and finally felt clean when she dried off.

Maggie had spent the remainder of the night on her couch, and Brinna could hear her moving around, so she knew her friend was also up. When she left her room, she saw that Maggie was on the phone, checking to see if there was anything new on Rick. The night before, they'd decided to go back to the hospital if Brinna felt well enough. She stretched and decided she felt okay—not great, but okay for someone who was pulled out of filthy rain runoff.

Coffee was already made—she could smell it—so she meandered into the kitchen and poured a cup. On the phone, Maggie nodded and answered in the affirmative from time to time. When she finally hung up, Brinna looked her way, hoping to see relief, but saw only more worry.

"Well?"

"He's in surgery. They're trying to relieve pressure on his spinal column." She yawned and ran her hands through her hair. "Your mom called while you were in the shower."

"Did she want me to call?" Brinna's brows scrunched together; she wasn't sure she was up to a conversation with her mother. Though they'd grown closer in the time since her father's death three months ago, and had even ironed out some big problems, Brinna still found it difficult sometimes to be "mothered." She often needed to nurse her wounds alone first and then call Mom. Right now, in pain and floundering in guilt, she wanted only to sort through her thoughts, not Mom's opinion about things.

"No, I don't think so. She heard about the rescue on

the news and wanted to know what happened. I told her."
Maggie shrugged. "She was relieved to know you were okay.
You know—typical mom stuff."

"Yeah, I know." Brinna stared into her coffee cup. Mom
would pray, a response that was her answer to everything,
something that used to bother Brinna. But her attitude about
prayer had shifted a lot in the last few months. While she
often still had a difficult time asking for prayer for herself,
she had no problem requesting it for others. And as she swallowed more coffee, she decided maybe that was what Rick
needed—Mom praying to God that he'd be all right.

"Want to head over to the hospital after I shower?" Maggie
asked, interrupting Brinna's train of thought.

"Sure. How'd you sleep last night?"

"All right. Your couch is comfortable. How about you?
Still sore?"

"Yeah, I'm aching in places I didn't think I had places."

"I hope Rick can say that after he gets out of surgery."

17

"I NEED TO SPEAK with you *now*."

Magda turned from her client, startled by the sound of her native language. Simon, one of Demitri's goons, stood before her, looking as though he'd been up all night. His hair was wet and his face dark with stubble. His clothes were rumpled and he wore a scowl. Magda glanced at her client and saw that Simon's expression made her uncomfortable.

"May I finish with my—?"

"No, now." Simon gripped her arm tightly, and Magda felt the fear rise.

Smiling and nodding at her client, she spoke to the woman in the calmest voice she could muster. "Will you excuse me for a moment, my dear?"

"Sure," the woman replied as she backed away, nervously glancing between the two. "I'll just browse a little longer."

"Thank you." Magda's smile quickly faded as she faced Simon, teeth clenched. "What is it?" she hissed.

"Not here; your office."

Blowing out an irritated breath, Magda stalked to her office, Simon on her heels.

"I don't like this," she said, shaking her head. "You have no right bursting into my business in the middle of the day. Demitri and I have an agreement."

"I have a problem, and I need your help." Simon looked at her with fear in his eyes. Magda recognized the fear. Something had happened that would displease Demitri.

"What?" The word squeaked out as the terror that she too would face Demitri's wrath throttled her.

"One of the girls ran away."

Magda took a step back, banging into her desk as her breath left her. "How?" was all she could manage.

"It doesn't matter. I have to get her back. If Demitri returns home to find her gone, I'm a dead man."

His last sentence hit Magda like a bullet. Simon was not exaggerating. Demitri would kill someone for a transgression like this. Worse, this could impact them both. Her mouth suddenly felt like cotton. She licked her lips.

"Get her back? Do you know where she ran to?" she asked.

Simon pulled a paper out of his pocket. It was from the local newspaper's website, breaking news at the top. He pointed to a short article about a girl being pulled from the river. "I think this is her. Magda, you have to help me. Demitri will return in six days."

Magda took the printout and read the brief article. The police had pulled the girl from the water. She had no ID. They were asking for the assistance of anyone who might know her identity.

Magda didn't know her identity; she never knew any of the girls. But she knew now she had an opportunity. The police were involved. How could she help Simon with his dilemma and at the same time get rid of Demitri for good?

18

Brinna and Maggie entered Memorial Medical Center through the main doors. It was before noon and there were a lot of cops in the lobby, obviously milling around waiting for news about Rick. One of the guys told them that he was still in surgery. The admonishment "immediate family only" had not changed. They also learned that his wife, Molly, was somewhere in the hospital.

"I want to find her," Maggie said, chewing on her bottom lip. "How about we check out the cafeteria? Maybe she's down there."

"I could use some bad hospital coffee," Brinna joked and then glanced at Maggie to see if there was any hint of a smile on her friend's face. But Maggie was obviously preoccupied, her brow creased in concern. Brinna noted that Maggie had grown quieter the closer they got to the hospital and guessed that she wouldn't be okay unless Rick was. Partnership was like that—at least good partnerships were. Though Brinna loved working with Hero and hated the thought that she might lose that privilege, she sometimes envied the working relationship Maggie had with Rick. Nothing sexual or strange, they simply complemented each other. They could count on one another . . . and that was very important when things went crazy on the streets.

Brinna had had a small taste of that kind of relationship a few months previous with Jack O'Reilly. It had been rough at first, since neither of them wanted to work with the other, but by the end of their time together, they'd meshed. In addition to stopping a serial child molester and rescuing a friend's kidnapped twin girls, Brinna remembered their last night together fondly.

"Any unit to handle, a 211 silent—"

Jack was driving, and when he looked across at Brinna, she knew they were in agreement about handling the silent robbery alarm. He flipped on the lights and stepped on it, leaving off the siren so as not to tip the bad guys off. Brinna advised dispatch they were en route. The address given was a 7-Eleven, commonly referred to as a "stop and rob." Jack parked around the corner, and the two of them got out of the car to approach carefully.

Brinna remembered neither of them had to speak; they knew what to do and how to approach the situation. She moved for cover in the parking lot while Jack tiptoed up and peeked in the window. With sign language he told her he saw one bad guy with a gun and three customers. No way could they just rush in—too many potential hostages and innocent targets.

Using the car as cover, Brinna got her own eye on the

store just as the bad guy turned to flee. They could not have handled it better if they'd done it a hundred times.

Brinna had inched forward, gun on target, catching the crook by surprise. He jammed to a stop and stared at her. Her distraction gave him no time to react as Jack moved in and smacked the gun away with a baton. In three steps Brinna was right there to hold the man still while Jack applied handcuffs. The people in the store applauded.

She and Jack were to be honored in a few weeks at the annual police awards banquet.

Chewing on a thumbnail as she and Maggie walked down the corridor to the cafeteria, Brinna remembered that special "partnership" feeling and noted it had only been a couple of weeks for her and Jack. Maggie and Rick had been partners for three years. Maggie was facing the same kind of separation from her partner that Brinna was from Hero, albeit for a much more tragic set of circumstances.

She wanted to tell her friend that she understood, but did she? As valuable as Hero was to her, she knew their partnership was not the same complex dynamic as interaction with a human partner. Losing Rick as a partner would be closer to being widowed or divorced for Maggie. As she pulled open the door to the cafeteria, she realized she was now just as concerned for Maggie as she was for Rick. How would Maggie take it if Rick could no longer be her partner?

She didn't see Jack and Ben until she heard one of them call her name.

"Brinna!"

She turned and grabbed Maggie's arm, trying to ignore the

spark of attraction that flared when she saw Jack. He'd been on her mind a lot lately, and now, with all that had happened, she realized she wanted to talk to him, hear his perspective. "It's Jack and Ben. Let's go join them."

They left the concession line and walked to where the detectives were sitting.

"What are you guys doing here?" Brinna asked them both but focused on Jack. He looked good in uniform, but he was downright heart-stopping in a suit and tie. "Was there a homicide last night?"

Jack shook his head. "We were here earlier, hoping to talk to that girl you saved from the river. They told us to come back and we just got here. Now we're waiting on a translator." He turned to Maggie. "Sorry to hear about Rick. I understand the best neurologist in the country is working on him now."

"Where'd you hear that?"

"I saw Molly upstairs," Ben said. "I'm buying the coffee; have a seat." He stood. "How do you take it?"

"Black." Brinna sat next to Jack and wondered if she should remind him about the lunch he'd mentioned.

"I've had enough coffee; how about a Coke?" Maggie asked as she sat down.

Ben held a thumb up and went to get the drinks.

"That happen the other night?" Jack asked, pointing to Brinna's left arm.

Brinna nodded, warmth spreading inside from the concern in Jack's voice and eyes. "I got banged up a bit, is all. I'll have to go to occupational health and see how long this will keep me off work." She leaned forward, eager to change the subject before her face flushed red. "Why are you here about the girl? Does she fit into a homicide?"

"Not sure, but she's connected to Alice in some way."

Brinna sat back. "Connected to Alice? How?"

"She has the same tattoo on her hip. Remember the rose? And they think she's Bulgarian."

"I saw that tattoo," Maggie said as Ben returned and set down the drinks. "The dead girl had the same one?"

Jack nodded. "Sergeant Rodriguez made the connection. She'd seen a photo of the tattoo on Alice's hip and then the practically identical one on this girl."

"We heard you pulled her out of the water, Brinna. Bucking for a position on the swift-water rescue team?" Ben asked.

Brinna sighed. "I went into the water accidentally, nothing heroic. Then I blacked out, and the next thing I remember, I was in an ambulance."

"Accidentally?" Jack said. "And here I thought you were exhibiting signs of firefighter envy."

Maggie snorted. "At least he didn't consider that you'd exhibited signs of craziness."

Brinna shook her head and explained. "When I saw the girl, adrenaline took over. I tried to get close enough to the edge to grab her and fell in. It was stupid."

"Hear, hear." Maggie held her soda cup up. "She and Rick were connected by a leash. When Brinna lost her balance, so did Rick. They both went into the water, but he hit the rocks. Matt and Jeff grabbed him; then all of a sudden there were firemen everywhere. They had been en route; their timing was impeccable."

"So who did save the girl?" Ben asked.

Maggie sighed and frowned. "I think she grabbed hold of Brinna, because I remember seeing them come out of the water together. The rescue divers pulled them out at the same time. The poor thing was practically blue. She'd lost most of her clothes in the water, and that water was cold."

"Was she conscious? Did she talk?"

"She seemed delirious. What I did hear sounded like a foreign language," Maggie said. "After I saw that Brinna would be all right, I followed Rick's paramedic rig to the hospital. Other than the paramedics trying to assess her condition, I don't think anyone talked to the girl."

"We hope to get answers from her, find out who she is and where she came from," Jack said.

"I'd like to be there when you do," Brinna said, holding up her cast. "Since I don't have to go to work today." She glanced at Maggie, who gave a noncommittal tilt of the head.

"I still want to see Rick. But I don't want to take any time away from family visits. If nothing else, I hope to be able to sit with Molly for a while, provide moral support." Maggie turned to Ben. "You saw Molly where?"

"Second-floor surgery waiting room," Ben said. "I don't think Rick will be allowed visitors. Molly said that the surgery he's having is tricky, and when it's finished, he'll be in ICU for a while."

"I'll go up and see if she needs anything." Maggie stood.

"I hope the girl can tell you what happened." Maggie nodded at Brinna, then left the trio staring after her.

Brinna watched her go, frowning.

"Something wrong?" Jack asked. "I mean, besides Rick?"

"Rick is most of it. She's very worried about him. And I think she blames me for him getting hurt."

"You?" Jack choked on some coffee.

"Yeah, I shouldn't have gotten so close to the river's edge. If I hadn't slipped, Rick wouldn't be in this predicament. The swift-water rescue team was close; I should have waited."

"Did you *know* they were close at the time, or is this hindsight?"

"Well, hindsight, but—"

"Then don't blame yourself! It's unfortunate what happened to Rick, but you didn't slip on purpose. You could have been hurt just as badly."

But I wasn't, she thought. Brinna looked away and sipped her coffee, wondering what this escapade would say to the little girl who idolized her. *Have I let her down?* she wondered. *Will the reports call me reckless, and is that a good example to set for an impressionable mind?*

19

BRINNA LISTENED to Jack and Ben discuss aspects of their case while she finished her coffee. She realized then just how much she missed Jack. If she could be his partner, it wouldn't be so bad losing Hero. But he wasn't going to leave homicide to go back to patrol; it was obvious he was in his element as a detective. She wondered if that also meant he was over the death of his wife and then squirmed when she recognized that she was sizing him up as a date.

"Arm hurt?" Jack asked.

"What?"

"The way you were fidgeting, I thought maybe the arm hurt."

"No, I was just thinking about Rick."

He held her gaze and Brinna could have melted. Ben's phone buzzing with a text interrupted the moment.

"Translator is in the building," he said as he read the message.

"Then let's go," Jack said.

They all left the cafeteria and headed for the elevator.

The girl, labeled Jane Doe as far as the hospital was concerned, was on the fifth floor. On the ride up, Brinna found herself glad to be hitchhiking into part of this investigation even if it was only to watch. Harvey would not like it, especially since she was officially off with the injured-on-duty status, but she had no plans to get overly involved or disobey any direct orders. Thinking about the investigation muted the unease that hospitals gave her. She thought of Rick, no doubt facing a lengthy hospital stay, and hoped his experience here would be a positive one.

Helpless, she thought, *I feel helpless. That is what hospitals do to me. The feeling is compounded by the fact that there's nothing I can do for Rick but hope the doctors can fix him.*

She thought about her mom and mentally chastised herself about not asking for prayer for Rick. She'd have to do that after they spoke to the girl.

Brinna envied the peace her mother's calm reliance on prayer gave her. When Brinna picked up the Bible, she wanted to believe that same peace could be hers, but so far she'd only seemed to glimpse what her mom had an overabundance of.

She chewed on a thumbnail and frowned. *I've seen prayers answered, like when Jack and I got to the twins in time. But in Rick's case, is it better to trust prayer than a skilled physician?* She knew that her mother would say yes.

The elevator opened, and Brinna nearly ran into her friend and local FBI agent, Chuck Weldon. He'd just come around the nurses' station with two women Brinna didn't recognize.

"Chuck? What are you doing here?" Jack asked before Brinna found her voice.

"Probably here for the same reason you are. Jane Doe from the San Gabriel River. She's become a federal issue." Weldon turned to Brinna. "I hear you're a swimmer."

"More like a sinker." She shook her head and changed the subject. "Why is the FBI involved with our Jane Doe?"

"A tip." He nodded to the stocky, dark-haired woman standing next to him. The woman looked official in a tailored suit, with an intense expression on her face. "This is Helena. I can't pronounce her last name. She's a translator from the Bulgarian embassy. They received an anonymous phone call telling them that the girl from the river is a Bulgarian national and was brought into this country illegally and held against her will."

Brinna's ears perked up. This was a big-time felony. "You mean she's run away from kidnappers?"

"We think she's a victim of human trafficking."

"Human trafficking?" Brinna repeated the term as the translation reverberated in her mind: *modern-day slavery.* Anger swelled. Though men could be victims, vastly more women and young girls were trafficked here in the US and in Western Europe. Often they were forced into the sex trade, but they could be trafficked for just about any type of exploitation.

"Yep, if the tip was good, this girl and several others were smuggled into the country and kept in servitude somewhere nearby as either house servants or prostitutes." He pointed to the second woman, who looked less serious, softer in a way than the translator. She reminded Brinna of her mom. "Which brings us to Elisa Duggan. She is an independent counselor called in by ICE. If it turns out that Jane Doe is a victim, she'll have to be evaluated in order to assess her needs before she's placed in a shelter. State law requires we bring in a nongovernmental agency to protect the victim while we gather evidence."

"I hope we can find a shelter to place her in; most of the ones I work with are full," Duggan said.

"I had no idea this was happening so close to home," Brinna said. "For some reason I thought it was mostly closer to the border, and that the victims were largely Hispanic and Asian."

"Unfortunately it's an equal-opportunity crime. It's prevalent in parts of Europe and spreading just about anywhere. The bureau is investigating cases all over the country involving all nationalities. The common thread is that the people being brought here genuinely believe they're coming to the land of opportunity. Instead, the traffickers imprison and exploit them."

Jack snapped his fingers. "You know, we just received an e-mail alert about a big case of trafficking in San Diego. A patrol officer dispatched to a domestic violence call stumbled on a human-trafficking ring." Jack turned on his tablet and tapped the screen. In a few minutes he had the alert up.

"Here it is." He held up the tablet for all to see. "Several women and young girls from the Philippines were brought to California supposedly to meet husbands. Once here, they were kept locked down and forced to be prostitutes. All of them were housed in one large room with only curtain partitions for privacy. The owner of the house brought johns in and made a lot of money."

"And the cops went there on a domestic violence call?" Brinna asked.

Jack nodded. "Yeah, the man's wife found out what he was hiding in the back room and the fight was on. Neighbors called the police."

"Human trafficking is more prevalent than we might want to think, and it's growing faster than drug trafficking," Chuck added. "You figure, once a kilo of cocaine is sold, it's gone; the dealer has to replenish his supply to make more money. Unfortunately human traffickers have discovered that human contraband is a reusable resource. Their victims can be exploited over and over. No break in the flow of money."

Chuck tapped Brinna on the shoulder. "Brin, little kids are becoming a big part of it. This is something you'll want to sink your teeth into."

"I'll start a file. Like I said, I'm surprised it's happening in our backyard, but I'll be no less ready to deal with it."

"How are these people getting into the country?" Ben asked.

"Sometimes legitimately—on visas or with valid passports. That's why we don't believe this girl was kidnapped. She probably came here willingly. But once here, the trafficker confiscates her ID, tells her the police in this country are not to be trusted, and then puts her to work, keeping her prisoner. Sometimes they're smuggled across borders as well. Our northern and southern borders, along with many ports, can be off-loading sites."

"Excuse me."

Everyone turned at the voice. A tall, gray-haired woman with wire-rimmed glasses stood in the hallway. The white coat and stethoscope gave away her profession.

"I'm Dr. Rachel Kallen. The young lady is awake and alert. I can give you a few minutes with her."

"Thanks." Chuck nodded, and all of them started for the girl's room.

"One caution." Dr. Kallen held a hand up. "She's badly frightened. Aside from the physical abuse, there are signs of sexual abuse as well. She responds better to women than men, so go easy."

Ben looked at the doctor and shook his head. "There are too many of us. Jack, I'll let you go in. I'll head back downstairs and find Maggie and Molly. Come get me there when you're done." Ben turned back to the elevator.

Jack nodded and cast a glance at Brinna as they made their way to the room. "Maybe you should take the lead here."

"Let's see what she has to say to the translator first," Chuck said.

20

THE GIRL WAS OBVIOUSLY FRIGHTENED—and young. Brinna wanted to say she looked all of twelve or thirteen years old. Pale except for the bruising along her jawline and neck, she seemed to try to shrink into the bedding as everyone filed into the room. One did not have to be a trained observer to realize that the girl was especially apprehensive about Jack and Chuck.

Chuck motioned to the translator, and the woman stepped close to the bed. She began speaking in Bulgarian. The girl's eyes kept darting from the translator to Chuck and back again.

Helena kept talking, her voice soothing. The girl nodded once or twice but said nothing.

"She is Bulgarian but afraid," Helena said after a couple of minutes, looking at Chuck.

"Make sure she knows she's not in trouble here. She's the victim. We want to help." Elisa Duggan held her hands out and smiled at the girl.

Helena relayed the message. The girl shook her head violently, and tears began to fall. Words came out in sobs. Helena reached out and patted her shoulder. The girl cringed.

Brinna wondered what they could do, what it would take, to convince the girl they were on her side.

Helena stepped back. "She doesn't believe you will help her. She says that police don't help people like her. She really believes you'll kill her or return her to her prison." Helena folded her arms. "This is common. In Bulgaria the police often assist the traffickers if the money is right."

"Can you impress upon her that this is America and the police don't work that way here?" Brinna asked. "I mean, that's why she's here in the hospital."

The girl looked at Brinna, then jabbered something to Helena.

Helena smiled. "She recognizes you and has asked me about your arm."

Brinna held up her cast, amazed the girl could remember her after the chaos in the water. "I'm okay. It's just a slight fracture. She remembers me from the river?"

Helena spoke to the girl, who seemed to calm down.

The translator smiled at Brinna. "She tells me that you saved her from death. She wants to thank you."

Brinna jabbed a thumb at Jack and Chuck. "Tell her I'm a police officer just like these two guys and I was doing my job, which is helping people. We all want to help her. No one in this room wants to see her hurt anymore."

Helena translated. The girl looked down at the blanket she had gripped tightly in both hands. To Brinna, it seemed as though there was a monumental struggle going on inside her: give in to fear or open up to trust. A wave of understanding flowed through her like a warm Santa Ana wind. The young girl had known nothing but abuse and victimization since she'd come to America. She'd been wrenched from the familiar into a horrible nightmare, like all the young girls Brinna dedicated her life and career to rescuing.

Brinna felt a strong bond, a connection to the pale, battered foreigner. Whether or not the girl would ever feel the connection Brinna now felt didn't matter. Brinna knew she was bound to do whatever she could to help her and bring the creep who did this to justice.

Finally, still looking down at her hands, the girl spoke in heavily accented English. "Ivana . . . my name is Ivana. Please, where is my sister, Villie?"

21

"YOU MUST GO to the hospital and find out about her." Simon paced the warehouse. Magda had convinced him that any conversation about the girl was better held in a private place. In part that was true, but it was also a stall. She'd needed time to think about the situation before making any comment on what she would or wouldn't do.

He'd waited here at Demitri's warehouse on the water until she could get away for a late lunch, and from the looks and smell of the place, he'd smoked a case of cigarettes. She had used the intervening hours to think and to make a phone call. Her mind swirled with schemes—how to in some way use this situation to her advantage.

"I will not. I'm sure there are police everywhere. Your mistake must not jeopardize my business or my life." Hands behind her back, fists clenched, Magda forced herself to stay ramrod stiff. She'd never dare talk to Demitri this way. But Simon must know that he did not have the same power, the same measure of control.

"Magda, Magda, I don't have to tell you what Demitri is capable of." He grabbed her shoulders, eyes desperate and pleading. But absent were threats or bullying. Simon seemed to accept that he was here at Magda's mercy, not the other way around. "Please, it was an accident. I don't want to die for an accident."

She held his bloodshot gaze, both pleased and relieved to see that she did have some power here. Part of her did feel for Simon. She knew all too well how Demitri expressed displeasure. Vivid reminders were ugly purple scars that remained on her husband's back from Demitri's ordered beating. But another part of her lusted for revenge. This current situation was a chink in Demitri's armor, a soft spot vulnerable to attack. And Magda would exploit it for all it was worth.

"Calm down. You can't think straight when your head is swimming with fear." Magda pushed his hands away. "We need to wait. To determine what the girl says to the authorities and how the authorities react."

"But we have only six days!" He pounded his fists into his thighs.

"Think, or you will waste all your time groveling in fear."

Simon sighed and threw his hands up in resignation. "What would you have me think about? My life is over if Demitri finds out about the girl."

Magda let herself relax. She had the reins now. It was simply a matter of directing Simon where she wanted him to go. "Maybe it is not as bad as you think. First, what exactly can the girl tell the authorities when they ask about where she came from? Will she be able to lead them back to the house? Does she know your name?"

"I'm not sure." He rubbed his forehead. "I guess she doesn't know much." His eyes brightened ever so slightly. "She was brought to the house in a panel van, kept in the back room. I don't believe she could tell them how to find it. When she ran, it was raining."

"Where is this house, this place where you keep the girls?"

"In Hawaiian Gardens. It's on a dead end, near the river." He shook his head. "It would have been better for me if that stupid girl had drowned in that water."

"Look." This time Magda grabbed Simon's shoulders. "This is what we will do. You will go back to the house and wait for me to call. I will look into American law. I don't think this girl can tell the police much. She will simply be a mystery to them. I don't think they will put her in jail. Maybe in a couple of days it will be possible for you to get her back."

"That's cutting it very, very close."

"Trust me, Simon. You must think very carefully before you do anything. It will be better to cut things close than to make a mistake by rushing in without considering the consequences." Magda held her breath and watched as Simon considered her words. He had to believe her. He had to let things proceed slowly, to give her time.

Finally he spoke. "Okay, what you say makes sense." He held her gaze with haunted eyes. "Just don't make me wait too long. Please."

22

THE INTERVIEW WAS GRUELING. Ivana spoke for herself, with Helena standing by in case she was needed. Jack felt the girl's pain spoken in her own words. She kept her gaze downcast as he asked the questions. When she did look up, it was to one of the women present—Helena, Brinna, or Elisa.

"Why did you agree to leave Bulgaria and come here?"

"Demitri promised us jobs and a new life."

"Did he tell you where you would work?"

"He made many promises."

"When did you realize he was lying?"

"When the boat docked. He took our papers and then gave us both beatings."

"And after that?"

"He took us to that house where the men . . ."

She broke down as she recounted rape sessions—usually with one man at a time, but once or twice she and her sister were forced to endure gang rape. Any resistance or show of attitude to the men resulted in beatings. What she'd been through in the time she'd been in the United States was heart-wrenching. Even more so when she told them all the promises this Demitri character had made her: money, a good job, a wonderful apartment, expensive clothes, clubs every night, freedom.

She'd walked willingly into hell, thinking it would be heaven.

The girl's strength as she shared impressed Jack but angered him at the same time. That someone like Demitri could so use these women and treat them so harshly made him wish he had the man in front of him.

And the frustration set in as he realized that while they had a list of crimes to charge Demitri with, and a strong witness in Ivana, she could offer them no solid way to find him. She couldn't even tell them the location of the house that she ran from.

He saw how the girl's story touched Brinna as well and wanted to hug both of them to assure them the monster would be stopped. Was that chauvinistic? he wondered.

"That was rough," he said to Brinna after they finished. All in all, they'd been with Ivana for an hour and a half. Jack felt as though he'd run a marathon.

"Yeah, it was." She leaned against the wall next to the elevator and looked sapped of strength. "But the tone of your voice seemed to help a lot, Jack. You didn't scare her like Chuck did."

"She was afraid of her own shadow, poor thing. I know Chuck wasn't trying to be scary."

Brinna nodded in agreement.

"Hey, I think I owe you lunch." Jack wanted to make her smile. Did her face brighten? He hoped so. "Right now I want to get all my reports to the DA. I'll call you later and we'll make arrangements for sometime soon, okay?"

"Sounds good." He got the smile from her he wanted when they parted ways in the lobby. Jack mentally scrolled through his schedule, hoping to make time for the lunch date.

* * *

"Everything the girl said fits trafficking," Jack told Ben as they drove back to the station. "She was promised legitimate work here, but once she arrived, she was forced into prostitution."

"Too bad she couldn't be more clear about where she was being held."

Jack sighed. "Yeah, bad luck that. But then she was terrified, running for her life, so it's not surprising she can't describe the house." He rubbed his chin, chest still tight as he thought about the vicious deception.

Surprisingly she wasn't as young as she looked; she was eighteen, an adult—a cruelly exploited young adult. Her missing sister was four years older. When she'd described her sister, his heart had sunk with the realization that their Alice was most likely Villie. He'd decided to wait until Ivana was stronger before bringing a picture to her for a positive ID.

"How long will they keep her in the hospital?" Ben asked.

"Another day, then Immigration and Customs Enforcement will take over. Since she's a victim of trafficking, Elisa is searching for a women's shelter and will keep her whereabouts confidential."

"Is that the best idea? She's a possible witness for us on Alice. Will we have access if we need it?"

"They just want to keep her safe and make her feel secure, and a women's shelter is a perfect nongovernmental agency. But I can see how it might be hard to reach her in a hurry if we need to." Jack drummed on the dash with his fingers and thought for a minute. "We need another viable alternative." He snapped his fingers. "I've got it."

"What?"

"Brinna. She's off work; she's got room. What say we talk her into taking the girl in, watching her for a bit? ICE shouldn't have a problem with the victim being released into the private home of a cop. And Brinna's address should be safe from discovery," Jack wouldn't admit that this line of reasoning was also selfish. The more Brinna was involved with the case, the more he had an opportunity to be around her.

"Yeah, but Brinna might not like it. She's all for protecting kids, but—"

"This affected her; I could tell. I bet she was thinking about all the teens she's been involved with who ran away from home because someone promised them something, only to be exploited or murdered. She'll be up for it."

"Hope you're right, because it does sound like a good plan."

23

Brinna and Maggie left the hospital around two thirty. Maggie was so quiet during the ride to her condo, Brinna worried she was sick and asked if she felt okay.

"Not sick. Just restless and not able to sit still."

"What are you going to do? Go back to the hospital?" Brinna asked when they pulled into Maggie's complex.

"I'll be worthless until I know what's going on with Rick. At least if I stay at the hospital, I can help Molly if she needs anything."

"Do you want me—?"

"No. You're dead on your feet, Brin. Go get some sleep."

"Call me if you need me for anything at all."

Maggie only nodded and climbed out of the car.

Brinna sat in her car and watched her friend disappear into the condo. Nothing they'd heard about Rick's condition had been conclusive, and she knew that weighed on Maggie. Rick had come through the surgery all right, but his paralysis was still a question mark. It was the elephant in the room neither of them could bring up.

Yawning, Brinna headed home. When she arrived and before she got out of the car, she called her mother. Asking for prayer was not easy; it was still something Brinna was trying to learn. Somehow it was easier to just leave a message on her mother's voice mail.

"Mom, hey, I'm back home from the hospital. Rick, Maggie's partner, had some serious surgery on his back. Could you pray? I mean . . . well, I don't want him to be paralyzed, so . . ."

She kept the line open until there was a beep and then closed her phone, hoping Mom would understand. She trudged into the house feeling as though her shoes were made of lead. She wished with all her heart that Rick would recover completely. Surely the best doctor in the country could accomplish that, couldn't he?

Once inside, Hero wanted a walk, but she didn't have the energy to give him one. He had to settle for a trip out to the backyard. Trying to clear her mind, she lay down in bed. She closed her eyes, and sleep fell like a hammer.

* * *

The phone woke her around four thirty. Still sore after the power nap, Brinna moved slowly to pick up the receiver. It was her mother.

"Hi, Mom, what's up?"

"Just wondering how you're doing. When I spoke to Maggie this morning, she said you and Rick had been through an awful lot. I got your message, and of course I'll pray."

Brinna felt herself flush—not sure why—but she was glad her mother was on the phone. A feeling rolled over her that she didn't want to admit having. A feeling that in the past she would have beat out of herself by engaging in a heart-pumping kayak paddle or a knee-crushing run. One look at her cast reminded her that she wouldn't be out in the kayak anytime soon, and her aching bruises would preclude a run. Biting her lip, mindful that her mother waited for a response, she caved in to the fact that she couldn't deny the feeling.

She wanted her mom.

"I'm not doing so good, Mom. I ache all over, and I'm worried about Rick." And there was also the situation with Hero, which she hadn't yet told her mother about. Sighing, she leaned back against her pillow, receiver held tight to her ear. A solitary tear fell, and she wondered if her mom heard her voice break ever so slightly.

Rose's words were soothing, coming from the woman who had kissed boo-boos and washed hurts. "I know this is hard for you. I know how close the three of you are. Want some company?"

Brinna squeezed her eyes shut and whispered, "Yes. Yes, I do."

"Have you eaten? I just made chicken and dumplings. I could pick up some corn bread on the way over, and we can have dinner. How does that sound?"

Despite the feelings of hurt and frustration, the dinner offer made Brinna crack a smile. "Sounds great, Mom."

"Be over in about twenty minutes."

Brinna hung the phone up, allowing relief to course through her veins. Mom was coming, and she would bring comfort food. *One of my favorites,* she thought. *Creamy chicken soup with thick chunks of meat and plump dumplings topped off with warm corn bread spread with honey butter.* Where food was concerned, her mother never missed the mark.

Sitting on the edge of the bed, holding her face in her hands, Brinna hated admitting she needed her mom as much as she hated feeling helpless about Rick and Hero. A few months ago it would have been Milo she called, her mentor. Milo would have known what to say to give Brinna confidence that Rick would be okay. Milo would have known how to help her shake this helpless feeling.

But Milo was dead. He'd taken his own life, and while Brinna was forced to accept it, she would never understand it. She stood and walked across the hall to her office. Ten missing posters lined her Innocent Wall. She studied each face, an exercise that usually helped pump her full of anger and indignation, emotions that made her feel strong, made her feel like charging to the rescue.

But it didn't help. No matter what, she couldn't charge to Rick's rescue. Or Maggie's. Or her own.

"I hate this!" Brinna cried as she threw herself into her chair. The tears came, and she couldn't stop them.

When Hero padded softly into the room, Brinna fell to her knees and hugged him, letting the tears fall into his soft fur. Since there was no stopping the storm, all Brinna could hope was that it would blow over by the time her mother arrived.

24

A REPORT WAS SITTING on Jack's desk when he and Ben returned to the office. It was the lab analysis of the blanket Brinna had recovered from the first crime scene. Ben picked up the phone to call Chuck and run the Ivana-staying-with-Brinna scenario by him.

"Hey, look at this," Jack said, stopping Ben mid-dial. "This blanket is European, and the lab was even able to compile a list of possible vendors." He turned the report to show Ben. "There's only one place anywhere close to us, a place in Shoreline Village: Black Sea Folk Art and Collectibles. They import stuff from Bulgaria, of all places. Did you know that?"

Ben shook his head. "I'm not a collectible kind of guy. This may be a great lead. Usually immigrant people band together, stay close to things that are familiar. But if these girls were prisoners, they never would have been let near that shop."

"I'm not thinking they went anywhere near the shop; I'm thinking more that whoever smuggled them might go near the shop. Or—" Jack took a deep breath—"it's possible the

shop is the key, the front for trafficking. Maybe they don't stop at importing folk art."

"That's a stretch, partner. We'd need a lot more information to make that stick."

"Let's get it, then. Power up the computer and look up this place. You're better at the utilities search. I'll call Chuck."

"Okay, boss." Ben grinned. "It sure is good to have my partner back operating at 100 percent. Even giving orders." He slapped Jack on the shoulder and then sat and logged on to the computer.

Jack smiled, thinking it felt good to be back. It was hard to imagine that a few months ago he'd begged to be taken out of homicide. He dialed Chuck's number and quietly prayed a prayer of thanks for the person who'd helped bring him out of his pit of despair and send him back to work with a new mission and purpose.

Brinna Caruso.

*　*　*

The chicken soup was wonderful and therapeutic. Brinna had two helpings, with thick slices of corn bread drenched in honey butter. Afterward she was content to curl up on the couch, feeling stuffed to bursting, while her mother brewed some coffee. Hero trotted into the room, and Brinna did something she rarely allowed—she invited him up on the couch. As he made a spot for himself at her feet, she sighed, relaxing for the first time all day.

"Now I know you're having a rough time," Rose Caruso said as she slid into Brinna's recliner.

"What do you mean by that?" Brinna asked.

"Well, it's one thing to let me bring you dinner; it's another thing entirely for you to let me make the coffee. You're incredibly territorial about how your coffee is brewed. You must be distracted if you trust me to do it right."

Brinna smiled and realized her mom was right. But she was just too tired to argue over coffee and knew that whatever her mom gave her would be fine.

"Yeah, yesterday ranks up there among the worst days of my life. I almost got myself killed; I put myself out of commission by breaking my wrist, and by the time it's healed, Hero will likely be gone; and—" she sighed as she sat up and faced her mother—"my best friend's partner may be paralyzed for the rest of his life, and it's my fault." As the words spilled out, the helpless feeling roared back with a vengeance.

"You can't blame yourself for what happened to Rick. Both of you took a chance. Both of you believed you were doing the right thing for the person in trouble at the time."

Brinna groaned. "That doesn't make me feel any better. In fact, I hate to admit it, and I'd never say this in front of Maggie, but I'd probably do the same thing again. The result was, the girl is alive." Grabbing a pillow, Brinna hugged it to herself and rocked forward as pain gripped her chest in a vise. "Still, I can't help but think about Rick's family. He's got kids, a wife. This can't happen to him."

Rose stood and moved to the couch, sitting between Hero and Brinna and resting a hand on her daughter's shoulder. "I wouldn't wish that kind of injury on anyone. And I cringe inside when I think about some of the decisions you make.

But the bottom line is, in this case, by making a dangerous decision, the two of you succeeded in saving a life. Second-guessing the consequences of that decision will get you nowhere."

The coffee beeped its completion, and Brinna sucked in a breath, fighting for all she was worth to hold her composure. *I've cried enough today. If I start again, I might not stop, and it will solve nothing.* She flung the pillow aside and headed for the kitchen. "I need some caffeine," she called to Rose over her shoulder.

Hands shaking as she poured, Brinna considered her mother's words and her own thought process. She thought back to her smug response to Maggie after the Henry Corliss pursuit. She'd been proud of the fact that she'd beaten the odds, saved Nikki, and arrested Corliss without anything bad happening. Nikki was safe; that was all that mattered to her then. Now, today, Ivana was safe, but Rick had been crippled.

I don't feel so smug today.

How do I reconcile these two feelings? We kept her from ending up in the ocean. Could we have let her sweep by to her death?

Brinna knew the answer would be no for Rick, just like it was for her. Taking several deep breaths, she calmed some of the emotion raging within. Carrying her black coffee and a cup for her mother with cream and sugar, she went back to the living room.

Handing her mom the coffee, then taking a sip of her own, Brinna sat down again and picked up the conversation where they'd left off. "You're right, Mom, but that doesn't make it any easier. Why did this have to happen to Rick when he saved a life? It was a worthwhile risk, but why does the good guy have to get hurt doing the right thing?"

"I can't answer the why," Rose said softly. "I wish I could. But you know things happen for a reason. Even bad things. Maybe we can't see it now, but God is in control."

"Sometimes I think I get that, but other times . . ." Brinna threw her injured hand up and then flinched because the movement caused a stab of pain through her wrist. "I really want to ask God why he lets horrible things happen to good people."

"Ask. He answers." Rose smiled. "Bad things happen to everyone. No one by their behavior can store up any immunity from disaster or tragedy. All any of us can control is how we respond when tough times come. This does not diminish God or his sovereignty in my mind."

Brinna bit her lip and tried to wrap her mind around something she'd heard from her mother and her brother, Brian. She had to admit their faith seemed rock solid; they never freaked out, no matter what.

It came back to the defining incident of her life. Something she refused to let rule her life but something that was nonetheless always in the background. When she trusted herself to speak, she looked at her mother and worked to keep her voice level. "Why did he let me be abducted and molested? I was only six. How is a six-year-old supposed to respond to something like that?"

A stricken look crossed over Rose's face, and her shoulders stiffened. Letting out a breath of air, she swallowed and held Brinna's gaze. "I can only say this about what happened to you all those years ago. Look at how it has shaped you—made you compassionate and caring, made you the crusader for children that you are, and made you willing to lay your life on the line for others." Rose wiped the tears that began to spill down her cheeks.

"When I became a parent, I wanted to shield my children from every pain. I'm sure when you have kids, you'll feel the same. That one incident proved to me how truly powerless I was in that regard. But as horrible as it was, and as much as I wish it had never happened, I can't deny that some good has come from it. And for the good, I thank God." Rose sniffled and grabbed some Kleenex.

A lump grew in Brinna's throat, and she looked away. The doorbell saved her from further confrontation. She rose to answer it, wishing under her breath for good news on this dark day.

25

Brinna opened the door to a beautiful bouquet of flowers.

"Brinna Caruso?" the delivery woman asked.

"That's me," Brinna answered, surprised almost to the point of speechlessness. She was conscious of her mother's presence behind her.

"Oh, Brin, they're beautiful. Who are they from?" Rose inquired.

"There's a card, if you'll just sign here." The woman pushed a clipboard at Brinna.

Brinna handed the flowers to her mother so she could sign for the bouquet.

"Enjoy," the delivery woman said as she left.

Back inside the house, Rose placed the arrangement on the dining room table, plucked out the card, and handed it to Brinna.

"You haven't mentioned anyone in your life lately," she said, managing to sound hurt.

"That's because there isn't anyone. I have no clue who these are from." She studied the envelope and frowned.

"Only way to find out is to open the card," her mother said impatiently.

Rolling her eyes, Brinna did just that.

To Brinna, the Kid Crusader, from Dave the paramedic. I hope your aches and pains heal quickly, and you're back on the job soon. All my best, Dave.

"Dave the paramedic?" Her mother regarded her with raised eyebrows.

"Yeah, he took me to the hospital yesterday. I've met him a couple of times. He's a nice enough guy, but we've never gone out or anything."

"From the look of this bouquet, he'd like to change that."

"Oh, don't jump to conclusions. He's probably just being nice." Brinna waved her cast toward her mother with a nonchalance she wasn't sure she felt. Dave was cute, no denying that, but when it came to flowers, she found herself a bit disappointed that they weren't from Jack.

"Harrumph" was Rose's response.

Brinna glared at her mother only to have any reply interrupted by a second assault on the doorbell.

"What now?" She set the card on the table and answered the door. Jack and Ben stood on her porch.

"We were in the neighborhood, visiting all the sick, lame, and lazy cops in the area," Jack teased with a grin.

"Ha-ha. The fat, dumb, and happy detectives visiting the

sick, lame, and lazy? Sounds like the start of a fairy tale to me. Especially since your shift is over." She stepped aside and invited them in.

"You know the saying—no rest for the weary." Jack chuckled.

"Didn't know you had company." Ben nodded to Rose. "Hello, Mrs. Caruso. We can come back if this is a bad time."

Brinna made a face and waved her hand. "It's my mom, not company. You guys want coffee?"

"Coffee is always welcome, and today I feel as though I've had five gallons," Jack said. "Nice to see you, Mrs. Caruso."

"It's good to see you both, and please, it's Rose. Stop making me feel like the middle-aged matron I am," Rose said. "I'll get the coffee. You guys have a seat." She cast a glance at Brinna. "Since my daughter never gives me much insight into her life, I think I'll enjoy hanging around and eavesdropping for a bit."

As her mother headed for the kitchen, Brinna shrugged. "I don't mind if you hang out, Mom. You always find ways to get insight into my life anyway. At least today it will be firsthand and not what you manage to wring out of Maggie." She motioned for Hero to get off the couch, and Ben and Jack sat down.

"I'm guessing your visit has to do with Ivana," Brinna observed as she relaxed in the recliner.

"Good guess," Jack said, accepting a cup of coffee from Rose. Rose then pulled a chair from the dining room and joined them.

"Ivana is the girl Brinna pulled from the flood control?" Rose asked.

Jack nodded and looked to Brinna.

"You can fill her in," Brinna said.

Jack gave Rose the Reader's Digest version of everything they knew about Ivana so far. Brinna noted that even though he was gentle, Rose was understandably horrified.

"We figure the odds are good that Alice is Ivana's missing sister." Jack turned to Brinna when he finished updating Rose.

Brinna sucked in a breath, hoping they wouldn't ask her to break the news. "I considered that connection as well. Too close a description."

"We didn't want to hit her with it while she was in the hospital, but once she's out, we'll put together some pictures and hopefully get a positive ID," Jack continued.

"How much more horrible can this get for that poor girl?" Rose interjected. "Just when I think I can't be disgusted any more by the evil in this world, I am."

Jack gave Rose a look that said he understood and agreed. "I don't want to inflict any more indignity on her by putting together a weak case."

"Amen," Ben agreed.

"Right now Ivana is our only witness to the traffickers and, if Alice turns out to be her sister, our only connection to Alice and perhaps to a murderer. We'd like to keep her accessible," Jack explained.

"ICE wants her in a women's shelter since their addresses are closely guarded," Ben continued. "You know how that works. Keeping her whereabouts secret is important for her safety, but we might have a difficult time getting to her when we need her."

"I can see that," Brinna agreed. "But what does this have to do with me?"

"How'd you like a temporary roommate?" Jack asked.

Brinna's eyebrows arched, and she searched the two detectives' faces for signs they were pulling her leg. She saw none.

"Me?" She pointed back to herself with her thumb. "You want me to let her stay here?" The suggestion caught her by surprise. She'd felt a connection to Ivana and would do everything in her power to catch the bad guy, but she was totally out of her element with the thought of having to nurture the girl.

"ICE is overworked and stretched thin. I have to believe that they would be okay with having her stay here. Chuck is checking for us. Strictly speaking, your house is a nongovernmental entity. And you're off work for a bit, so this would be a perfect place to stash her." Jack looked around the living room.

"Yeah, but I'm not sure I like the idea of being a Holiday Inn. I—"

Rose cleared her throat, and the trio looked her way. "I have a nice spare guest room. There's nothing I'd rather do with my home and free time than make a poor, abused girl welcome and comfortable." Rose smiled, her tone pleasant, nothing in what she said meant as a chastisement for Brinna.

"You?" Brinna leaned forward and stared at her mom. She knew her mother liked to have people stay in her guest room, but this girl was the victim of a serious and brutal crime.

"Of course. I'm very nongovernmental. Since your father died, I've had several houseguests the church has sent over. I house missionaries home on furlough, so I'm used to taking care of strangers. I'd be more than happy to offer safe haven to this young woman."

Brinna sat back and watched as Jack and Ben exchanged glances. She could tell they were considering the idea as a positive solution. She almost objected and then wondered why the proposal bothered her. Ivana did need to be accessible and safe. And she would be more comfortable in her mother's guest room than on a couch in Brinna's living room.

"Thanks, Rose," Ben said. "That's something we hadn't considered. We'd need to run it by Chuck. We could put a decoy up in a shelter and then send Ivana to you through the back door."

"Actually," Brinna cut in, "it's a great idea. Tracy Michaels has my address, and everyone knows that once a reporter knows something, there's a good chance other people do too. My mom's place will work much better."

"Of course it will work." Rose preened and Brinna stifled a chuckle. Rose would be in her element fussing over a guest in her home. "And I'll get everything ready as soon as I get home tonight."

"Mom, make sure you consider that this could be a long commitment," Brinna said, "and we really know nothing about this girl. Be comfortable with every aspect before going forward with this."

"The only thing that's important to me is the one concerning Ivana's well-being. I very much want to help." Rose held Brinna's gaze, and Brinna saw peace and resolve reflected there. Oddly, that one look gave Brinna peace as well. Suddenly she knew. The best place for Ivana would be with Rose Caruso.

She smiled and nodded at her mother.

"By the way, we got a lead on that blanket you found." Jack's voice took her thoughts away from Mom, and she gave him her full attention. "There's a possible vendor down in Shoreline Village."

"Shoreline Village?"

"A place called Black Sea Folk Art and Collectibles. Ever heard of it?"

Brinna shook her head, but her mother spoke up. "I have. I've been there several times," Rose said, frowning. "It has a lot of interesting knickknacks. You don't think they're involved in this horrible trafficking mess, do you?"

"We're not sure. We stopped by on the way over here, but the owner wasn't there. We left a card and hope she'll contact us tomorrow."

"Even if the killer bought it at this shop, it doesn't necessarily mean the shop is involved," Brinna told her mother.

"I certainly hope not." Rose rubbed her hands together. "I've met the owner. She's a lovely woman. I couldn't imagine her being involved in anything this distasteful."

"Sometimes appearances are deceiving." Jack shrugged. "I never take preconceived notions with me into an interview. We'll see what she has to tell us. Hopefully it will be a useful lead that points us to the killer."

26

MAGDA'S EYES BURNED from reading the computer screen. She rubbed her temples, trying unsuccessfully to erase the headache pounding there. She'd perused every government website she could find, wanting to ascertain what the lost girl's status would be. While she had absolutely no intention of helping Simon retrieve the girl, she needed to know if there was any way she could use the girl's status to her advantage.

She'd already made one call, an anonymous tip to the embassy, and fear crawled through her belly because of that. Paranoia from the time Communism permeated her country lurked in Magda's consciousness. She remembered as a girl listening to her father talk about how there were no secrets from the government. Their eyes and ears were everywhere, especially where you least expected it, he'd said. Magda had never seen the American government as threatening. But if they somehow discovered she was the one who'd called and then Demitri found out . . . She shivered at the thought.

She'd learned what the authorities called the crimes Demitri committed: *human trafficking*. She was familiar with the concept. Anton had a cousin who'd been lured from her small, squalid village to the brothels of France two years ago. He'd spent months trying to help the girl's family find her and bring her home.

The French authorities were no help. They seemed to turn a blind eye to information that the trafficking of human beings might be occurring in their country. Even so, they did locate the girl for the family but took her word that she had come to the country willingly, never considering that perhaps she'd been coerced. Finally Anton began spreading money around and smoked out someone who was able to help. He ended up buying the girl's freedom and sending her home, but she was never the same. She died of a drug overdose within months of arriving back in her native country.

More guilt infused Magda. She'd tried to ignore the broader implications of her involvement with Demitri, but it was all punching her in the face at the moment. She feared the strain would tear her apart before anything could be resolved.

27

First thing Tuesday morning Brinna reported to occupational health. The note they gave her said she'd be off work for at least three weeks. After that time she would be reevaluated and perhaps given a modified duty position until the doctors released her for full duty. She tried not to think about Rick, still stuck in the hospital, as she considered her forced hiatus.

What it meant to Brinna was that she had even less time to work with Hero, if, in fact, she did lose the grant. Stepping into the sunshine in front of the OH office, she took a deep breath and forced herself to look at the glass as half-full. The grant funding could stay in place. She punched in Sergeant Rodriguez's number as she walked to her car.

"Brinna, good to hear from you. How's the arm?"

"I'm off duty for three weeks, per occupational health."

"Sorry to hear it, but do try to rest. Don't go off on any searches; you might hurt yourself worse since you're not 100 percent."

"I wasn't planning on doing any searches, but I was wondering if you'd heard any more about Hero's grant money."

"Not a word, sorry."

Brinna thanked her and hung up, disappointed on one hand, but energized by the fact that now she'd have extra time to help Jack and Ben, even if her help was unofficial. She climbed into her car for the ten-minute drive to the station.

The occupational health paperwork needed to go to personnel. Once that task was done, Brinna wished she could turn around and go home. But even before hearing from OH that morning, she'd gotten a call from internal affairs. It was time to face the music for ignoring Lieutenant Harvey's order when she chased Corliss. After leaving the paperwork at personnel, she would meet a union rep at IA, where she'd hear the entire complaint against her and be interviewed about the incident.

I'll just tell them the truth, Brinna thought. *I'm not ashamed of the outcome, and if there are consequences for my actions, so be it.*

* * *

Magda nearly fainted when she saw the note left for her at the cash register. She'd arrived to work late after being up most of the night and had had to call a clerk in to open for her. The business card with the Long Beach Police Department logo might as well have been a dagger in her chest.

They know, her mind screamed as she sank into her desk chair, heart pounding. She clutched her chest and tried to calm down so she could think.

How could they know? she asked herself finally and

concluded that, in spite of her fright, they couldn't. The card must just be some horrible coincidence. The note her clerk had left said only that the detectives dropped by to ask her some questions. They wanted her to call and let them know when the most convenient time for them to contact her was.

Convenient time to talk to the police? Magda blew out a breath and grabbed a Kleenex to dab the perspiration from her forehead. It was not warm in the shop; she'd yet to turn on the heater. But the fright she'd experienced had caused her to break out in a cold sweat.

As her heart rate slowed and her thoughts cleared, Magda decided that this card, this request from the police, might work in her favor. Her mood brightened considerably as she thought that maybe she could use this police contact to her advantage. She just had to think carefully about what she would reveal when she called them back and most of all when they came to ask her their questions.

Conversely, it might not have anything to do with the poor girl who ran from Simon. It might be totally unrelated. *Then again, I was the one who placed the call to the Bulgarian embassy,* she thought. *What if they've discovered that?*

No, they couldn't have, she decided. She'd used a pay phone—the only one she knew of—and she'd had to drive to San Pedro, where she paid cash. They couldn't know it had been her.

Magda stood and straightened her skirt. *No matter. Whatever comes, I will find a way to work this to favor me. I knew when I called the embassy that there was no turning back. Now I will ride the wave my action has created.*

28

Sergeant Sutton, the internal affairs investigator assigned to Brinna's case, read the complaint filed by Lieutenant Harvey while Brinna and Maria, her peer representative, listened. It was long, but the part that bothered Brinna the most was the summary of the most recent incidents at the end. "'Officer Caruso shows a consistent disregard for the chain of command. We witnessed that three months ago when she took off against orders, and we saw it again a week ago when she disobeyed my direct order to terminate a pursuit.'"

"No formal complaint was filed regarding that incident with the twins," Maria jumped in, but Brinna barely heard.

Consistent disregard.

That stung because she considered herself a disciplined cop, a good cop. But a good cop did not show "consistent disregard."

"Yes, I was getting to that. What happened three months

ago is not an issue here," Sutton was saying. "When Lieutenant Harvey issued the order to terminate the pursuit, what did you do?"

"I turned off my siren—not right away, but I did eventually turn it off. But I kept following."

"Were you obeying traffic laws?"

"My focus was on the fleeing sex offender. I didn't look at my speedometer," Brinna said truthfully. "I did stop for stop signs and red lights, unlike Corliss."

"You did not terminate the pursuit?" Sutton asked.

As painful as the whole truth was, Brinna had to tell it. "Technically, no."

Sutton sat back in his chair. "Tell me everything from your perspective, beginning to end."

Brinna took a deep breath and related the entire incident, beginning with the dispatch that told her Corliss had just kidnapped a little girl a couple hours previous.

Sutton nodded, took notes even though the session was taped, asked one or two questions for clarification, and let Brinna talk. When she finished, he noted the time the interview ended and turned off the recorder.

Brinna and Maria both stood, and as they turned to leave, Sutton said, "While the lieutenant's complaint is broad, the only incident we are concerned with here is the pursuit of a week ago. You'll receive a letter of the disciplinary board's findings, and any discipline, in about a week."

Brinna left internal affairs feeling a little wobbly. It bothered her that Harvey seemed to have a problem with her entire career, a career she believed she'd spent doing good. Harvey was out for blood, bringing just about every action Brinna had ever taken into question.

Sutton she couldn't read, but he had a reputation for being fair.

Am I such a hothead? Such a rogue? she asked herself, and an answer popped into her head immediately. *I'm a good cop, aggressive but good.*

How do you get from aggressive to "consistent disregard"? Anger swelled as the full weight of Harvey's complaint sank in, and she looked at Maria.

"It sounds like Harvey wants my head," she said as they stepped onto the elevator.

"Yes, it does," Maria concurred. "But ultimately the decision is the disciplinary board's and the chief's. The chief will be sure to study both sides. And there is a lot going for you. You've never been in trouble like this before, and no one is going to consider other incidents that have never been formally addressed."

"I just want to protect kids," Brinna said between gritted teeth as she leaned against the back of the elevator.

Maria smiled. "I know that. I also know that most good cops bend the rules from time to time. It might not be right, but it happens. It's difficult for hard chargers to pull back sometimes. Harvey is by the book. He wants the letter of the law obeyed; remember that."

When the doors opened on Maria's floor, she paused before she stepped out. "A word to the wise, Brinna. Everyone knows how important these kids are to you. Well, chain of command is just as important to a police organization.

Unless the order is unlawful, we're supposed to obey." She leveled her gaze at Brinna before exiting the elevator. "Even the Kid Crusader. Got it?"

Brinna nodded. As the doors closed, she sagged against the back of the elevator. *Chain of command and rules* are *important,* she thought. *I agree. Where am I going wrong?*

She'd intended to go home but leaned forward and hit the third-floor button, deciding to get off on the homicide floor and see if Jack was in. *I really want to talk to Maggie, but she hasn't returned any of my calls, and I'm out of options.*

Her spirits lifted as soon as she saw Jack at his desk. His face brightened with a smile when he looked up and caught her eye.

"Hey, nice surprise. To what do I owe the honor?"

"I've been to occupational health and to internal affairs, so I thought I'd cap the day off with a friendly face." She slumped in a chair across from him.

"IA, huh?" Jack folded his hands in front of him. "Is this for jumping in the river?"

Brinna couldn't help the wry chuckle that escaped her. "No, something else."

"Something else?" Jack lifted an eyebrow. "Sounds like we can't put off lunch any longer. I have time now; do you?" He stood and grabbed his jacket.

"I knew it was a good idea to come visit you." Brinna grinned.

Together they left the police station and walked to a local coffee shop that served sandwiches.

Brinna ordered ham and cheese while Jack chose pastrami.

They found a table by the window and sat with their sodas and sandwiches.

"So tell me what happened," Jack said as he unwrapped his sandwich. "I've heard rumors there was drama, but I try not to pay attention to rumors."

Brinna sighed, took a fortifying sip of her Diet Coke, and then launched into the story of the Henry Corliss chase.

Jack rubbed his chin after she finished. "I can see why you kept going, but I can also see why Harvey is so upset."

"I know we had his address and there was no place for Corliss to hide, but the girl was in immediate danger. Corliss's MO said he'd take his victim to a remote location to molest her. And these guys generally get progressively more violent, so it could have been worse for Nikki." Brinna leaned forward, suddenly feeling as though it was important that Jack agree with her.

"Hey, I'm just saying I can understand both sides." He held his hands up. "I might have even done the same thing you did, but that doesn't mean we aren't both wrong."

Brinna blew out a frustrated breath and sat back in her chair while he went on.

"Harvey aside, think of how horrible you would have felt if Corliss had crashed and the girl were seriously hurt or killed," Jack said. "Yes, it turned out okay—this time. But, Brin, after we found the twins, you promised to stop thinking it was all up to you, remember?"

"Yes, I remember and I agree, but . . ." She placed both hands flat on the table. "Let's say it was you, and you were given the order to stop. How could you live with yourself if, by stopping, you allowed the guy to molest and murder the girl?"

"That might not have been the outcome. We had a BOLO out on Corliss; his face was plastered everywhere. He couldn't hide."

"So you would have stopped and just *hoped* someone else got him?"

"Honestly, I would have prayed that someone else stopped him. I would have prayed with all my heart that God would intervene."

Brinna sat back. "I'm trying to learn how to do that—honest, I am. Why is it so easy for you and so hard for me?"

Jack smiled the smile Brinna had grown to love, then reached across the table to grip her hand. Warmth spread through her entire body from his touch.

"Just keep working on it. I promise it will click."

For a long second their gazes held. Brinna felt such a strong connection to him; his eyes held hers, and she felt strength and comfort there.

"Then I promise to keep trying," she said. "You and my mom keep saying the same things; you can't both be wrong."

Jack laughed and took his hand away, but his touch lingered. "We're both right. Because we have faith that God loves us and wants the best for us and he listens to our prayers. Brin, sometimes bad things happen in our lives. I think I know that better than anyone." He paused and sipped his soda. She knew he spoke of the death of his wife, who was killed by a drunk driver.

"I don't have to remind you—you know it as well as I

do. The point is, though painful, these things often make us stronger." He played with his straw. "Adversity is not always a bad thing. You seem to think life should always be hearts and flowers."

"Guilty. I don't like seeing innocent people hurt by bad people. I admit I sometimes still get angry with God; he should stop the bad."

"But that works both ways. If he is a good God, why would he stop something in your life that will make you stronger, make you a better person?"

Brinna considered this argument she'd just heard from her mother. Her mentor, Milo, used to say the same thing a different way: *That which doesn't kill you will make you stronger.* She felt close enough to Jack to ask the question that popped into her head.

"Do you believe that your wife's death has been something that made you stronger, a better person?"

"Absolutely," Jack said without hesitation, surprising Brinna. "I miss her every day, and I'd rather she'd lived, but I do know, as painful as losing her was, that God has my best in mind." He sighed. "Brinna, we can't see the whole picture, how our life will unfold, but God can."

29

Jack's phone rang before Brinna could respond. She could tell from his side of the conversation it had to do with her mother. They'd both finished their lunch, and she could admit she was disappointed that her time with Jack was almost over.

"News?" she asked when he disconnected.

"That was Ben. We got the okay from ICE for Ivana to stay with your mom. But it was a fight and it's temporary. None of their shelters have openings, and the hospital is preparing to release her. She has to go somewhere."

"What will the press be told if they ask?"

"The official information will be that a women's shelter has stepped in to house the girl. Your mom's name will not be on any paperwork. I've got to get back to the station."

"And I think I'll tell my mom; is that okay?"

They both stood.

"Absolutely."

"Thanks for lunch, Jack, and the conversation. I always appreciate what you have to say."

"My pleasure." He brushed her shoulder gently with his hand. "Let's do it again—soon."

They walked back to the station together, arms occasionally touching and Brinna feeling a tingle each time they did.

When they said good-bye, Jack promised he'd call with Ivana's release date and time.

Back in her car, Brinna found herself looking forward to another visit with her mother and was glad for the feeling. Not long ago she would have tried to shut her mom out. Now she was happy to have Mom in her corner, no matter what—and after IA she needed someone in her corner. Besides, Mom was taking a baking class and experimenting a lot with sweets. There was a good chance she'd have something scrumptious for dessert.

Brinna stopped by her house first and picked up Hero. He was full of energy, and she knew he'd appreciate a game of fetch in her mom's large backyard. She'd gotten approval to take him to K-9 training every week, in spite of her injury, in order to keep him sharp, but the next session wasn't for several days. She'd have to do some exercises with him at home. She could tell he was bored, and he'd appreciate just about anything.

Hero bounded up to her mother's front door, and Rose gave him the obligatory pats.

"What brings you by today?" Mom asked as she gave Brinna a kiss when she walked in.

"I have some news about the girl from the river."

"Good news, I hope."

"Depends. It's okay with Chuck and with ICE if she stays here, but it's only temporary. They can't find a bed at a shelter, so you are the best alternative until one opens up. Ben and Jack firmly believe she'll be more comfortable here than at a shelter. They hope it will help her relax and remember details that could help the investigation."

Rose chuckled. "That's all well and good, but I'm more concerned about her personal well-being than the investigation."

"So am I. I just happen to think both things are related. Won't her well-being get a boost if the man who victimized her is arrested?" Once in the house, Brinna inhaled and smiled. Mom was baking, and whatever it was would be delicious.

Rose shrugged and gave Brinna a half smile. "Yes, it will help her sense of well-being if that man is no longer a threat. But I'm also concerned about her spiritual health. You should know that."

"Yeah, I do. I just had a pleasant conversation with Jack about that. I hope the girl understands English well enough to get your message clearly." She then cut to the chase. "Smells great—what's cooking?"

She got the desired result. Rose loved cooking for her family now as much as she had when her husband was still alive and her children lived at home. She happily led Brinna to the kitchen for dessert.

"Have you had lunch?" Rose asked, and Brinna nodded. "Good. This is a cocoa cake with caramel. I was just about to glaze it."

"Smells like heaven. I love caramel."

"Start some coffee?"

Brinna nodded and set a pot to drip. She leaned against the counter and watched her mother drizzle caramel over a dark-colored cake. The entire kitchen smelled like a bakery.

When the coffee and the cake were both finished, Rose cut two slices while Brinna poured coffee. Together they sat at the table, and as they ate the cake, the conversation stayed on Ivana.

"The poor thing is scared to death of men," Brinna said. "Nonthreatening, homey surroundings may help her relax and begin to trust—us at first, and then Jack and Ben. If she realizes none of us mean her any harm, maybe she'll remember more information that can help the investigation."

"Being here, in a home—" Rose waved her hand around— "will help a great deal, and not just what she remembers regarding the investigation. From what you've told me, and what I've read about her in the paper, Ivana has been through so much. Being deceived into coming here, promised a job that never existed, and then being forced into prostitution, losing her sister." Rose shuddered. "She needs to know she has friends. Anyway, the guest room is ready." Mom cleared away the dirty dishes and refilled her coffee. "She'll probably need clothes, shoes, everything."

Brinna stared at her mom, realizing with a jolt that the gift of being hospitable was definitely not an inherited trait. "Uh, yeah, I guess I hadn't thought about that—or even that far ahead. You want to go shopping?"

Rose shook her head. "Not yet. The church has a huge

closet filled with donated clothes. First I'll pick up a few things, and then whenever she's comfortable, I'll take her there and we'll see what we can find in her size. When will she be released?"

"Jack is supposed to call with that information."

"By the way—" Rose smiled and put a hand on Brinna's shoulder—"I forgot to mention the article in the paper last week. It was a nice human-interest piece. How does it feel to have a fan?"

Brinna frowned and then remembered. "Oh, Gracie." She sighed. "What a responsibility. Now I know how Milo felt."

"He never let you down, did he?"

"No" was what Brinna said out loud, but she couldn't help thinking, *Once. He let me down only once . . . when he took his own life.* "But how can I be sure I won't let Gracie down?" she asked her mom.

"You won't."

Brinna's cell phone rang and she jumped for it, suddenly embarrassed by the expression on her mother's face and the emotion that was threatening her own. "That's got to be Jack." She answered and was correct. As promised, Jack was calling to relay information about Ivana.

"She'll be signed out tomorrow, probably about eleven thirty. Chuck will meet you there to facilitate the girl's release." Jack's voice sounded strained. Brinna remembered that particular timbre from their time as partners. It had been there when he was hurting over the loss of his wife.

"Thanks for the information." She frowned. "What else is bothering you?"

Jack cleared his throat. "It will never cease to amaze me how perceptive you can be." He paused before continuing. "I hate to be the bearer of bad news, but it will be all over the local newscasts later today. This just came down from the chief. It's about Rick. . . . His spinal cord is severed; he'll never regain the use of his legs."

30

MAGDA PACED her small office, which was a confined achievement. Two steps one direction and one and a half the other. She'd called the detectives named on the card and now awaited their arrival. She'd also told Simon about the note and immediately regretted it. Afterward it took a good thirty minutes trying to calm him down.

The detective she spoke to was pleasant but wouldn't say what they wanted over the phone, so there was nothing Magda could tell Simon to put him at ease. Back home, Magda had considered all police to be corrupt, either in one organization's pocket or another's. A well-placed contribution in Varna would make just about any problem go away. But here in America, she'd tried to avoid that which she didn't understand, and that meant avoiding contact with the local authorities.

She remembered talking to Long Beach Police detectives after her husband's beating and the break-in at their home. They all seemed helpful, concerned, but she knew they could never get to Demitri before Demitri could assassinate her entire family, so she'd stayed quiet. One of them seemed to sense she was holding back information, but he'd never threatened or frightened her in any way like a Bulgarian officer might have.

Sighing, she stepped out into the showroom and stood by the window. They'd be here soon, and then, as the Americans said, for Magda it would be showtime.

*　*　*

"I've found one entry on our database for the shopkeeper, Magda Boteva," Ben said as he and Jack prepared to leave for Shoreline Village.

"What's that? A traffic ticket?"

"Nope, a home invasion robbery from two years ago. It's still open. Want to walk down to robbery and see if they remember it? Welty was the primary."

"Darryl Welty?" Jack asked, happy with the news. Welty was one heck of an investigator. He'd be able to give them good insight on this Magda if he'd spoken to her after the robbery.

"Yep. You ready?"

"Let's go."

They took the stairs down to the robbery office and found Detective Welty at his desk.

"Black Sea Folk Art and Collectibles." Welty sat back in his chair and rubbed his chin. "Good-looking Bulgarian woman, Magda. She kind of reminded me of Angelina Jolie in a mature, understated way. I remember that case." He turned to his computer and punched up a screen that allowed him to recall crime reports. In a few minutes all three detectives were scanning the narrative of a home invasion robbery report.

"Seems Mrs. Boteva came home from work to find her house ransacked. Some jewelry missing but not worth enough money for all the damage that was done. The worst of it were her two kids and her husband, Anton. He was severely beaten, then left in the living room trussed up like a Thanksgiving Day turkey. The kids—twins, as I recall—were tied up and shoved into a closet. I think they were seven or eight at the time."

"Sexual assault?" Ben asked.

Welty shook his head. "No. In fact, other than being scared to death, the kids weren't hurt. The husband took the brunt of it. He was whipped with a belt; it laid his back open. But the attackers wore masks and never said a word."

"Leads?"

"Zip." Darryl held his hands out, palms up. "I always thought that scene looked more like a shakedown than a robbery."

"Shakedown? You mean, because of her business?" Jack asked.

"Maybe." Welty frowned. "It resembled a couple of cases I handled up on Anaheim, in the Vietnamese district. Asian gangs were shaking down merchants for protection money. They'd go after families all the time. You remember we had a rash of home invasions there. This Magda was so frightened. I had the feeling she knew more than she was willing to tell us."

"I'd be frightened too, if I came home and found my husband beat up and my kids traumatized," Jack observed.

"It was more than that. I'd have bet money she knew who was responsible for the crime. But whoever it was had accomplished what he wanted—scared her enough to keep her mouth shut."

"Did you look into the intimidation angle? Check to see if there was evidence she was being extorted?"

"Whenever I had time, for about a year after, I went back to that case. I looked at every lead I could. Her business is clean, on the up-and-up. Whatever the beating was about, it had nothing to do with that. What's going on with her now?"

"Her shop is connected to a homicide because of a piece of cloth we found at the crime scene. Nothing rock solid, though. Then there's the nationality angle." Jack explained about the dead girl.

Darryl rubbed his chin. "As I recall, Magda had a young Bulgarian girl working for her. Immigrant communities generally do stick together, so you might be on the right track. Just remember: over there, the cops are no better than mobsters. Pressing hard will get you nowhere. Time for good cop/good cop."

* * *

"You've been awfully quiet," Ben said as he and Jack drove to Shoreline Village.

"Just thinking about what Darryl said."

"About Magda and the break-in?"

"That, and about how Ivana was so scared of me and

162

Chuck. Both women come from a totally different culture. Like Darryl said, the cops are corrupt in a lot of those post-Communist countries. I hear the Mafia or the Eastern European equivalent has a lot of power over there. That angle might be playing here."

"Bulgarian Mafia?"

Jack hiked his shoulders. "I think we need to consider it as a possibility. And be prepared for this woman to play it close to the vest. If the mob is involved in some way, she'd sure have a reason to be frightened."

"I guess you're right. Unfortunately something else just popped into my head. Human trafficking would be just the kind of thing a Mafia-type organization would be involved with."

"And if Ivana ran away from the Mafia . . ."

"I'm way ahead of you. I'll call Chuck."

31

MAGDA SAW THEM get out of their car. Police detectives obviously, they were both tall and professional looking in suits and ties. She could tell they were armed, and she fought the rising panic in her chest. Glancing around the shop, she was happy for once there were no customers at the moment. Laura, her morning clerk, was busy dusting. She had been born and raised in Long Beach and had shown no alarm whatsoever when Magda had told her the police were visiting.

I should take my cue from her, Magda thought. *She doesn't fear these detectives; maybe I shouldn't either.*

"Laura, it looks like the police are here," she said.

An instant later the bell on the door jingled as the two officers walked through.

"We will be back in my office," Magda said. Laura nodded, and Magda turned to the officers. "Detectives O'Reilly and Carney, I presume?"

The taller one with dark-reddish hair answered. "Yes, I'm Jack O'Reilly, and this is my partner, Ben Carney."

They shook hands all around, and Magda found it hard to meet their eyes. In particular, O'Reilly's piercing gaze had such a searching look, she was certain he could see right through her.

"Can we go into my office? It's small but more private than talking out here in the shop."

The two men nodded and followed her back to her tiny office space.

Magda braced for their questions. "I will admit your call surprised me," she said as she sat, working hard to keep her tone light and unaffected. "How could I possibly help the police?"

"We've come across a few coincidences with a case we're working that originate in Bulgaria," O'Reilly said. "And since you import from Bulgaria and other parts of Eastern Europe, we're hoping you might help us clarify some things." He set a briefcase on her desk and clicked it open. "We found this at the scene of a crime." He held up a plastic bag containing a dirty piece of cloth.

Magda didn't have to take the bag or look closely; she knew what it was. The pattern, the colors, were unique to handwoven blankets she purchased in Varna, from a woman who worked for Demitri. There were none in stock now, but she knew that if she'd gotten blankets from the woman, so had Demitri. Her throat tightened as panic threatened to destroy her facade. She moved her hands to her lap, where the officers couldn't see them shake.

"Yes, I know it. I have sold such blankets in the store." She worked hard to keep her voice level. Neither neutral face gave any clue about the crime that involved the blanket or what her admission might mean to them. She saw nothing.

"Is there any way to trace the sales of these blankets?" the one named Carney asked.

Magda shook her head. "I don't see how. These blankets are made by an old woman. Each one is different; they are only marked with a flimsy 'Made in Bulgaria' tag. And I don't charge much for blankets like this. It's not unusual for me to give one away when someone makes a large purchase."

She watched as the detectives exchanged glances. Beneath her desk her fingernails dug into her palms.

"I also have some photos I'd like you to look at." O'Reilly laid the plastic bag on her desk, and Magda could clearly see what looked like blood on the fabric. When he placed a photo in front of Magda, she nearly screamed.

"Is that young woman . . . *dead*?" She felt the color drain from her face and hoped the detectives took it as shock at the photo and nothing else.

"Do you know her?"

Frantically Magda shook her head. A half-truth. She'd seen the girl with Demitri, but she never knew her name. "No, no. But what has happened to her? She looks brutalized." She jerked her eyes from the photo.

"We pulled her out of the river. Look closely, please. We have no idea what her name is, and she is a Bulgarian national."

Magda couldn't and didn't even try to conceal her surprise at that statement. How could a dead girl tell them where she was from?

"Bulgarian? How do you know this?"

"Actually, dental work told us. She was obviously a poor girl who saw dentists with limited resources. The plastic crowns gave it away. Look again at the photo," he prompted gently.

Reluctantly Magda lowered her eyes to the photo. After a long moment, she looked up again. "No, I don't know who she is."

"She also had a unique tattoo on her hip. I wonder if you've ever seen anything like this." He placed a picture of the rose tattoo Magda knew Demitri had designed. Her throat tightened. The day he'd shown it to her, he'd told her he marked all his girls with it. It was his brand, he'd bragged.

"I've seen this before," she began, not certain she could tell a bald-faced lie without giving something away. She might get away with another half-truth. "Back home, I think, but I'm not certain."

Again, the detectives exchanged glances.

"We have another photo to show you. This girl is alive. If you read the papers, you might have seen an article about her." O'Reilly fished around in his briefcase.

Here it comes, Magda thought, and she decided to face this head-on. "Are you speaking about the girl from the river? I read a short paragraph about her."

"Yes," O'Reilly said, sliding a third photo toward her.

Magda forced a concerned frown across her brow as she looked down at the photo. A young girl with pale-blonde hair and frightened blue eyes stared back at her.

"How is this girl related to the other . . . uh, the first girl you showed me?" she asked, hoping her face looked legitimately confused.

"They are both Bulgarian, and they both have the same tattoo," Detective Carney said. "Have you ever seen this girl?"

"No." This time there was no lie in Magda's answer. She had never seen this girl, but if she had Demitri's tattoo, she was certain this was the girl who had escaped from Simon.

"Well, thank you for your time. If you can remember exactly where you saw that tattoo before, or anything else you think might help, will you call us?" O'Reilly asked. Magda nodded, and he continued. "Do you mind if we show the photos to your clerk? Perhaps she might have seen one of the girls in your shop or know something about the tattoo."

"No, I don't mind. If Laura can help you, I would be grateful." Slowly Magda's panic subsided.

"Is she your only clerk?" Carney asked. "Do you have a clerk here who is Bulgarian?"

Again Magda worked to hide her surprise. "I have a total of five clerks, and yes, one is Bulgarian. But Anka is out of town right now." She sucked in a breath, thankful they would not be able to speak to Anka right away. "I can give you all their names if you need them."

"We will," O'Reilly said.

He and Carney asked her a few more questions about clientele and the local Bulgarian community while she wrote down the names and phone numbers of her clerks for them. Magda relaxed under that type of scrutiny. She knew nothing about a Bulgarian community in California, if there was one. When she'd moved to California with her family, she'd thrown herself into assimilating. Magda wanted to be American. It was the only subject she and Anton argued about. *"Be proud of your heritage,"* he'd say. *"It will be important to our children someday."* It wasn't that Magda hated Bulgaria; it was more that she wanted to embrace all that was American and instill in her children an appreciation of the optimism and opportunity she'd found in this great country.

She did breathe easier when O'Reilly pushed the piece of blanket back into his briefcase and closed it, leaving only the photos out.

"Thank you for your time," he said, and he and his partner headed out to speak to Laura.

Magda could only nod. Later, alone with her thoughts, she realized how gentle and professional the officers had been. There was no threat or implied threat in their interview, no hint that they wanted money.

Perhaps I can trust them, she thought. She tried to think of some way to get back to them, to implicate Demitri without in any way implicating herself. *I know now is my chance. And it may be my only one. I can't waste it.*

32

THE NEXT DAY, Brinna and her mother arrived at the hospital a little before eleven thirty. They'd stopped by Rose's church and picked up an assortment of clothing. Brinna had been amazed at the selection of clothes. She'd expected a bunch of ratty hand-me-downs but found instead a lot of trendy fashions. Some even had the price tags still attached. Ivana would be pleasantly surprised, she thought.

As they waited for the elevator, Brinna took a deep breath and made a difficult decision. The anger she'd felt after hearing about Rick had faded and been replaced with bitter guilt and regret.

"Mom, I'll meet you upstairs. I want to stop by and check on Rick, okay?" She didn't turn to face her mom, not wanting to see the sympathy there. The last thing Brinna wanted was to enter Rick's room choked up and teary. She'd kept her emotions in check while around her mom, and she certainly wasn't going to break down in front of Rick.

"A good idea, I think," Rose said. "Don't rush your visit.

You know that I have a lot of clothes for Ivana to try on, and it will probably take a while for her to decide what she wants to wear."

The elevator arrived, and Brinna hit floor number two for her and five for her mother. When she got off on two, there were several officers in the main waiting room—some in uniform and some in plain clothes. Brinna recognized most of them as guys from Rick's academy class. They were huddled over paperwork on a table, working on something. Jack had mentioned there was already a plan in place to make Rick's house wheelchair accessible.

That kind of thing was common in the police force. When an officer was hurt on duty, people stepped up to the plate quickly. Guys offered up whatever skills they had to make life easier for a wounded fellow officer. It was something that made Brinna very proud to wear the blue suit. Absentmindedly she fiddled with her cast, realizing she wouldn't be able to help with any manual labor. *I'll have to think of some other way to help,* she thought.

"Is he up for visitors?" Brinna asked one of the guys.

He nodded. "I think so. His wife is in there. His brother went out to get some lunch."

Brinna thanked him and walked down the hallway to room 243. Though the door was open, she knocked on the doorframe before entering. A female voice told her to come in.

Rick wore a thick brace, much like a body cast. What Brinna could see encased his chest up to his armpits and then disappeared under the blanket. His shoulders were bare and visible above the blanket. He was hooked up to various IVs and monitors, but his expression was calm, peaceful. *Drugs?* Brinna wondered.

She cleared her throat. "Hey, buddy, how are you doing?"

Rick's wife, Molly, was seated by the bed. They both smiled.

"Just laying around, Brin." In spite of his confinement, Rick's voice sounded strong and confident. "Actually, I'm doing well. I've gotten more feeling back in my arms, and most of the scrapes and bruises are healing." Brinna watched as Rick bent his elbows and wiggled his fingers.

Brinna grinned, hoping it didn't look plastic. "Great news!"

"I'll come back; I promise," he said. "Iraq didn't get me. Neither will the San Gabriel riverbank."

She cleared her throat, wondering at his upbeat demeanor. Jack had said the paralysis was permanent. Was he mistaken?

"I love hearing the confidence in your voice. How are you holding up, Molly?" Brinna stopped at the foot of the bed, meeting Molly's gaze.

"I have my husband. We can work through just about anything as long as we're together." She smiled and squeezed Rick's shoulder.

"I'm gratified you guys are so positive . . ." Brinna felt her throat clog and coughed to clear it. The guilty emotions she fought so hard to keep back threatened to overflow. "I wanted to . . . Well, gosh, Rick, I feel a lot responsible for what happened. I, uh—"

Rick stopped her with a wave of his hand. A frown crossed his brow. "Stop it. This wasn't your fault. I wanted to save that girl as much as you did. And we did. I'm proud of that. I have no regrets. Not one bit of regret."

Brinna couldn't speak or move, she was so afraid she'd lose it. He'd be confined for the rest of his life, and he didn't regret it.

Molly spoke up. "God has his hand in everything—we have to believe that. Nothing facing us will be easy, but we'll get through it and something good will come out of this."

Brinna nodded and wiped her eye with her good hand. She remembered Maggie talking about Rick and Molly going to church. She hadn't known that they were in the same league as her mother and Jack. But maybe that was a good thing. After all, their life from now on would never be the same, and her mother always said that faith helps people through the tough times.

According to Jack, a good God could make Molly and Rick stronger through this. *I hope that's what I'm seeing. They will need one another for the challenges they'll face in the future.*

"Do you need anything?" she asked when she trusted herself to speak. "Is there anything I can do for you?" She held up her cast. "I'm off work for a while, so I've got some free time."

"Thanks for the offer." Molly exchanged glances with Rick and then continued. "If we think of something, we'll ask. But the chief has released Maggie to hang out with us, watch the kids, that kind of thing. She's been a big help."

"By the way, where is Maggie?" She'd tried to call Maggie that morning; maybe that was why her friend hadn't answered.

"Babysitting," Molly said. "The boys are too young to

be allowed up here to see Rick right now. It's good knowing they're in Maggie's hands."

"Maggie loves kids." Brinna smiled. Maybe her friend wasn't mad at her after all.

"Hey, how's the girl?" Rick asked.

"She's doing okay. Her name is Ivana," Brinna explained. "In fact, that's why I'm here. This is confidential, but she's going to stay with my mom while we sort out her situation and wait for a spot in a shelter."

"I guess she's a pretty brave kid," Rick observed. "Maggie said she'd been trafficked here and ran away from a house where she was forced into prostitution. She's ready to leave the hospital?"

"Yes. Mom's upstairs with her now."

Rick's upper body shifted in bed and he frowned. "I can't blame her for jumping in the river. Would you do me a favor?"

"Anything."

"I'd like to meet her, put a face to the victim, and pray for her. When you think she's up to it, will you ask her if she'll come talk to me?"

Shrugging, Brinna could think of no reason to say no. "Sure. Right now she's wary of men; she's only opened up to women. She has about zero trust in the police. Once she learns she can trust us, I'll ask her."

"Great." Rick flashed a smile.

Brinna visited for a few more minutes, listening as Molly and Rick described the medical plan for him. When she left the room, bewilderment creased her brow. She seemed to feel worse about Rick's paralysis than he did. His life as he knew it was over, so how could he possibly have a positive outlook? She needed to speak to Maggie and hoped her friend would eventually return her calls.

33

IVANA WAS A WISP of a girl/woman. Her shoulder-length hair was blonde and stringy, her eyes a pale blue. A good three or four inches shorter than Brinna's five feet seven inches, she couldn't weigh more than 105. A bandage covered one side of her head where there'd been a gash. Her jaw, neck, and arms all bore bruises of varied colors and ages. She'd chosen a pair of jeans and a white cotton shirt to wear. She and Rose Caruso were trying to decide among the pairs of shoes Rose had brought with her when Brinna arrived.

Brinna raised a surprised eyebrow at the other people already there when she entered the room. Jack had said that Chuck would be there and he was, along with ADA Swift.

"Hello, Chuck, Counselor. Hope there aren't any problems."

Chuck smiled and shook his head. "Nope, we're here to ensure all goes smoothly for your mom. And to make sure Ivana understands her status. She's not a criminal; she's a victim."

"I'll do everything in my power to make her feel at home,"

Rose said, smiling at the girl. "I'm just amazed she speaks such clear English."

"Yeah." Brinna frowned. "Where'd you learn your English, Ivana?"

Ivana spoke without meeting Brinna's gaze. "The missionaries came often to the home where I was raised, the orphanage. I take the English classes."

"Imagine that," Rose said.

Brinna suppressed a grin. Her brother, Brian, was a missionary in South America. He'd talked once or twice about going to Eastern Europe but said the languages were difficult to learn. She could bet her mother was already thinking about how to get Brian involved in some way.

She switched her attention to Chuck. They'd worked together on many missing-child cases, and Brinna looked forward to working with him on this case as well. "Can we have a word?"

Chuck nodded and motioned to Swift. The three of them stepped out of the room.

"Will ICE want to talk to the girl at all?" Brinna asked.

"You worried about her immigration status?"

"Yeah, I guess I am."

"Don't be. Because Ivana is a victim, her immigration status is immaterial," Chuck said. "We don't want her to fear us, because we're going to need her help."

Swift spoke up. "We're hopeful there will be an arrest and prosecution in this case, and we'll need her testimony. She needs to clearly understand that there is no fear of deportation."

Brinna nodded. "Will do." She turned to go back into the room, but Chuck held the door closed.

"Before we go back inside, Brinna, I need you to be aware of something."

"What is it?" Brinna asked.

"We're working a new angle on this case," Chuck began. "It's possible there's an organized crime involvement with the girl. Jack and Ben have suspicions, and I spoke to an agent I know back East. It seems they've had quite a big problem with the Russian Mafia and human trafficking back there."

"Russian Mafia? Is my mom in any danger?" Anxiety stabbed at Brinna with an intensity she wasn't prepared for.

"Don't jump ahead," Swift cautioned. "This is only a theory. We have no solid proof of a connection at this time, but we're looking at all angles."

"We've taken the steps needed to ensure your mom's name and address stay out of the loop. An acceptable shelter bed could open up at any moment, but in the event Ivana is with your mother for an extended period, we'll keep tabs on them both, so tell your mom to expect a government car in the neighborhood," Chuck added. "Maybe not today, but for sure first thing in the morning."

"The most important thing right now is that we build a relationship of trust with Ivana," Swift observed. "You're the only person of official capacity that she will even look at, much less talk to."

"Yeah, I realize that." Brinna crossed her arms. "But if this arrangement puts my mom in danger, I'm going to want more than a government car in the neighborhood." She shot a pointed look at Chuck.

"Understood, and I'm working on it. You have to trust me to keep your mom safe, just like I trust you to gain that girl's confidence."

Chuck and Swift left, leaving Brinna alone with her thoughts. She stood outside Ivana's room for a moment. She'd never had any contact with organized crime. Other than the horrors she'd seen perpetrated on TV or read about in books, she had no frame of reference. Long Beach might have its crime problems, but the Mafia wasn't one of them. Could they really have reached an arm in here now?

* * *

After all the hospital release paperwork was signed, Brinna stepped back into the girl's room. She watched Ivana make final clothing selections and noted that Rose's friendly tone and motherly demeanor were more successful than any interview techniques Brinna knew for putting someone at ease. Though shy, Ivana responded to Rose in a very positive way. Brinna paid attention, knowing that it would only be by making the girl feel comfortable and safe that an environment of trust could flourish.

Ivana's face brightened as she picked out a pair of leather flats. She held them up and ran her hand over the top of them. A smile played on her lips as she slid them on and found they fit as if they were made for her. Rose then gave her a jacket to complete the outfit, and they were ready to leave.

"Are you hungry, Ivana?" Brinna asked. "We can stop somewhere and pick up lunch on the way home."

Ivana looked at Rose and shrugged shyly. Rose placed a hand on the girl's shoulder. "It's okay. Remember you're with friends. I'd guess that you're hungry. We're taking you out of here as lunch is being served. Do you have a favorite food?"

Nodding, Ivana said in a soft voice, "I would like to try something American. And thank you. You are very nice."

"Why don't we try that new barbecue place in Seal Beach," Rose suggested. "I've heard only good things about it, and barbecue is very American."

"Good choice," Brinna agreed.

They left the hospital with Rose draping an arm over Ivana's shoulder in a protective manner. Brinna fought a strange uneasiness as she looked around the busy parking lot. *Organized crime*—those two words had really spooked her, and she wondered if they were being watched. Almost as quickly as the thought entered her head, she felt foolish. They'd reached the section of parking lot where the car was when Brinna's cell phone rang, interrupting her paranoia episode. She opened it, hoping it was Maggie.

"Hey, Brinna." The unfamiliar voice caught her off guard.

"Hello?"

"It's Dave the paramedic, just calling to see how you're feeling today."

"Uh . . ." Brinna fumbled for words. David's sudden interest in her took her by surprise. And all she could think was *Jack*. "Hi, Dave. I'm okay. Up and around, anyway. Thanks very much for the flowers, by the way—they were beautiful." Brinna turned away from her mother's inquiring gaze.

"No problem. The sentiment was sincere; I hope you get back to duty soon. I was wondering if you'd be interested in going out to lunch or having coffee sometime."

"Uh . . ." She paused. Lunch with Jack the other day had been awesome, but had he made peace with his wife's death? "Thanks for asking, David. Not sure about that. Right now I'm a little tied up."

"That's fine. I'll call you in a couple of days. Maybe then we can set up something."

"Okay, bye." Brinna closed the phone, knowing she was blushing under her mother's scrutiny. David was a nice guy from what she'd seen. But as she stood, phone in hand, she realized that his invitation had only served to cement the fact that she wanted Jack to be the guy she dated.

"The guy who sent the flowers?" Rose asked.

Brinna nodded as they reached the car. They'd come in her mother's since it had a more comfortable backseat than Brinna's truck.

She didn't say anything further so as not to fan the flames of her mother's imagination, just opened the door and motioned for Ivana to hop in the back.

Rose was quiet as she got into the passenger seat, but Brinna knew she wasn't going to let the matter drop. It was going to be a long afternoon.

34

"What do you think?" Jack asked Ben as they got back into their plain car.

"She's hiding something." Ben confirmed what Jack had surmised.

"I agree." Jack thought about the way Magda's face had blanched when she saw the first two photos, Alice and then the tattoo. It could have been shock over the girl's appearance, but he doubted that was the only reason. "I'd bet money that she knew Alice, and she knows something more about that tattoo."

"Yep," Ben agreed. "But how to dig that out of her? We have nothing but the tenuous link of a blanket."

"Not sure, but I think we played it right by not pressing too hard today. This is one person we'll definitely get more out of with sugar."

Ben nodded. "We should see if Ivana is ready to talk to us. She might know about Magda and this shop. And it's time we got a positive ID on Alice. Make sure she is, in fact, Ivana's missing sister. If it turns out she's not, the investigation might go an entirely different direction."

Jack pulled out his phone. "Good idea. I'll call the hospital and see if she's been released yet." He punched in the phone number and quickly discovered that Ivana had left. It gave him another excuse to talk to Brinna, maybe spend some time with her. "Ivana is with Brinna's mom now. Let's give her a little time to get settled in. I'll call Brinna later today."

* * *

Magda fled the shop after she was sure the detectives were long gone. Her cell phone rang several times, all calls from Simon, but she had no desire to talk to him at the moment. She rubbed her clammy palms together, then yanked a handkerchief from her pocket to dry them. Her hands shook, and her heart felt as if it would race from her chest. She wasn't certain she'd convinced the officers of anything. And she wasn't sure she wanted to. There had to be some way she could point them to Demitri without Demitri knowing the tip came from her.

But how?

Magda strode purposefully along the walkway that paralleled the marina. There was a chill in the air and a strong onshore breeze, but no rain. Magda felt nothing. Her golden opportunity was here, and she couldn't figure out how to make the most of it.

How can I say I know who killed the girl? And that I know the same man brings many girls here and exploits them? And I help him? He uses my legitimacy to enhance his illegitimate endeavors. She stopped at the end of the walkway and leaned her elbows on a railing. The ocean was dark-blue and choppy, and the sting of salt was in the wind.

If I weren't a coward, if I weren't so afraid for my family, I would tell the truth and Demitri be damned. Memories of the day Magda had been told that both her parents were dead and she was alone in the world played in her consciousness. She survived that day because she was young and fearless. But youth disappears with time, and fearlessness fades when one realizes just how much there is in the world to fear.

She knew she couldn't survive a loss like that again; she couldn't bear losing her family to Demitri. *I've come to see him as invincible,* she thought. *Maybe there is no chink in his armor.*

As her tears began to fall, Magda felt her golden opportunity dwindle away like foam on a whitecap. Demitri's grip grew stronger, as if he were next to her, hands around her throat, squeezing the life from her body. Her hand came to her mouth to stifle a sob as the realization hit that she was powerless to do anything.

35

ONCE THEY ARRIVED in Seal Beach, Brinna drove down Main Street to Ocean and turned slowly, giving Ivana time to look at the ocean, the beach, and a little of the town. Ivana wanted to get out into the sunshine but admitted to being tired and not up to it at the moment. Brinna was glad for that because ever since they'd left the hospital, she felt uncomfortable with the idea of the girl out in the open. Though there was no real reason for the lingering paranoia at the moment, she trusted her instincts and just wanted to get to her mother's house and inside.

"How beautiful!" Ivana noticed the quaint wooden pier that extended from the end of Main Street out into the ocean.

"When you're feeling stronger, we'll take a walk out onto the pier," Rose promised. The two of them chatted about the sights.

Brinna doubted the girl would be with her mother long enough to include touristy things in the plan but said nothing.

Her mother had called in a take-out order while they drove, so once Brinna parked, she just had to walk up to the window and pay, and then lunch was ready. The food smelled great all the way to her mother's.

As they spread out the meal on her mother's table, Ivana seemed to blossom. Color returned to her face, splashes of rosy red on pale cheeks, and Brinna hoped bad memories were fading. The girl alternated from delight to wide-eyed wonder as they piled her plate high with tender brisket, tangy short ribs, sweet potato fries, and coleslaw.

Rose said a blessing and they enjoyed their lunch. As Rose told stories about church, Ivana giggled and for a bit seemed like a normal American teenager, not an abused and exploited young woman. Brinna couldn't stop her thoughts from drifting to all the kids she'd seen in her career who'd had their innocence shattered, including herself at six.

How many of us bounced back, able to deal with the scars and lead normal lives? she wondered.

I don't know what the future holds for Ivana, Brinna thought, *but I'll do everything I can to help her move on. My mom was right about one thing: what happened to me has helped me to be more empathetic. It also made me stronger, and I hope the same happens for Ivana.*

36

MAGDA HAD BEEN so preoccupied with the police, she'd forgotten that Anton planned to meet her for lunch that afternoon. The time was 12:30 on her watch, and she was halfway back from the end of the marina walkway when she remembered. Bringing a hand to her mouth, she uttered a frustrated grunt and stepped up her pace. Anton would arrive at the shop at one, and Magda had to freshen up so he wouldn't know she'd been crying. For a brief moment she wondered if the wisest course of action would be to tell Anton everything and enlist his help. But he knew nothing about Demitri and the loan—nothing.

As much as she wanted—no, *needed*—her husband's support in most aspects of her life, fear that Anton would despise her for taking Demitri's help had kept her quiet about the alliance all the years she had known Anton.

She'd met her husband in Varna, where her first shop flourished. He wasn't Bulgarian; he was Albanian. Retired from the army after losing his left leg to a land mine, he'd come to the seaside village of Varna to recuperate. He was hurt and alone, and that appealed to Magda. Their relationship blossomed to love quickly.

Now he spent his time caring for their children while Magda supported the family. The arrangement worked perfectly for both of them. Anton was a pillar of strength in the home for Magda. She couldn't bear to disappoint him and tell him that he was beaten and humiliated and their children endangered because of a choice she'd made so many years ago.

I've put our family's very existence in peril and have stood by and watched as Demitri brutalized other people's children. The despair rose so thick in her throat, Magda nearly choked. Swallowing the tightness, she fought for control, fingernails digging into her palms. *The crying must stop, and I must be composed before Anton arrives.*

Slowly she felt a calm smoothing over the panic and guilt. Anton did that for her. Because of his very presence, she could believe that everything bad would, ultimately, be all right.

And then she reached the shop, only to see a man waiting for her at the door. But it wasn't Anton. It was Simon.

Here was the source of her angst, at her doorstep, much too close to the time Anton would arrive. Magda nearly screamed, the sight too much to bear just now. Panic jolted her as she knew she could never explain Simon if Anton arrived early. She must get rid of him. Fast.

"I have called and called. Why haven't you answered?" Simon demanded, striding toward her.

"I haven't had the time," she hissed, motioning him away from the front of the shop. "What are you doing here?"

"I need to know what the police wanted." He gripped Magda's shoulders, and she saw the fear in his eyes. "Time is running out. You must help me."

Magda ripped away from his grip. "I'm trying to help. But you can't haunt my shop like this. You have to give me an opportunity to think of a solution to this problem. And I can't think with your constant badgering."

Simon jerked a package of cigarettes from his pocket and uttered a string of curses in their native language as he pulled one out and lit it. Magda watched as he took a deep drag on the cigarette, shoved the pack back in his pocket, and blew out a puff of smoke.

"I'm sorry," he said after another drag on the cigarette, "but time is short. What did the police want?"

Magda folded her arms. "They not only asked me about the girl who ran away; they came to me about a dead girl. You told me nothing about a dead girl."

"A dead girl?" Simon groaned as if thoroughly distressed. "I didn't realize they had found her. That was Demitri!" He cursed some more. "I hate this. Demitri, he lost his temper with that girl." Pacing back and forth, sucking on the cigarette as if it were oxygen, he told her how Demitri had beaten the girl to death, then dumped her in the river, hoping the body would be carried out to sea and never recovered.

"I told him to be careful. He wouldn't listen. You know him, Magda; does he listen to anyone?" Simon stopped his pacing, and his tortured eyes held Magda's. She couldn't help feeling sorry for him. He was right. Demitri only listened to Demitri.

"The police knew that the two girls are Bulgarian, so they came to me." She left out the remnant of blanket. "They have connected them, and Demitri is solely to blame for that. He branded them both." She spit the last words out, and realization shone in Simon's eyes.

He swore. "This nightmare gets worse and worse. Has Ivana told them anything?"

Magda covered her ears. "No names! I don't want to know them. I don't want to be any more involved than I already am. And if the girl has told them anything, they did not tell me."

Simon rubbed his hands together and mumbled under his breath. "We tell the girls over and over again that they can't trust the local authorities and that they will be sent to jail for entering the country illegally. Since we keep their papers and prevent them from going anywhere, that is an easy thing to make them believe." He straightened his shoulders. "I have someone watching the hospital for me. When the girl is released, I will find out where they send her." Simon tossed the cigarette on the ground and smashed it with his heel. "Unless you have other ideas, I plan on getting her back. He should call soon." Immediately he lit another cigarette.

Magda sighed and shook her head. "Then you are on your own. I can't help you. I will not jeopardize my business and my life over this."

They stared at one another, and for a few seconds Magda feared Simon would force the issue. Then a light of understanding showed in his dark eyes, and he gave a slight tilt of his head. "Will you tell me if the police come back? If they make any more connections between the dead girl and Iv— uh, the one they found in the river?"

Magda frowned. "Is there another connection between the two girls besides Demitri?"

"The girls are sisters."

Magda blanched. The girl in custody would not stay quiet for long. Her sister was murdered, so how could she keep from telling the police what she knew? Everything in Demitri's organization would be exposed, including Magda.

"This is worse than I ever expected." She grabbed Simon's arm. "You must tell Demitri. Tell him to stay in Bulgaria. Then you and however many girls you have here must leave as well." Magda's mind raced. "He's ruined this place for his business; even he must admit that."

By staying away, Demitri might not get what was coming to him, but at least his reach to America would be severed.

"Are you mad? Demitri will not blame himself; he will blame me." Simon tore his arm from her grasp. "I would be signing my own death warrant. The only possible solution is that I get the missing girl back before she says anything."

Magda hugged her arms to her chest and shook her head vehemently. "Then I will not help you, and I demand you stay away from my shop. You've destroyed yourself. Please don't take me with you." She glared at Simon until he looked away.

Finally he stomped out his second cigarette and shoved both hands in his pockets. "Things were so much easier at home. The police could be bought with a minimum of trouble. I think Demitri made a mistake coming here. It may well be the end of him, but I can't be the one to tell him that." He turned on his heel and strode toward the parking lot.

Magda watched him go, fervently hoping that Demitri would realize he'd made a mistake expanding to the US. If there was a God in heaven, she prayed he'd let this incident forever sever the hold Demitri had over her.

37

Rose Caruso lived in a quiet section of East Long Beach. The family had moved to the house when Brinna was seven and her little brother, Brian, was five. Brinna thought that maybe her mother would downsize from the three-bedroom, two-bath house after her father died. But Rose wanted to stay in the house and use the space as an opportunity to help people who needed a temporary place to live. Brinna knew her mother liked company and enjoyed helping, and she also realized her mom needed someone to fuss over. Better others than her. Brinna's old room went from sewing room to guest room, and Brian's old room became the sewing room.

Ivana settled in quickly, thanking Rose over and over again for the spacious room that would be hers and the peaceful location of the house. Now certain that Mom's house would be the best place for Ivana to heal, Brinna decided it was time for her to head to her own home. She was about to leave when her cell phone jingled with a call from Jack. Ivana was in the bathroom when Brinna hung up.

"That was Jack," she told Rose. "He wants to come by and talk to Ivana."

"And? Your expression says there's more to it."

Brinna blew out a breath, conceding the fact that keeping anything from her mother was impossible. She glanced down the hall to make certain Ivana wouldn't hear her. "He's bringing pictures of the dead girl from the river—the one he thinks might be Ivana's sister. They have identical tattoos."

Rose grimaced. "I know it's important they identify the poor girl. But I can't help wishing for a different outcome." Wringing her hands, she continued. "At least I'll be here when she gets the news. I'll do my best to help her through this. Was there more?"

"Yeah, Jack hopes Ivana can describe Demitri so we can put out a press release with a sketch."

Rose settled in on the sofa. "That would be a good thing. What did you tell him?"

"That I'd ask you both. I know she's had a rough time, but the sooner we get the information out, the better chance we have of catching the creep."

"I agree. I hope she's not still too fragile. We'll ask—at least give her the chance to say yes or no."

A few minutes later Ivana joined them in the living room.

"Thank you, Mrs. Caruso. The room is beautiful."

"My pleasure. You are welcome here, and I want you to think of this house as your home. Help yourself to anything you want."

Ivana smiled. "Never in my life have I imagined such a

nice home. It would have been a place my sister, Villie, would have loved." Her eyes misted over.

Brinna saw her mother stiffen at the mention of Ivana's sister. Rose motioned for Ivana to sit on the couch. Once she was seated, Rose took the girl's hands in hers. "Ivana, another policeman wants to talk to you, to go over the statement you gave in the hospital. And to talk about your sister. He wants to come here. Do you feel up to talking to him?"

Ivana's gaze flitted from Rose to Brinna and then down to her hands. Brinna held her breath, hoping she wouldn't freak out. There was so much they needed to ask her, and the sooner the better.

Finally she nodded. "Yes, I will answer his questions." She looked up into Rose's eyes. "You'll stay with me while he is here?"

Rose smiled. "Of course. I'm not going anywhere."

Brinna called Jack and was told he would be right over. Ben opted to stay at the station because he didn't want Ivana to feel in any way intimidated or overwhelmed. In preparation for Jack's visit, Brinna went to her mother's kitchen and put some coffee on, checking her cell phone for messages while the coffee brewed, though she knew it hadn't rung.

Still no call from Maggie. Even if she was angry, it just wasn't like her chatty friend to ignore messages. Brinna punched in Maggie's number one more time and left a third message. After closing the phone, she said under her breath, "Call me, Maggie . . . please call."

The coffee had just finished when Jack arrived. Rose and

Ivana sat on the couch, where Rose had begun teaching the girl how to crochet.

"Glad to see you're feeling better," Jack said, smiling at Ivana. "The color has come back to your face. You look well."

Ivana returned the smile and nodded, but Brinna noted that she would not look Jack in the eye. She also kept a firm grip on Rose's hand.

Jack sat on the coffee table across from Ivana. He held his hands out, palms up. "I'm not here to frighten or intimidate you. I'm here to help you; I promise." He placed a digital recorder beside him on the table. "This interview will be taped so everything we say is recorded accurately."

Jack wore no cop face today. His expression was friendly and soft. It said, *You can trust me.* Brinna felt such a warmth inside as she watched him. He was professional and courteous, and she bet he could put anyone at ease. He started recording, first stating the date and time of the interview and persons present before he addressed Ivana.

"I'm afraid I have to start with some unpleasant business." He pulled a manila envelope out of his briefcase and opened the clasp but didn't take anything out. "I have a picture here of a young girl we found murdered about a week before you were pulled out of the river."

Brinna watched as Ivana stiffened perceptibly. For the first time since he'd come into the house, she raised her head and looked Jack in the eye.

"My sister, Villie?" she asked in a low but firm voice.

"I don't know. I need you to tell me," Jack said quietly. "The pictures aren't pretty. Are you ready to take a look?"

Ivana squared her shoulders and nodded. Jack took two pictures from the envelope and showed Ivana the top one. Her eyes closed and tears leaked out the corners.

"Yes, that is Villie, my sister," she said without hesitation. Rose put an arm over her shoulders and squeezed.

"I'm sorry, Ivana," Jack said, tone calm and soothing. "But now that she has a name and you are here to tell me what you know about what happened to her, we are that much closer to catching whoever did this to her."

"I understand, and I want to help." Ivana wiped the tears away with the back of one hand and again looked at Jack. "Demitri killed her; I'm certain." She held his gaze as he began to ask questions.

"What did Demitri do that you saw?"

"He beat her when she defied him. When girls defied him, he would take them from the house. He said it was to give them to a brutal man as punishment. This happened once before to Villie and she came back, but—" She sputtered and stifled a sob, and Jack gave her a minute before continuing.

As Brinna sat across the room and listened, she found herself surprised and impressed by Ivana's strength. The girl kept her composure as she told about their life in forced prostitution.

Brinna said nothing, not wanting to interfere or interrupt Jack's line of thought or questioning. She couldn't help but be inspired by his style. Jack was all about making Ivana feel at ease, and Brinna gave him points for being professional and nonthreatening.

"The tattoo that you both have." Jack pointed to a close-up of the rose tattoo. "What does it signify?"

"It was something Demitri insisted we all have done before leaving Bulgaria. He said it was his mark, and it was important that all his girls have one, whether they wanted one or not. I want to get mine off!" She made a fist and pounded the air.

Jack asked her about how they came to America, and Ivana explained that they first flew to Canada—Vancouver. It was still an adventure then. Demitri hadn't yet revealed his true intentions. In Vancouver they had boarded a ship. She and Villie and four other girls shared a square, window-less room on the ship. They were not allowed out until they reached California.

Ivana had to pause for a second. She asked Rose for some water. After drinking half a glass, she continued. The quarters were cramped and stifling and the passage difficult, but all the girls were excited about the prospect of America and the jobs Demitri had promised them. Things were fine until they approached the port of Long Beach. That was where things started to go sour. Demitri confiscated everyone's passports and gave Villie her first beating. Ivana, Villie, and the other girls were taken straight from the ship to a large warehouse.

Villie got her second beating when she asked Demitri why they weren't entering the United States legally since they had passports. It was in the warehouse that Demitri told them all what their jobs would really be. Ivana's expression hardened, and her eyes wandered to the manila envelope Jack still held in his hands.

"Liar," she spit out. "He lied to us all."

Jack nodded in agreement. "We'll stop him. Tell me as much as you can remember about the men who came here with you."

Ivana described four men besides Demitri. The only other names she knew were Simon and Sergei. And she only knew first names. She'd never heard last names from the men. There was always one man with Demitri, but he never stayed at the house, so she didn't know his name. Simon was the man who ran the house where she was kept. He was the man she ran away from. Ivana's voice faltered, and tears began to fall anew.

As Ivana related the horrors she and the other girls were subjected to in that warehouse on their first day in America, Brinna's fingernails dug into the recliner and anger surged. This Demitri was as bad as any child predator. He needed to be stopped, and Brinna planned to do everything in her power to stop him.

There was a pause in the interview as Rose began to cry with Ivana. Jack shut the recorder off and glanced at Brinna.

"Water?" Brinna asked Jack, and he nodded.

She couldn't help but notice that Jack's eyes were moist as well, and she was touched. *He feels Ivana's pain,* she thought as she stood to get the water. *But then, am I surprised? He's a good cop—a great advocate for victims.*

After more water and a lot of Kleenex, Ivana was ready to continue. She explained why she and Villie were so eager to come to America and why it was so easy to believe everything Demitri had told them.

In a halting voice, Ivana told him how Demitri had

approached her at the orphanage in her hometown. She explained that on her eighteenth birthday she had to leave the orphanage whether she was ready to go or not. Her first plan was to join her older sister, Villie, who had a job sweeping the city streets in Sofia. The job didn't pay much, but it enabled Villie to rent a room in the city, a room she shared with two other girls. Ivana felt certain she could get the same job and then live with her sister. This was better than sleeping on the streets, which happened to many other orphans.

Then Demitri came to visit. He was a prosperous businessman, he said. Tall, with broad shoulders and dark hair, gray at the temples, Demitri had a winning smile. He came to the orphanage interested in all the young women who would be turning eighteen. He spun stories about America, how the girls could find good jobs and live in nice houses. One time he visited with a girl he introduced as his daughter, not much older than Villie, who had moved to America, had a job, and told stories about endless opportunities. Ivana could get one of these jobs, Demitri told her. She wouldn't have to sweep streets and share a bedroom in someone else's house.

At first Ivana said no. She told Demitri she could not leave her sister. Demitri then wanted to meet Villie. One afternoon he took Ivana from the orphanage, and they met Villie at a restaurant. Demitri fed them better than they had ever been fed and told them he would take them both to America and find them wonderful jobs, perhaps working for a movie star who needed a nanny for her children.

It was here Ivana broke down. She sobbed for her sister.

"She was so excited about coming here. It's my fault. If we had stayed in Bulgaria, Villie would still be alive."

Jack shook his head. "Don't blame yourself. The only person to blame is Demitri. He took advantage of both of you in the worst way. It's my job to see that he pays for that and that he never takes advantage of another young woman again."

When Ivana calmed down, Jack turned the line of questioning to the house where Ivana and the other girls were kept. She couldn't tell him much about the place. She and the other girls had been brought there in a van without windows. On the evening she ran away, it had been dark and raining. She accidentally found the river and thought she could swim across, but the current was too strong.

No, she didn't think she'd recognize the place if she saw it again. She would drive with Jack through the neighborhoods but wasn't certain she would recognize anything.

"This is a lot for her to take in on one day," Rose said, interrupting Jack. "Maybe tomorrow would be a better day for her to take that drive."

"Sure, Rose, that's probably a good suggestion. One more question and then I'll go. Ivana, did you ever meet a woman named Magda? She owns a shop here in Long Beach called Black Sea Folk Art and Collectibles."

Ivana frowned. "I don't know the name, no. But the girl Demitri brought to visit the orphanage worked at a shop somewhere in California. If I saw the girl again, I would know her."

"Great. Thanks for all your help." Jack stood. "Now, you relax and get better. I'll check in with you tomorrow." He turned to Brinna. "Walk out with me, Brin?"

"Sure." Brinna opened the door and walked with Jack to the plain car parked at the curb. "She really can't help you much, can she?"

Jack shrugged. "I don't know. This lead about the girl who came to visit with Demitri to talk about working in America may be something. Ben and I spoke to this Magda, the shop owner. She has a Bulgarian clerk. And we both thought she may have been hiding something."

"You think she is involved in the actual trafficking?" Brinna shoved her hands in her pockets, brows furrowed. Though women often could be as vicious as men, it always surprised her when a woman was guilty of exploiting another woman or young girl.

"She's got a doorway: this import business of hers is thriving. Ben is crawling through any and all records he can get his hands on. For all we know, she's bringing girls in with her collectibles."

"Something to think about," Brinna agreed.

"Something else to think about—you free for dinner?"

"What?" Brinna felt a jolt, the abrupt change of subject a shock. She met Jack's gaze.

"Dinner—you know, that meal after lunch and before bedtime. I'm off in an hour, so why don't we meet in the Shore? Lunch the other day was just sandwiches, and I'd be honored to buy a nice dinner for the woman who inspires 'hero worship.'" His eyes crinkled with amusement.

Brinna felt his warmth and blushed. "I've got to stop giving interviews." She remembered David's invite. It had in no way elicited the same response as this inquiry from Jack. His second invitation . . . Was it safe to infer that he was ready to move on from his wife? "I don't have anything else planned. Legends?" She mentioned the first restaurant that came to mind.

"Great. See you there about five thirty." Jack smiled and patted her shoulder, then walked around and climbed into his car.

38

BRINNA SAT IN HER TRUCK for a few minutes before starting the engine and driving away. Lunch with Jack the other day had been great, but all of a sudden the butterflies in her stomach as she contemplated dinner were huge. *I need to be certain Jack is over his wife and ready to date, if that's what this is. Already I feel that I could fall hard for the guy.*

Dave the paramedic crossed her mind again. He was cute and interested and maybe a better prospect than Jack. Was it really a good idea to date someone you worked with?

She slapped the steering wheel. *You're being silly, Caruso,* she chided herself. *It's Jack, and you've never got along as well with another guy.* She pulled away from her mother's house, chewing on her bottom lip, doubt nagging. *What if I want more than friendship and Jack doesn't? What if he's just being nice?*

Blowing out a breath, she checked her cell phone. Still nothing from Maggie.

"I need to talk to you, Mags," Brinna said out loud. "First Dave, now Jack. You're the man expert—call me."

* * *

Brinna made a detour on the way home. Shoving thoughts of Jack, Dave, and Maggie from her mind, she decided to check out the Black Sea shop in Shoreline Village.

Rain started to fall again as she drove into the Village parking lot. Brinna pulled on a rain jacket, then hurried to the complex and found the Black Sea store with no problem at all. Slightly damp, water still dripping from her jacket, Brinna went in, working to look as little like a cop as possible.

Nothing in the store appealed to her at all. Brinna was not a trendy knickknack or folk-art type of person. It was going to be difficult to feign interest in these things, and she found herself again wishing for Maggie's company. Maggie was the decorator, the person with an eye for what would make a house look great. Sighing, she decided she'd think of something to tell the clerk if the question came up.

A tall, elegant woman approached her. "May I help you?" she asked in a slightly accented voice.

"Hi, yeah, I'm looking for a unique wedding present," Brinna said. "Something different."

"You came to the right place." The woman beamed and led her to a section of the shop decorated with tapestries, artwork, and pottery.

"These are beautiful," Brinna said, zeroing in on the only thing that caught her eye—some handmade coffee cups. "All of this is from Bulgaria?"

"Most of it." The woman nodded. "From the Black Sea area." She pointed to several items that were from other areas of Eastern Europe.

"Hmm." Brinna picked up the most expensive piece she could find. "I have to admit to being a little ignorant about that area of the world. Can you tell me a little about it?"

Because of her age and accent, Brinna guessed the woman was probably Magda. The woman smiled and began to talk about the Black Sea and the resorts there. Working hard to size her up, Brinna listened carefully. Giving Magda her attention was not difficult, since the information the woman had to impart was fascinating. Under different circumstances Brinna realized she'd probably like and admire this resourceful shop owner. She'd built a thriving business from nothing, and she had contacts all over Eastern Europe. As Brinna listened and looked around the shop, she realized what a perfect cover for trafficking this would be.

She found herself wondering if Jack and Ben had mentioned their suspicions to ICE. She was certain they had, but she made a mental note to speak to Chuck about whether or not this Black Sea shop was on their radar.

Though on the surface Magda didn't seem like the type of person who could exploit and imprison young women, Brinna cautioned herself. One thing being a police officer had taught her was that appearances could be and often were deceiving.

She asked the woman to put an expensive piece of pottery on hold for her and left the shop as the rain abated. Her plan was to return in the future for a more thorough investigation.

Tonight, she had just enough time to get home and change before meeting Jack in Belmont Shore. The dinner was a good idea, she decided. They had a lot of cop business to discuss.

* * *

Ivana opted for an early bedtime. She still did not feel 100 percent and found that she grew tired easily. Plus, the emotional interview she'd given Detective O'Reilly had drained her. She lay on the soft, comfortable bed and stared at the ceiling, almost afraid to close her eyes, afraid this was all a dream and she would wake up back on the filthy mattress with Ana and Galina taunting her.

Working to banish those images forever from her mind, she turned her thoughts to her host. *Rose Caruso is like an angel,* she thought, *like I've always imagined my own mother was. Even the police here are nice. Detective O'Reilly is a beautiful man, eyes so warm and calm.* She hugged her arms to her chest. O'Reilly was a man she and Villie would have dreamed of, handsome like a movie star and so kind.

Is this all real? she asked herself. And then the reality of Villie's death crashed down on her, and Ivana let the tears fall. It was tragically real. Villie would never again laugh with her, grab her arm and drag her into some adventure. Villie was gone forever, and Ivana realized that only seeing Demitri pay for what he'd done could ever make her feel any better. She'd never feel good, and she'd never get her sister back, but at least if Demitri were arrested, she'd know that no one else's sister would meet the same fate as Villie.

Rolling over, Ivana vowed that whatever she could do to help the police officer Jack O'Reilly she would do. It was now her mission to stop Demitri. And she relished the thought of seeing him arrested and humbled.

39

JACK FIDGETED with his tie after he parked. After looking around to make sure Brinna wasn't already in the parking lot watching, he leaned over to study what he could of his appearance in the rearview mirror.

Tie on or off? He loosened it, then tightened it, then took it off.

"Argh." He blew out a breath in frustration, not quite believing he was so nervous, but he was. The invitation to dinner had slipped glibly off his tongue, but as five thirty approached, he realized this was perilously close to a date. He liked Brinna, admired her, looked forward to any chance he got to be around her, but was he ready to date her?

For that matter, was she ready to date him? Where was she at with her faith?

Jack righted himself in the driver's seat and drummed his fingers on the steering wheel. He'd come to grips with his wife's death and knew the last thing she would have wanted was for him to pine and stay hidden in the house for the rest of his life, so this nervousness was not because of her.

No, this nervousness was because he didn't know what Brinna would think of the two of them stepping from a working relationship to a personal relationship. What if she didn't feel the same way he did?

Only one way to find out. He squeezed the wheel before letting it go and then got out of the car and walked into the restaurant. He only had to wait a few minutes before Brinna arrived. And when she did, even in casual attire— jeans and a pale-green sweater—she took his breath away. Jack knew there was no getting around it; he wanted a personal relationship with her. He wanted to know everything about her and be an integral part of her life. Praying that she returned the feeling, he stepped forward and got her attention.

* * *

Legends was a popular Long Beach sports bar and restaurant. Brinna walked in and looked around until she heard Jack call her name. She turned and saw him in the waiting area. He'd taken off his tie and loosened his collar but still wore his suit jacket. A flash of nervousness enveloped Brinna. She worked to quash it.

"I hope I didn't keep you waiting."

He shook his head. "I was a few minutes early; you're right on time."

It was still a bit early for the dinner crowd, so they were seated quickly.

"Good choice," Jack said as they opened their menus. "I haven't been here in ages."

"Maggie and Rick and I come here a lot during football," Brinna said without thinking, and then she remembered Rick.

Jack looked up from his menu, and she could tell by his face he understood. "Ouch. I know it hurts about Rick, but there is still hope."

Brinna set her menu down. "Yeah, I'm beginning to believe that. My mom always says it. And when I went to see Rick, he was unflaggingly upbeat. I imagine he'll be okay no matter what happens."

"A step forward for you, I think, seeing hope in a tragic situation."

Their eyes held for a moment, but the waitress approaching the table sent their attention back to the menus. Brinna ordered a hamburger and fries and Jack, a sirloin steak.

When the waitress left, Jack sat back and regarded Brinna. "You're an easy date. Just a hamburger?" His gray eyes teased.

Brinna wondered at his choice of words. "Is that what this is? A date?" she asked, cocking an eyebrow.

"Yes, I guess it is." He leaned forward, the teasing gone, warmth and curiosity in his gaze.

Brinna's breath caught in her throat, and for a minute she lost her voice. She kept her eyes on Jack's and sensed the connection they had when they were partners. This was what she wanted—the easy camaraderie she had with him during their partnership. But suddenly it all felt unsure.

"Jack, I like you. I like the way you look at things, and I like being around you, but . . ."

"I was afraid there was a *but* coming."

"It's just that . . . well, when we worked together, your wife still weighed heavy on you. . . . Boy, did that sound lame."

Jack smiled and shook his head. "I know what you mean. I will always love Vicki, but I am ready to move on. Maybe I didn't realize how ready until I started spending more time with you. The case, lunch the other day . . . I enjoy being with you. I hope you can say the same about me."

Brinna felt the heat start to rise in her cheeks, and she played with the napkin in her lap for a moment. "I can. You were a good partner, and I miss our chats."

"Only as a partner?" The twinkle was back.

She smiled and struggled to find words that didn't sound odd. "No, I guess I can think of you as more than a partner. Is that where we're going?"

He cleared his throat. "I'd like more, Brinna. I would."

Warmth bubbled through Brinna, and the heat she'd felt rising a minute ago flooded her face. This was what she wanted, and he wanted the same thing. "Then we're on the same page in more ways than one."

Their eyes locked, and he reached his hand across the table. Brinna put her hand in his and relished the strength she felt there.

40

SCRAPE, EEEK, scrape, thump . . .

Ivana lay holding her breath, listening to the noises coming from outside her window and trying to convince herself it was only her overactive imagination. Her efforts were rewarded with a few moments of silence, and then the scraping started again. She'd awakened from a sound sleep to the noises at the window and was now wide awake, completely unable to go back to sleep.

What would make that type of noise? she wondered, gathering the blanket in her hands closer around her neck, afraid to turn toward the window. She'd seen very little of this country to have any frame of reference for the sound. At home the noise could have been the branch of a tree or one of the other girls' suitors tapping on the pane to get the attention of his beloved. She hadn't seen enough of Mrs. Caruso's yard to know if there was a branch near enough to scrape the window. As for suitors . . .

Her room was in the rear of the house with a large window

overlooking the backyard. Mrs. Caruso's room was toward the front of the house. As Ivana listened, the sound grew louder, and fear crept into her gut like a hunter stalking its prey. She imagined someone was at the window picking the lock, and when she forced herself to turn toward the window, she saw a shadow.

Jumping up from the bed, Ivana grabbed the new robe Mrs. Caruso had given her earlier in the day. She scrambled into it as she fled the dark room and hurried down the hall. Pausing at Mrs. Caruso's door, Ivana froze. She hadn't even noticed the time; Mrs. Caruso might be sound asleep. And what if she were only imagining things? Would the woman think she'd taken in some timid thing that cringed at every shadow?

Glancing back down the hall, Ivana knew she wasn't jumping at shadows. Someone had been at her window; she was certain. She knocked on the bedroom door.

"Come in" came a clear but sleepy reply.

Slowly Ivana opened the door. Rose Caruso had turned on a bedside light. She looked at Ivana in the semidarkness, concern in her eyes. "Is everything okay? Did you have a bad dream?" she asked as she threw the covers off and got out of bed.

"I heard something scratching at the window in my room. It frightened me." Ivana looked over her shoulder. "I'm sorry to wake you."

The older woman donned her own robe and took Ivana's shoulders. "Don't apologize. One benefit of having a police officer for a daughter is knowing I can call the police anytime I think I have a problem." She walked to her nightstand, picked up the phone, and punched in a number. Motioning toward Ivana, Mrs. Caruso indicated she could take a seat on the end of the bed.

Ivana complied and felt the anxiety in her stomach calming while she listened to Mrs. Caruso talk to the police. She told them that she thought there was a prowler outside the house and that she wanted a patrol officer to come and look in the yard. There was a bit more to the conversation, and then Mrs. Caruso hung up.

"There—they'll send a patrol car by to check things out. Does that make you feel better?" Mrs. Caruso sat next to Ivana and put an arm over her shoulders.

"Yes, thank you. I'm sorry to be so frightened. You must think me a weak little mouse." As she sat in the cozy room with Rose Caruso, Ivana's panic seemed foolish, and she believed the noises and the shadows were figments of her imagination and nothing more.

"I said, don't apologize. And I think only that you are a young girl who has every right to be fearful. Now, since we're up, how about we go to the kitchen and have some tea?"

Ivana nodded and followed Mrs. Caruso into the kitchen. The woman flipped on the hall light, the living room light, and all the kitchen lights, and Ivana smiled. The brightness made her feel better, safer somehow. And when the kettle was on the stove with flames glowing under it, Ivana felt normal again and as safe as she had ever felt in her life.

She took a steaming cup of tea and turned to sit at the table. Instantly a scream tore from her throat, and the teacup fell from her hands, shattering on the floor.

As fear pounded in her ears, Ivana heard Mrs. Caruso behind her. "Wha—?" was all the woman managed.

The masked man in the doorway moved forward quickly. He pointed a gun at Ivana and in her native tongue ordered her quiet.

Mrs. Caruso stepped forward and tried to push Ivana behind her, but the man's hand came up quickly and caught the left side of Mrs. Caruso's face, sending her backward against the kitchen counter and then down to the floor.

"No!" Ivana cried, leaping for the man despite her fear. He was there for her—she knew it. Somehow Demitri had found her. Rushing forward, she ignored the gun and grabbed the mask, jerking it from the man's head.

"Simon!" The shock of recognition stunned her.

Simon jammed the gun into her midsection with a curse. "Now look what you have done. You've signed your friend's death warrant." He shoved Ivana to where Mrs. Caruso was now struggling to her feet. Stepping to the door, he unlocked it and pulled it open. Two more masked men rushed in.

"Take them both," Simon ordered in Bulgarian. "The woman has seen my face. I can't leave her here." He turned to Mrs. Caruso and Ivana, this time speaking in English. "If either of you makes a sound, I'll kill you both."

The men moved quickly. One grabbed Ivana, and the other, Mrs. Caruso. Ivana struggled to no avail. The man who held her had a grip of iron. Her heart filled with worry for Mrs. Caruso, who still seemed dazed from the slap. A thin line of blood ran down her chin. A sack was yanked over Ivana's head, and everything went black.

Pulled from her feet, Ivana was carried out into the cold night. Shivers racked her body, both from the cold and from fear. Her ears distinguished the rumble of a car motor and the door of a van being pulled open. She was pushed inside and, a second later, felt Mrs. Caruso come to rest beside her. The door slammed, and the van jerked backward into the street, then forward. Horror gripped Ivana's heart as she realized she was responsible for her benefactor being taken to the same hell she thought she'd escaped.

No one would know they were being taken. They were at the mercy of Demitri, and he would punish them both for Ivana's transgression.

Ivana expelled rib-shaking sobs, certain the van was taking her and Mrs. Caruso to their deaths.

41

BRINNA WASN'T ASLEEP when the phone started ringing. She'd been lying in bed, stroking the slumbering Hero, feelings alternating between anxiety and anticipation. The situation with Hero, wondering if the city would pick up his cost, caused the anxiety; and this new thing with Jack caused the anticipation. She'd really enjoyed the dinner with him, more than she could remember enjoying a night out with a man. She even looked forward to Sunday and attending church with Jack. That would knock her mother for a loop.

But Brinna couldn't say she'd ever been good at relationships. The last guy she dated had been nice enough, but he couldn't understand Brinna's mission, her need to rescue children. She and Jack had more common ground, common interests, and common concerns. Would all that commonality help them make a relationship work?

When the phone rang, Brinna frowned. She was still hoping Maggie would call but knew a call at this time of night was unlikely to be from her friend. She glanced at the clock and the time gave her pause. It was a little after 2 a.m. No good news ever came this late. She answered the phone on the nightstand as Hero stirred.

"Yes?"

"Brinna, it's Debbie from communications. Sorry to wake you." Brinna recognized the voice of one of the dispatch supervisors.

"I was awake. What's up?"

"Do you know where your mother is?"

Brinna sat up and swung her legs out from under the covers. Her frown deepened, and a knot of fear formed inside her.

"I assume she's home in bed. Why?"

She heard Debbie sigh. "She called us about forty-five minutes ago, saying she thought she had a prowler. She didn't indicate it was urgent, so we didn't enter the call as a priority one. Anyway, a graveyard unit is at her house now, and there's no sign of her. All the lights are on in the house and the kitchen door was open, but your mom isn't there."

The knot of fear inside Brinna exploded like a hand grenade, and she sprang to her feet. "I'm on my way over there now. Is there a sergeant on scene?"

"There will be by the time you get there. I'll also notify the watch commander."

"Thanks." Brinna could tell by the tension in Debbie's voice that she would treat this situation very seriously. She hung up the phone and grabbed some clothes. Dressing quickly, she whistled for Hero, and the two of them sped to her mother's house.

* * *

There were three black-and-whites in front of the house when Brinna arrived—one sergeant and two patrol cars. Every light in the house was on, and through open blinds Brinna could see officers standing in her mother's living room. A dread tightened in her stomach, very similar to the feeling she'd had the day she herself was snatched off the sidewalk twenty years ago by a monster. He'd wrapped her in a blanket and wedged her under a table in a camping trailer. She'd felt like she would suffocate back then and she felt that way now. Her throat tightened, and her hands shook as she jumped out of the truck and jogged to the house. Her injured wrist throbbed. She left Hero in the truck with the motor running and the air on until she knew exactly what she was dealing with.

"What's going on?" she asked the first officer who caught her eye, a rookie she knew only as Bates. He was acting as scribe at her mom's kitchen door.

"Not sure yet," he said as he put pen to paper to write down her name. "Sergeant Klein is inside, waiting for you." He stepped aside and Brinna leaped past him.

Once in the kitchen, Brinna took a deep breath and surveyed the scene, struggling for a police officer's detachment. Klein was there, along with Donovan, another graveyard officer Brinna figured was training the rookie outside. She saw the broken teacup on the floor, the gas burner on the stove still burning, and the chair turned over on its side, but other than that, there was no blood, no bodies. Her breath came out in a whoosh.

"Brinna." Klein put a hand on her shoulder. "We don't know what we have here, but it doesn't look good."

"What can you tell me?" were all the words her tight, dry throat could manage.

"Forced entry through a back bedroom window." Klein waved his arm around the kitchen. "And this. I'd be willing to bet your mom isn't in the habit of leaving the stove on or dropping cups on the floor and then disappearing at two o'clock in the morning."

Brinna shook her head, trying to clear thoughts muddied by fear. "Is her car still here? And what about the girl, Ivana?" she rasped, swallowing as her voice threatened to break completely.

"The girl?" Klein's expression told Brinna he knew nothing about Ivana, and she remembered that her mother's role in housing Ivana was not supposed to be on any paperwork. The question *How did they find her, then?* shot through her brain like a bullet train. She breathed deeply and composed herself before briefly explaining to Klein about Ivana staying with her mother.

"Car is in the garage. No sign of this Ivana. I have officers at St. Mary's in case maybe a neighbor took your mother to the emergency room. Nothing yet. Officers are knocking on doors."

Brinna felt her knees weaken, and she moved to the archway between the kitchen and living room to lean for support. She knew Klein and Donovan were watching her.

"Debbie said that my mom called about a prowler."

"Yes," Donovan spoke up. "We caught the call. She didn't

use 911; she called the seven-digit line. The computer shows it took us sixteen minutes to get here. We could have gotten here quicker, but dispatch didn't make the call a priority because your mom didn't act like it was an emergency." His contrite posture told her he regretted not hurrying over. But Brinna couldn't fault him. Cops couldn't be clairvoyant, and if her mother didn't say it was urgent, there was no way Donovan could know.

She closed her eyes and tried to think without having fear crowd in at every turn. But concentration eluded her. There was also Brian to consider. Brinna had no idea how to get ahold of him in South America and tell him what was going on. He should be told, but she decided that notifying him would have to wait. There was too much else to worry about at the moment.

Folding her arms tight around her midsection, she wished this were a nightmare that she'd wake up from soon. She might as well have been on a rough sea the way her insides pitched and her temples pounded. She took another deep breath.

I have to think clearly, she told herself, *have to be a cop now. That's the only way to help my mother. No garden-variety prowler abducts two people from a house this cleanly.*

"Call O'Reilly," she said finally.

"Jack O'Reilly?" Klein asked.

Brinna nodded and swallowed. "This case, the homicide Jack is working on, and the situation with Ivana, the girl— there are possible organized crime ties. Jack and Ben have been working that angle." *And I want Jack here. I need his strength.*

"The girl you pulled out of the river is tied to a homicide?" Klein frowned.

"Yeah, she's a victim of human trafficking, possibly brought to this country by organized crime. Since my mom doesn't have any enemies that I know of, that's the only angle I can think to work."

"Sounds like a sensible theory." Klein pulled out his handheld radio and asked dispatch to call O'Reilly. He also asked for a priority lab.

Brinna surveyed her mother's kitchen again, the realization hitting like a baton blow. This was now a crime scene.

42

Jack sat at his kitchen table, Bible open in front of him, cup of tea steaming on his right. He hadn't had trouble sleeping in a while. Months ago he'd struggled with insomnia and had trouble closing his eyes because all he'd see were visions of his dead wife, Vicki. But lately he'd been sleeping well. There'd been no ghosts invading his dreams, no nightmares about Vicki's accident.

Tonight his sleeplessness had nothing to do with Vicki. Instead, his thoughts were on Brinna. She touched his heart like he'd never thought it could be touched since Vicki. It made him giddy. He was certain the goofy grin on his face would never fade.

And Brinna was coming around to a solid faith in God, and that made him happy. Gone was the antagonism toward prayer and the faith he and her mother shared. They'd made plans to go to church together on Sunday, and he found he could hardly wait. She still had a lot of questions, but they'd be able to work through them as a couple.

She hated the fact that innocents suffered and that God

allowed bad things in a person's life. He studied Scripture and prayed for answers, for insight, for a way to help a woman he truly cared about understand that a good God existed and that he loved her and her kids even more than she did.

Taking a sip of tea, he settled back in his chair. *The Lord causes the rain to fall on the just and the unjust,* Jack thought, not remembering the exact verse. He could quote many other verses that told the Christian to expect adversity, trials, and all sorts of trouble in this life. Life in this world would never be perfect.

Brinna wanted perfection—perfect justice and a perfect world. She wanted to be able to save all the innocents in the world. Jack could understand the desire she had to protect the innocent. That same desire had drawn him to police work many years ago. But he'd been grounded in the belief that God was real and directing his steps, guiding his life.

He rubbed his face with both hands and prayed that the answers he shared with her would reach her and help her on her faith journey.

The ring of the telephone interrupted him.

Debbie in communications was on the line, and she quickly and concisely explained the situation with Brinna's mother. Jack groaned.

"It's always tougher when it's one of our own. This is horrible for Brinna, isn't it?" Debbie said.

"I'm sure it is. Tell them I'll be there as soon as I can." Jack dressed quickly, praying for Rose, Ivana, and Brinna and wondering where this crisis would push Brinna and her views about God.

43

When the van came to a stop, Ivana and Mrs. Caruso were jerked out of the back and half carried, half dragged into a building. Ivana struggled to clear her mind as confusion and disorientation twisted her thoughts. Though the hood was still in place and she could see nothing but black, she could tell they weren't at the house she'd run from. The cold night air, the smell of salt water in her nostrils, and the sounds of waves told her they were close to the ocean.

The odors and sounds dredged up the memory of when she and her sister had first stepped onto America's shores. They'd been dumped in a dingy warehouse, and immediately Demitri told them the truth of why he'd brought them to America. Ivana had just recounted the horrors of that day for Detective O'Reilly, and these noises and smells brought the memory of that bleak day back anew.

She heard Rose Caruso protesting, threatening that her daughter was a police officer. Simon told her to shut up or be slapped again.

The screech of metal scraping metal as a heavy door was opened caused Ivana to flinch. Then Simon yanked her hood off, and Ivana blinked as her eyes adjusted to the presence of light. Mrs. Caruso stood next to her, looking just as disoriented but not frightened, and that surprised Ivana. Ivana herself was terrified. She recognized this place. It was the warehouse, the horrible place where they'd found out what Demitri wanted of them. Here was where Villie had received a horrible beating.

All of their captors had their hoods off, and they spoke in low tones in Bulgarian. Ivana had seen all of them before, but it was only Simon whose name she knew.

"Simon, please, let this woman go. She is no threat to you. Don't punish her because of me," Ivana pleaded, also speaking in her native tongue. She ignored Mrs. Caruso's questioning gaze.

Simon grabbed her elbow and pulled her toward the small room in which she and Villie had stayed with the other girls before they'd been taken to the house. "You should have thought about that before you ran away." Simon was furious. "I will not face Demitri's wrath because of you."

He shoved Ivana into the room, and one of the others thrust Rose Caruso in after her.

"You men, I warn you—you are making a huge mistake," Mrs. Caruso protested. "What exactly do you plan to do with us?"

"You will stay here for a few days," Simon answered in English. "My employer will answer your questions when he returns." He glared at Ivana when he said *employer*, and she knew he meant Demitri.

Simon tossed a bag into the room. "Some food and water for you." He stood in the doorway and lit a cigarette. After the first puff he pointed at Ivana. "There is no way out of here. You can scream all you want; no one will hear. You will be here until Demitri returns, so sit quietly and behave."

With that, he turned on his heel and slammed the door behind him.

44

NEEDING TO DO SOMETHING to feel useful in some way, Brinna got Hero out of the truck. She asked him to find her mother. The dog caught the scent leaving the kitchen but the trail ended in the driveway, where he circled a bit, then finally stopped and looked at her as if to say, *"I got nothing."* He whimpered a bit as he sat at her feet, and Brinna fought back tears of frustration. Her mother and Ivana had most likely been put into a car and driven away.

After the brief search, all she could do was pace and wait for Jack. While she waited, she phoned Chuck, expecting his voice mail. Instead he answered, and at the sound of his voice, the tale of her latest nightmare tumbled out in a torrent.

"Whoa, Brinna, slow down. What do you mean your mom is gone? How is that possible?"

"I wish I knew." She took a deep breath and held her fractured wrist up, hoping the throbbing would ease. "Her house is empty. No sign of her or Ivana."

"I can't believe this. The surveillance car would have been

in place at 6 a.m., in just a few hours. I don't know what to say." He paused a moment. "What's happening on your end?"

Brinna explained that Jack was on the way, and right now LBPD lab personnel were processing the scene.

"Look, I'll get over there as soon as I can. Hang in there. We'll find them both."

Brinna closed her phone and watched the street for Jack's arrival. As he parked his car and walked up, she struggled to keep her emotions in check, convinced that every cop on scene regarded her with pity. She looked to Jack for strength and wisdom, knowing from past experience she could count on his insight. If he regarded her with the same pity as everyone else, the ragged walls of control she'd been struggling to erect would implode and crumble like pixie dust.

Jack nodded her way, but in his eyes Brinna saw what she had hoped to see: cop resolve. He first conferred with Klein, and Brinna listened in as all the information she already knew was repeated. The only new bit came from one of the officers who'd been knocking on every door in the neighborhood. Someone had seen a white panel van in her mother's driveway. The woman, an elderly neighbor, had thought the sight unusual, but by the time she'd finished in the bathroom and looked back out the window, the van was gone. This only confirmed to Brinna what Hero had told her—her mother was long gone.

Up to date on all that was known at the time, Jack regarded Brinna with an indefinable expression. "I'm so sorry," he said. "I can't understand how this could happen. I know great pains were taken to keep your mother's address out of the public domain. I'm not certain how anyone could have gotten it this fast . . . or organized this type of assault."

Brinna willed her voice to stay steady. "For all we know, we were followed home from the hospital. I felt uneasy, but I didn't see anything and thought I was just being paranoid. Maybe I led them right to Ivana and my mom."

"Hey." Jack reached out and gripped her shoulder. "No time for any blame game. We had no information indicating something like this was a possibility. The course of action now is to concentrate on finding them." He held her gaze, and she had to look away as her eyes started to fill.

Just then a light sprinkle began to fall, and Brinna felt as though it was the last straw. "I want to find them. But Hero has already been in the driveway searching. The trail ends here." She stomped on the spotted driveway. "We have no trail to follow." Her jaw tightened and her good hand formed a frustrated fist.

Jack stepped close. "Listen, before I came out here, I called Ben and filled him in. He had an idea that might help. We know Ivana ran from a house somewhere in Hawaiian Gardens, right?" When Brinna nodded, he continued. "Well, Ben thought about driving up to the sheriff's office in Lakewood; they handle Hawaiian Gardens. He's going to review all their nuisance complaints. If Ivana was held in a house with other girls for the purpose of prostitution, it's possible a neighbor noticed a pattern of excessive traffic and made a complaint about the house."

Brinna considered that line of thinking. It happened at drug houses all the time. Neighbors would get angry because a constant stream of customers to the drug house would increase traffic and noise in the neighborhood and monopolize available parking spots. Complaints often gave officers a heads-up about the problem and many times led to probable cause for a search warrant.

"That could work," she conceded. "Given the location Ivana went into the river, we have a reasonable amount of ground to cover." Though for Brinna, she knew she would knock on every door in Hawaiian Gardens if it would help find her mother.

"Exactly. Maybe officers went out and checked a complaint but didn't have enough for a warrant. In any event, it will be worth the time and effort to recheck any house we can."

For the first time since she'd realized her mother was gone, Brinna felt a spark of hope. If Ivana's captors had taken her mother, the odds were good that they took her to the house Ivana escaped from. If they could find that house, and find it fast, her mother's chances were better.

"Maybe I can go and help Ben out—" Brinna stopped and followed Jack's gaze. She groaned and covered her mouth with her hand. A news van had just pulled up. Her mother's plight would be all over the morning news shows. This would be a great development if it helped find her mother. But it would be horrible if the heat made her mother's captors decide that Rose Caruso was a liability.

45

Chuck parked behind the news van as Jack and Brinna were just about to leave for Lakewood. He had with him a federal forensic team. Without a word, he gave Brinna a hug.

"Telling you we dropped the ball on this probably doesn't help," he said after a moment.

"Hey, blame right now isn't going to help anything." Brinna nodded toward Jack. "He just told me that."

"I guess he's right. We need to concentrate on the bad guys." Chuck shook Jack's hand, and Jack told him where he and Brinna were going.

"Good idea. Keep me apprised."

As they left, Chuck and the forensic team disappeared into Rose's house. Brinna wondered what her mom would have to say about all the traffic in her house. She hoped she'd have the chance to complain about it.

Brinna dropped Hero and her car off at her house in order to drive with Jack. The trip to Lakewood took fifteen minutes, and the pair rode in silence. Brinna was as grateful for his company as she was for the quiet. In all her searches for missing kids, there was usually an emotional component because she'd been through the same thing. Kidnapped at six and rescued two days later, she knew what they were going through, yet she was able to maintain a professional detachment and do her job.

But now that it was her mother, all bets were off. Every wall she built seemed to be like rice paper, delicate and easily destroyed. Even a Kevlar heart, the shield she would erect around her emotions, eluded her.

Child molesters, perverts—when they snatched a kid, it was often without a thought or a plan. They invariably made mistakes that tripped them up. If an organized crime syndicate had snatched her mother, what if they didn't make any mistakes?

Brinna worked hard to concentrate on the task in front of her, not on all the what-ifs her overactive imagination could conjure up.

They found Ben in a conference room at the sheriff's department. His expression told Brinna he had good news.

"What have you got, partner?" Jack asked.

"I've been able to narrow our search down to four homes." He handed each of them a report form. "These four are in the same general neighborhood. The complaints are about excessive vehicular and foot traffic to the homes, and none are far from the flood control channel."

Brinna glanced over the report she'd been given. The deputy who cleared the call noted that while he'd been on scene, he'd not observed any excessive traffic but recommended the address be forwarded to narcotics for further investigation. She figured it was ditto for the other houses. Four addresses would be relatively easy to check out, and Brinna was ready to get going.

"Great, Ben. How do you want to work this?" she asked.

"We'll have to coordinate with the deputies. All of the houses are in their jurisdiction. How about we just start with the closest and work our way through the list?"

"Are the deputies on board?"

"I'll set things up with the watch commander," Ben said. "Do you want to notify Chuck?"

"He's at Rose Caruso's now. I'll call and give him an update," Jack said. He pulled out his cell phone and dialed. As he finished the call and closed his phone, Jack turned to Brinna. "How about you and I wait for Ben outside?"

"Sounds good."

Once outside, Brinna fairly vibrated with the urge to get going and knock on doors. She anxiously tapped on the hood of the car, imagining it was the sound of every wasted second ticking away.

"I sure hope the sheriff doesn't tie us up with a lot of red tape," she told Jack.

"They'll want a car to stand by while we do our knock-and-talks. We'd do the same if deputies were in our city." He shoved his hands in his pockets. "How are you holding up?"

Brinna shook her head and sighed. "I feel like I'm ready to jump out of my skin. I truly wish I'd let Ivana stay with me. Then my mom wouldn't be in this predicament."

"Yeah, we might be looking for you." Jack smiled while

Brinna glared at him. He tilted his head, reaching out to touch her shoulder. "We can't go back and do it over—you know that."

"You're right, but I can't help feeling responsible. And everything I've read about foreign gangsters—if that is who we're dealing with—is that they are ruthless." She stopped and took a deep, painful breath. "I couldn't handle it if something happened to my mother just because she was doing something to help us." Her fingernails dug into her palms, and she barely held the tears back.

Jack put a hand on her back. "We'll find her."

She couldn't meet his eyes, and the warmth of his touch almost pushed her over the edge.

What saved her was Ben, coming out of the station with a uniformed deputy. They were ready to go.

And Brinna was ready not only to knock on doors, but to kick them open if the need arose.

46

MAGDA AWOKE to the aroma of coffee brewing and smiled, pleased that she should be so fortunate to have such a thoughtful husband. He'd left a half hour ago to take the twins to school but had ensured that Magda would awake to a fresh pot of coffee by setting the timer for her. That pleasant aroma and the love she felt for Anton made it easy to rise from slumber and to push thoughts of Simon and Demitri from her mind.

She went to the kitchen and poured a cup. Fortified by a couple of sips, she carried the coffee with her to the bathroom. After showering and dressing, she took the empty cup back to the kitchen, refilled it, and turned on the TV to keep her company while she made herself breakfast. She was about to break an egg into a mixing bowl when the words the newsman spoke smacked into her mind.

". . . Rose Caruso, mother of a local police officer, has apparently been abducted, along with a young girl Officer

Brinna Caruso saved from drowning in the flood control channel four days ago."

Magda dropped the whole egg into the bowl and turned toward the television screen. The news camera panned the front of a house bustling with police activity. This was too much of a coincidence. How many young girls were plucked alive from the flood control channel?

She hugged her elbows and fought the growing dread in her stomach, struggling to remember what Simon had said. He'd told her he would handle it, that he had someone watching the hospital, waiting for the girl to be released. Had Simon found the girl and been stupid enough to not only grab her but to take this officer's mother also?

Transfixed, Magda watched the TV screen, listening to the police and their official statement. Photos of the police officer and her mother were flashed across the screen. Magda gasped. She'd seen both women before—they'd both been in her shop. The mother had visited several times, but the police officer—why, she'd come in just the other night.

Feeling as if she were going to throw up, Magda rushed to the bathroom and splashed water on her face, not caring that it would destroy her freshly applied makeup. There was no escape now. If Simon had kidnapped the mother of a police officer—or worse, if Demitri did something to the woman— the authorities would not rest until they solved the crime.

Magda had a lot more respect for American authorities than she did for Bulgarian authorities. Everything would be exposed. As much as she wanted Demitri stopped, this was a disaster. She knew that somehow, some way, she would be connected to this mess. A vision of being dragged out of her house in handcuffs in front of her children flashed through her head and she retched. All of the coffee she'd just ingested came back up, twice as bitter.

As she wiped her mouth, a horrible realization dawned. She had to come clean; she had to tell the police what she knew or those two women would most certainly die.

But first, she had to tell Anton.

Glancing at the clock, she realized he'd be back soon. He'd be surprised because normally she was gone to work before he got back. But not today. And he'd be doubly surprised when she told him all about the vile things she'd been a part of for their entire married life. He was certain to see her as a monster, and that would be the end of their marriage.

Tears fell freely as Magda's fears grew. What if a never-ending nightmare was just beginning? Would she ever awake to a normal, happy life again?

47

HAWAIIAN GARDENS was a small bedroom community tucked in between Long Beach, Lakewood, and Cypress. The largest landmark in the community was a gaming casino. A sheriff's deputy led Brinna and Jack through a maze of residential streets that were almost indistinguishable from what she might see in Long Beach. Besides Ben, a uniformed Long Beach unit was also in the caravan.

Brinna shook her head as they passed tract home after tract home. "Why in the world would anyone consider a residential neighborhood the place to open a brothel?" she asked Jack.

"I wondered about that as well," Jack said. "According to Chuck, it's a disturbing trend. The crooks are trying to shroud themselves in respectability. They figure cops are less likely to kick in doors in quiet neighborhoods. And they hope to attract a wider, more affluent clientele."

"You figure less dirtbags and more average joes visit brothels in suburbia?"

Jack chuckled. "I don't know about that. But it's all about money. These creeps will try anything if they think it will increase revenue. Not even suburbia is safe. But it gets worse. Sometimes it's not large scale. Sometimes it's a wealthy person exploiting a maid or nanny; they keep the individual a virtual slave. Back East they've busted prominent people who've brought young kids here from places like Indonesia and kept them isolated in servitude in their mansions."

Brinna looked at Jack and all she could do was shake her head.

The first two addresses were dead ends. They were rentals to college students who obviously liked to party and entertain, hence the nuisance complaints. They gave the group of officers typical young adult lip but were obviously not human traffickers. It was the third address that rang warning bells in Brinna's head.

"Look, Jack," she said, grabbing his arm as they drew close enough to read the house numbers. "A white van."

Backed into the driveway was a white panel van. The front passenger windows were tinted dark—an illegally dark tint, Brinna noticed. There was no front license plate to run a records check on; she'd have to check around the rear of the van.

"I see it," Jack answered as he pulled to the curb and parked the car. By now it was early morning and the sun was competing with rain clouds for domination of the sky. People in the neighborhood were beginning to rise and start the day. One man on the way to his car paused to regard the police vehicles curiously.

They followed the same routine as with the first two houses. Ben and the deputy would knock on the door while Jack and Brinna surveyed the outside, looking for anything out of the ordinary that might indicate the house was being used for illicit purposes. Brinna knew in this case the first thing she would do was run a check on the van's license plate.

The tract house itself looked like a perfect hideaway. A tall brick wall encircled the backyard, and dense shrubs hid the front windows. As Brinna walked toward the van, she noted that the rear windows were black, as if painted. She tried to look into the yard, but the view was blocked by more dense foliage. If the gate were open and the van moved farther up the driveway, no one from the street would be able to see who got in or out of the vehicle.

"You here to tell these people to clean up their yard?"

The voice startled Brinna, and she jumped, looking left. "What?"

"Didn't mean to scare you," the woman said. Standing on the neatly manicured lawn of the house next door, she peered at Brinna. She held a newspaper in her hand and wore a thick fleece robe.

"The house is an eyesore," she continued. "All the other neighbors take pains to keep their landscaping neat and clean looking. Not these people." She waved her hand in disgust. "Yard is a jungle. I suppose I should be happy they at least mow the lawn in front, what little they have."

"Actually, we're here regarding a nuisance complaint," Brinna explained as she watched Ben and the deputy approach the front door. "Someone called to complain about excessive vehicular traffic coming and going from this house."

"That was me." The woman nodded. "Don't know what is going on in there, but on the weekends there's a steady stream of men going in and out. All hours."

"Have you ever met the people who live here?"

"No, I've only seen a couple of guys—one real big one. You know, he looks like he could've played football. They're foreign."

"Foreign?" Brinna's heart jumped in her chest. Ben and the deputy had knocked on the front door, but as yet there had been no response.

"They speak some other language. It's not Spanish; I speak Spanish. I don't know what it is. I've only heard them once or twice. They don't make a habit of standing outside talking."

"Thanks. We'll handle it."

"I hope so." The woman gathered her robe tightly around her and turned and walked back into her house.

Brinna wrote the van's plate number on a piece of paper, stuffed it in her pocket, and headed for Ben. Not only did she want to hear what the residents of the house told the deputy; she also wanted to tell him what the neighbor had said. From her angle on the front door, she could see the deputy lean forward as if to speak to someone inside.

"We're here to ask a few questions," Brinna heard him say. "Why don't you come out and talk to us?"

She couldn't hear the response of the person inside the house.

Ben stood on the other side of the door closest to Brinna.

She knew the person inside would not be able to see Ben unless he or she stepped onto the small landing. When Brinna saw him pull his jacket back to uncover his gun, she tensed, reaching for her own weapon, a small automatic she carried in a fanny pack.

"Open the door!" the deputy yelled suddenly, lunging forward.

Brinna leaped toward the landing just as Ben and the deputy leaned into the door. She saw Jack sprinting toward the door from the other side of the house.

"Get around back!" she yelled to the two uniformed Long Beach officers. She knew they'd heard but she didn't wait to watch them move. She reached the front door just as Ben and the deputy forced it open. Someone shouted in a foreign language.

And then a gunshot . . .

Ben hit the ground half inside the door and half on the landing. The deputy retreated and took cover behind the doorpost, yanking out his radio and yelling, "Shots fired! Shots fired!" to his dispatch.

Brinna stayed low and put a hand on Ben's back. "You okay?"

"Yeah. I think he shot himself." He rose to a knee and peered into the house. Brinna tried to do the same, but the interior was dark and shaded.

"We should stand down and call SWAT," Ben said. "We have officers at the rear; the scene is secure."

"I don't agree," Brinna hissed, hand tensing on her gun. "There could be another guy in here with a gun. Ivana said there were other girls being held. Their lives may be in danger."

"I agree with you," the deputy said, nodding toward Brinna. "These guys might decide to kill anyone who could provide us with evidence."

Jack, on the other side of the door, next to the deputy, also nodded in agreement. "I don't want to see any more dead girls."

"Then I'm in as well." Ben stood and motioned the deputy in first.

The deputy nodded and went in, moving immediately to the left. Ben followed to the right, with Jack and Brinna right behind.

* * *

Magda heard the garage door open. Anton was home. She got up from the couch to check her image in the mirror. Her eyes were puffy from crying. She knew that even if she wanted to, she could not keep the truth from her husband any longer. The faces of the two kidnapped women on television haunted her. No matter what, she couldn't sit by and do nothing any longer. It was time to step up and be her sister's keeper.

48

By noon the house in Hawaiian Gardens teemed with all manner of law enforcement personnel. There had been only one dead man recovered, the male who opened the door to the deputy's knock. He had, indeed, killed himself. After that, Brinna and the others found three padlocked bedrooms, each containing frightened young women. One bedroom held two women; the other two held four each. They were all young and of Eastern European descent.

There was no sign of Ivana or Brinna's mother.

Chuck arrived with his forensic team. A short time later ICE pulled up with translators. All of the women were in the process of being interviewed. Brinna paced in frustration. None of the women spoke any more than broken English, so she was forced to rely on translation as each interview was finished.

She cursed after reading the transcripts. Waiting patiently had accomplished nothing. Down to the last interview, none of the women knew anything. Their stories were the same as Ivana's. They'd come to the US after being promised jobs by a man named Demitri. Once they arrived, they were forced into prostitution. All they knew of the US was the small bedroom they were imprisoned in. Two of the women knew Ivana, so that was at least confirmation that Ivana had run from this house. But none of the information the women shared would help locate Ivana and Rose now.

"Hey, what do you say we go get something to eat?" Jack appeared at Brinna's shoulder. "Chuck will clean this up. It's his mess now."

"I'm not hungry." Brinna crossed her arms, jaw tense.

"Brinna, half the day is gone. I know you haven't eaten anything. I'm starving; you must be also."

She blew out a breath and faced him, brows furrowed. "I can't eat while I'm this worried about my mom. Jack, you know the odds of her still being alive decrease with each passing hour." Her voice broke. She brought her fist to her mouth and sucked in a breath. Dread covered her like a shroud.

Jack stepped forward and grabbed her shoulders. "You're dead on your feet. You need a break, some food, and a separation from this." His gaze held hers.

Tears fell uncontrollably, and Brinna jerked away from him and wiped her face with the backs of her hands. She needed a few minutes and was thankful that Jack gave them to her. After she felt composed, she turned back to him.

"Okay, let's go." Together they walked toward the car. "There's certainly nothing more for us to learn here," she said.

* * *

When the heavy door shut and locked them in, Ivana felt as though her throat were closing. The only light in the room was a dim bulb, no brighter than a child's night-light. A chair, a beat-up table, and a small couch were the only furnishings. Though Ivana had sobbed the entire way here in the car, as she hugged her arms to her chest, closed her eyes, and threw her head back, the tears ran down her cheeks anew.

"I'm so sorry, Mrs. Caruso," she sobbed. "This is all my fault."

Mrs. Caruso came behind Ivana, turned her around, and hugged her tight. "Oh, sweetheart, of course this is not your fault. You've been the victim in all of this."

As the older woman stroked her hair and held her as though she were a child, Ivana sobbed harder.

After a while Ivana's tears finally ran out. She wiped her face with a sleeve and looked up to see Mrs. Caruso regarding her with a soft, loving expression. There was no hint of fear.

"Do you feel any better now that you've gotten all that out of your system?" Mrs. Caruso asked.

Ivana shrugged. "Maybe, but I'm still frightened. And you're not. You don't know these men; you—"

Mrs. Caruso shushed her and cupped her face in her hands. "Ivana, I have faith that we'll be rescued. I don't need to know these men. I know my daughter and the people she works with. They will find us."

"Oh, I wish I had such faith." Ivana pulled away and glanced around the room. "This is the place I told you about, the place where Demitri brought us—Villie and me—when we first came to this country. He promised us so much, and here is where he told us it was all a lie."

"All the more reason you should know, beyond a shadow of a doubt, that you are not the one at fault here. The evil is Demitri." She put an arm around Ivana's shoulders. "Now I've told you about my faith in God, and you've told me you've heard about him, yet you don't trust him."

Together the two women sat down on the soiled couch.

"How about you let me pray?" Mrs. Caruso continued. "It will give me a measure of peace, and maybe that will help you as well."

Ivana sniffled and nodded, already gaining strength from Rose Caruso's closeness and her composure. Mrs. Caruso began her prayer and Ivana listened very carefully, hoping something in the words would infuse her with some of the strength and faith she felt emanating from the woman.

49

Jack and Brinna had just pulled into the parking lot of a Coco's when her cell phone went off. She grabbed it, hoping it was good news about her mother. It was Maggie. Disappointment mixed with relief as she flipped the phone open.

"Mags," she breathed into the receiver.

"Hey, Brin, I just heard about your mom. I'm so sorry."

"Thanks. I'm glad you called. I thought you'd given up on me." She could hear Maggie sigh.

"I was mad at you. I needed time to think. It really bites what happened to Rick." Maggie's voice broke. "I can hardly look at his kids without choking up." There was a pause.

Brinna felt her own throat tighten again.

"Anyway," Maggie continued, "I realize it's not your fault, and I can't lose my best friend *and* my partner over this. Rick would have jumped into that water no matter what. That day, the 'what' just happened to be you."

"And you know I'd change it if I could."

"Yeah, but neither one of us can. So we just need to move on and make the best of what we have left."

"Are you with Rick now?"

"No, his mom and dad flew in this morning. It's all family now, which is probably best for the kids. I'll check in with them from time to time, and they can always call me. Where are you at?"

Brinna looked up, suddenly remembering where she was and who she was with. Jack sat quietly in the driver's seat, watching her.

"Uh, I'm with Jack. We're at Coco's on Lakewood. We just came from the house we believe Ivana ran from before she jumped in the river."

"Lakewood? I heard that call on the scanner. It went crazy when the deputy put out that shots-fired call. Is this related to your mom?"

"Yeah, we'd hoped to find her at the house. . . . No such luck." Brinna rubbed her temple with the index finger on her injured hand, the dull ache there and in her wrist seemingly permanent.

"You need to bring me up to speed. I've been out of the loop."

"Want to join us? We haven't gone in and ordered yet."

"Sure, I'd like that. I'll be there in twenty."

Brinna took a deep, cleansing breath and closed the phone. At least one part of her personal life had realigned itself.

"Good news?" Jack asked, jolting her back to the most jagged part of her life.

"Yeah, Maggie doesn't hate me. She's had time to cool down and she's going to join us. Do you mind?"

"Not at all. Like I said before, what happened to Rick was not your fault." He reached across the car and tugged on her sleeve. "Rick made up his own mind to go into the water."

"I don't know." Brinna shook her head and looked away. "My falling in might have pulled him in as well. If we hadn't been attached by that leash, I probably would have been the only one in the water."

"This is all second-guessing. If I remember right, you told me that your mentor had a word for second-guessing scenarios you can't change and for second-guessers."

Brinna leaned back and frowned at Jack, who lifted an eyebrow and regarded her with an amused expression.

"I told you that, did I?"

"Yep. Come on now; how did Milo put it?"

In spite of everything, Brinna felt a smile tug at her lips. "He used to say that second-guessing was donkey dung and the second-guessers the donkeys. And I cleaned that up a lot."

"Right. I never met the man, but I agree with him today. Now, how about we go have a seat and order some coffee while we wait for Maggie?"

"Good idea." Brinna felt her mood lift somewhat. Being reminded of Milo was a good thing. Though accepting his death had been painful, enough time had passed and now memories of him made her feel warm and happy. He never would have wallowed in unproductive second-guessing. *"Onward and forward,"* he would have said. *"Just catch the bad guys."*

But thinking of Milo also brought her mother to mind. And her mother's faith. Milo had spoken with Rose at length about her faith, and the fact that Milo had come to accept it was what had caused Brinna to relax and let go of the irritation her mother's beliefs seemed to engender.

My mother's faith, Brinna thought as she and Jack took a seat in the restaurant. *Where does it fit into all of this? It will keep her strong. She'll not fall apart and do anything stupid; I'm sure of it.* Comforted by this, Brinna watched Jack as he yawned and stretched, and she knew he was the right person to be with when the conversation turned to faith.

The waitress arrived with coffee, pouring two cups and leaving a carafe. As the aroma wafted across the table, Brinna realized that in spite of the turmoil she felt, she was starved. Some food would probably even ease her headache.

"I have a question for you," Brinna said to Jack, after taking a long sip of hot coffee. She fixed a thoughtful gaze on him. "Here we are in another situation where the innocent are suffering at the hands of the evil. I want to believe God is good, and sometimes I think I'm almost there, but how can faith explain what has happened to my mom?"

"Just because bad things happen doesn't mean God isn't good."

Brinna bit her bottom lip. "I don't understand that. I can get behind evil people being jerked around, but why good people? My mom is truly good—she believes in God—so why would he let this happen to her?" She held her hands out, palms up. Her frustration with this old dilemma bubbled up like heartburn. She'd asked this question her whole life in terms of missing kids. Why were some kids saved and safe while others were brutally murdered? No child could ever be said to deserve that kind of treatment.

"I can't tell you why. All I can tell you is what the Bible says. No one is good. Everyone is considered a sinner in the eyes of God, and everyone is equal in his sight."

"Then how can anyone win? What is the point of having this great faith in God if you're still going to get smacked by something awful?"

"Brinna, God made man, but man made the society we live in." Jack's tone held such a firm confidence that Brinna gave him her undivided attention. "Evil is here to stay because man rejects God. You have to understand that God wants people to believe in him in spite of what's wrong in the world, not because of it. If he intervened—stopped things from happening or made people puppets—man would not have a free will. God recognizes that some will always reject him. He doesn't force anyone to believe or to be good."

"I've heard that from my mom so many times." Brinna leaned back in the booth and closed her eyes. "You have to believe of your own free will." She punctuated each word with her index finger, then opened her eyes and brought her head forward. "But if belief doesn't save you from calamity, what does it do for you? What's the point?"

"The point is, we can have peace in this world, no matter what our circumstances."

Brinna refilled her coffee cup. *Peace no matter what the circumstances.* "You think my mom has peace right now?"

Jack didn't look away. "I think your mom trusts God, and I think she will continue to trust, no matter what."

No matter what. Brinna ran her finger around the rim of her coffee cup, suddenly very tired. She knew Jack was right. God was the firm center of her mother's life.

"Will God come through for my mom?" Brinna held Jack's gaze.

"Of course he will." He rubbed the stubble on his chin. "But it might not be in a way you consider to be 'perfect.'"

"Figures. Nothing ever seems to work out perfectly." She glanced away for a moment, seeing Maggie heading to their table. "Here's Maggie."

The sight of her friend gave Brinna a jolt of adrenaline. She stood and embraced Maggie. "About time."

"Hey, I broke the land speed record getting here." Maggie's smile was warm, and Brinna felt that warmth to her core. It was good to have her friend back.

"Now," Maggie said as she sat, "why don't you guys fill me in on this human trafficking thing. I was happy to help Rick out as babysitter, but right now I need to be a cop again."

"I can relate to that," Brinna agreed.

Faith talk and God lingered in Brinna's mind as she launched into a narrative of the latest waking nightmare for Maggie's benefit. She'd always believed that work was the best place to be when the world seemed to tilt off its axis, but that was changing—it had changed, she was sure. She wanted the peaceful, sure faith of Jack and her mother. Here, with Jack, and with her mother in peril, she finally believed she'd get there.

50

"DEMITRI?" Anton's face turned red with rage. "That coward! All he knows how to do is exploit and use people." He banged one end of his cane into his palm as if it were a club. "He will pay for this, I promise."

Magda's fear for herself morphed into fear for Anton. She'd cried until she thought for sure every ounce of moisture had left her body as she'd told him about all the evil she'd let happen through the years. He'd listened, pacing the room, features stiffening with each detail she shared. Now this thought flashed through her mind: *What if he tries to confront Demitri?*

"He's a dangerous man—"

"He's an animal, a rabid animal who must be put down." He started for the door, and Magda leaped from her chair to grab his arm.

"What will you do? You can't stop him on your own; he'll kill you!"

Anton took her arm from his, then gripped her right

shoulder tight, left hand white as he leaned on his cane. His eyes were angry and pained. "I need to think. I need to pray. I will be on the porch for a moment. Leave me alone right now." He released her and turned to leave.

Magda felt a real pain pierce her through as she watched him disappear through the front door.

"Oh, God," she cried, "God, I'm not a good person like Anton, and I don't deserve anything, but if he leaves me, I will die. I will die." Her legs gave way and she collapsed onto the couch, tears springing from what she thought was a dry well. As she sobbed, alone and frightened, she vaguely realized that now that the horrible truth was out, she felt a modicum of relief. There were no secrets to keep anymore. If Anton would only forgive her, they could start life anew. She continued to cry out to the God she'd only given passing attention to until now.

After a while, Magda's tears ended. She got up from the couch and resisted the urge to open the front door to be certain Anton was still there. She went to the bathroom and washed her face, then returned to sit in her favorite chair in the living room to wait.

It was forty minutes before the front door opened. Anton entered and Magda forced herself to stay seated and not jump up and throw herself into his arms. She needed to know what decision he'd come to without her input. His face looked calm, peaceful, and she knew him well enough to see that he'd wrestled his anger away. He was in control as far as Demitri went, and some of the fear in her gut dissipated. But where was he in regard to her?

"Magda," he said, approaching her chair, "I wish you had told me all of this sooner, but I understand your fear. I knew something was wrong and have prayed that you would finally see your way free to tell me what it was."

"Oh, my love, I was so afraid." She stood, and he gathered her into him, kissing the top of her head and then resting his cheek there.

"I know that now. I had feared Demitri was making you smuggle drugs; never did I imagine he trafficked people."

"Oh, Anton, do you hate me? I've let this go on—"

He stopped her with a kiss. "No, I could never hate you. My heart breaks because you have been as much a victim in this as those girls. Demitri is the evil one behind this."

"He beat you because of me."

"I survived." There was no anger in his eyes, only love.

"I may go to jail because of all I've let happen."

"You will survive because I will be with you no matter what." He gripped both of her hands in his strong one.

"How can you forgive me? How can you still love me?" She stared into his eyes, almost not believing the depth of love she saw there.

"Because, my love, I have been forgiven much. And I know that the one who forgave me demands I forgive you. But again, I truly believe you are the victim. We must go to the police immediately and tell them everything."

"I know this is true, but I am so frightened. Demitri is powerful and evil. He has people everywhere. I fear for all of us."

"There will be nothing to fear once the police know

everything. It is time to trust them to stop Demitri and see that he is punished. God is in control. He will protect us."

"You'll go with me to the police?"

"I'll go with you. I will never leave you. I love you."

51

"Bulgarian Mafia?" Maggie asked after Jack and Brinna finished bringing her up to date on current events. She shook her head. "Here in Long Beach? Sounds like a bad movie."

"The worst movie," Brinna agreed.

"Have they made any demands? Ransom, anything?"

Jack and Brinna exchanged glances. "We're not sure what they want," Brinna said. She drained her third cup of coffee and frowned at Jack. "What if they do present demands, ask for ransom or something else?"

"I think we'd have heard from them by now if that were the case," Jack offered.

Brinna couldn't stifle a yawn. "You're probably right. I'm so tired right now I can barely think straight." She leaned back and closed her eyes while Maggie and Jack discussed events. Even the abundant caffeine couldn't halt the inevitable energy depletion crash.

When she opened her eyes again and checked her watch, she saw it was almost one in the afternoon. Her body now felt the consequences of lack of sleep, and she fought the fogginess that descended on her brain like sludge. Jack looked just as tired as Brinna felt. Only Maggie looked fresh.

"If they know that we know about them, what advantage would it be for them to hurt Ivana or Rose?" Maggie asked Jack.

"Why did they take them in the first place if it wasn't to hurt them, or at least hurt Ivana?" Brinna said before Jack could answer. "Everything I've ever heard about organized crime is that they kill people to send messages or make a point."

Jack drummed on the table with his fingers. "They were after Ivana. She was their captive and she ran away, so it's obvious why they took her. They wanted her back. Rose might have just gotten in the way. I can't see any upside for them to hurt her."

"Knowing my mom, I'm sure that she got in the way," Brinna said ruefully. "But what if she saw something she wasn't supposed to see?" Suddenly her throat clogged.

Maggie reached out and put a hand on Brinna's forearm. "If that were so, wouldn't they have just killed her and Ivana at the house? It's probably a good sign they were abducted—a sign they are still alive and needed for something. Maybe we're looking at this the wrong way. Maybe they do want money, and we'll eventually get a ransom demand."

"Could be. I would never rule ransom out," Jack agreed. "They might realize now that their operation has been exposed, and they'll want to use Ivana and Rose as leverage. If that's the case, negotiation could free them both."

Brinna toyed with her coffee mug. "I must be tired. That thought never occurred to me. That's a hopeful idea. We have some great hostage negotiators at the PD."

"Remember—" Maggie raised an eyebrow—"the glass is half-full."

Jack's cell phone rang. He answered it, and from the conversation, Brinna gathered he was talking to Ben. After a few minutes he hung up. "Well, all the girls we found at the house have been reinterviewed, but they still couldn't give us anything helpful. Chuck is digging through public records, trying to determine who owns the house and the van. Hopefully something will lead to a corporation or a man—or anything pointing to the place Ivana and Rose are being held."

He put his hand over Brinna's. "I think we both need to get some rest. I'm dead tired, and you must be too."

"I'll take the Crusader home," Maggie offered, looking from Jack to Brinna. "You can sleep, and I'll raid your fridge, make a mess, and listen for the phone."

Brinna couldn't suppress a grin. It was good to have Maggie back in this dark period of her life. "Okay, I can live with that. Besides, Hero needs some exercise. And—" she pointed out the window—"no rain. He might come in handy if we need a search."

Jack threw some money down on the table. "I'm glad we're in agreement. There are a lot of people on this." He held Brinna's gaze. "As corny as it sounds, there really is no place for the bad guys to hide."

Brinna nodded. "I'm sure my mom is praying right now.

No time like the present for me to try and join in. Hope I can pray the right way." She caught Jack's eye and hoped the comment didn't sound flippant.

Her mom would cling to prayers and so would Jack. *Maybe I should as well.* For Brinna, at this moment in time, she'd cling to anything that would bring her mom home.

52

MAGDA'S CELL PHONE rang as she and Anton were preparing to leave the house. It was Anton's idea to go directly to the police station and report what they knew.

"You must help me." It was Simon. The desperation in his voice sent a chill up her spine. She'd heard that flat, empty tone before. It was the main reason she'd left her native country. There were too many people there who had nothing and no means of changing their situation. They were lost and hopeless. Now that same chord rang in Simon's voice.

Magda remembered something her father had told her when Communism still ruled Bulgaria. Nothing was more dangerous than a desperate, hopeless man, he'd said. They were unpredictable.

Magda looked at Anton and grabbed his hand. "Simon, where are you?"

"Not important. I don't know what to do. They've found the house."

"The house?" Magda frowned and then realization dawned. "They? You mean the police?" She leaned into Anton, who wrapped his arms around her waist.

"Yes. The women are gone. Maybe Sergei has been arrested. I don't know. I am as good as dead. Please help me. Please." Again the monotone, hopeless voice.

Magda struggled for the right words that might get through to Simon. What did she know about him? Simon had never been violent like Demitri; he'd just been an obedient puppet. But without Demitri there to pull his strings, what would he do?

"Do you have the girl and that woman? The ones I saw on television?" she asked.

She heard an intake of breath and figured Simon was sucking on a cigarette, but he said nothing.

"You called me for help," she pleaded, "so now you have to tell me what's going on."

Still no response.

"Don't hurt them . . . please. End this without bloodshed."

"I'm tired, so tired. I can't run, and there is nowhere to hide. What do I do?" When his voice broke, Magda suddenly feared for the two women.

"Listen to me. Let the women go, and turn yourself in. Don't hurt them," she repeated. "Too many have been hurt already. It's time for all this to stop." She smashed the phone into her ear. Simon's breathing was all she could hear. "Simon?"

The connection was severed.

Magda hung up the phone and looked at Anton. "We must hurry."

* * *

Ivana awoke with Mrs. Caruso's arm draped over her shoulder. They lay on the filthy couch, huddled together for warmth. They'd been taken from the house wearing only pajamas and robes. There were no blankets in the small room and no heat.

"You awake?" Mrs. Caruso whispered.

Ivana sat up and stretched, managing a weak smile for her friend. "I dozed a little. You?" She didn't feel rested at all. They'd been taken from bed; now it was probably late morning. As she looked around in the dim light, she remembered what she and Mrs. Caruso were facing.

"The same. I'm hungry; my stomach tells me we missed breakfast." Mrs. Caruso patted Ivana's shoulder. "How about we take a look in the bag and see what there is to eat?"

"I'll get it." Ivana stood and went for the bag Simon had left by the door.

Mrs. Caruso stood and stretched. She walked to the wall and flipped on the single, dirty lightbulb. "That's a little better than nothing. At least we'll be able to see what we're eating."

Ivana placed the bag on the couch. Inside, they found some French rolls, sliced cheese, and two bottles of water.

"Dry, but nourishing," Mrs. Caruso said as she handed Ivana a roll. Ivana accepted it, amazed at how calm she felt at the moment. When they'd been brought to the warehouse the night before, she'd thought she would die from fear before Demitri had a chance to kill her. But when she saw Mrs. Caruso's calmness and heard the prayer she prayed, Ivana herself felt infused with peace. As this day began, she believed she could face anything if Mrs. Caruso were there to help her.

They munched on the cheese and bread, drinking the water sparingly. Ivana's roll was halfway gone when she heard a car pulling up outside.

"He's back," she whispered, fighting fear.

"Maybe he's come to his senses and decided to let us go," Mrs. Caruso said.

"I will follow your lead and think the best, good thoughts." Ivana sat back on the couch and held the older woman's hand. Together they listened as locks were undone and doors were opened. They could hear two men talking in Bulgarian in the other room. Ivana strained to make out the words. One voice belonged to Simon, she was certain, and maybe the second voice was one of the other men who had brought them to the warehouse the night before.

The voices became louder, angry all of a sudden. Ivana could hear and understand what was being said. The man whose name she didn't know wanted Simon to call Demitri for instructions. Simon, on the other hand, didn't want to tell Demitri anything.

"What are they saying?" Mrs. Caruso asked.

Ivana realized her jaw had gone slack. It was a revelation to her that Demitri was out of the country. All this time she'd been anticipating his presence, his cruelty, and now she knew he had no idea what was happening. She turned to Mrs. Caruso and translated what she was hearing.

"Demitri will send us more men, a plan, money, or better still, he will get us out of here," the nameless man said.

"No, no, no!" Simon insisted. "If we tell Demitri what is going on, we will be expendable. We don't know what Sergei told the police. He could have spilled his guts. With such news, Demitri will send someone here to eliminate us!"

"Sergei would never betray us. These weak American police could never make him talk."

"Without knowing exactly what is happening, telling Demitri anything would be risking suicide." Simon must have hit or thrown something because his last word was punctuated by a loud bang.

"Are we even safe in this warehouse? Perhaps we should kill the women and flee. I know people in Florida. That would be far, far away from here."

"We are safe here, provided Sergei has stayed silent."

The voices got softer as tempers seemed to ease. Ivana could no longer make out what was being said.

"I did not realize that Demitri was not in the country. I think this is why we are still alive," Ivana said to Mrs. Caruso. She crossed her arms, suddenly feeling the chill in the room deepen.

"We are still alive because the Lord is protecting us." Mrs. Caruso squeezed Ivana's shoulders. "Never forget that fact."

A key turned in the door, and it was jerked open. Light flooded the room and Ivana squinted. Simon and the other man stepped into the room and closed the door behind them. Simon had a gun in his hand.

"You." He pointed the gun toward Rose Caruso. "Come here."

Ivana felt her stomach roil and feared that the meager

meal she'd just eaten was going to come back up. Was all of Mrs. Caruso's faith misplaced? Was this the moment when both of their lives would end with a bullet each?

When Rose started toward Simon, Ivana tried to hold her back.

"It's all right." Mrs. Caruso smiled at Ivana, the peace in her eyes never fading. She removed Ivana's hands from her arm and continued toward Simon. "Yes?" she said, looking at the man with the gun.

"You said your daughter is a police officer?"

"Yes, she is."

He held up a cell phone. "Call her. Ask her what I tell you and only what I tell you." He gestured with his gun. "We saw the police at our house. We know everyone there was arrested. I want to know about Sergei. Where is he, and what has he said? You understand?"

"Yes, I understand."

"This phone is not traceable. You will say only what I tell you, or I will kill you." He touched the gun to Mrs. Caruso's temple, and Ivana held her breath, thinking to herself that if Mrs. Caruso's God was real, now was the time he needed to show himself and keep her levelheaded and calm.

53

BRINNA WASN'T SURE how long she'd been napping when she heard voices. One was Maggie's—of that she was certain—but the other voice she couldn't place. She sat up in bed and groaned as grogginess gripped her in a vise. It was only two thirty. She'd slept a bare forty-five minutes. How were you supposed to sleep when your mother's been kidnapped? The feeling in her gut was the same rigid knot she felt with any abduction, multiplied by ten.

Sliding off the bed, she stood and stretched, eventually making her way to the bathroom to splash water on her face. Hero wasn't in the room with her. *He must be out with Maggie,* she thought. She checked her reflection in the mirror as water dripped off her chin. *I look as bad as I feel.* There were dark circles under her bloodshot eyes, and her hair was a nightmare tangle. She worked with a brush and tried to smooth it out as best she could. When it was somewhere between Frankenstein's bride and passable, she gave up, grabbed a towel, and wiped her face.

"Time for coffee," she decided and tossed the towel in the sink. On her way to the kitchen, she peered in the living room and saw the source of the other voice—Dave the paramedic. He nodded to something Maggie said, but when he looked up and saw Brinna, he smiled.

"Hey, Brinna." He stood and shoved his hands in his pockets. Dave looked smaller out of his blue firefighter uniform, wearing jeans and a T-shirt. Brinna knew that every patch of skin on her face turned bright red. She was not prepared for a social visit, especially not a male social visit.

"Dave, what a surprise." A glance at Maggie revealed that her friend was amused by her discomfort. Hero, the traitor, was curled up on the couch with his head on Maggie's lap.

"I hope I didn't wake you. I saw the news, and I know what you've been going through. I just came by to, uh . . . well, show some support and to see if there's anything I can do to help." He glanced from Maggie to Brinna.

"I'm not sure if there have been any updates," Brinna said, eyebrows arched at Maggie. "Has anyone called?"

Maggie shook her head. "You just had a call from Rick, via Molly. They wanted you to know they were praying."

Brinna nodded, touched by how Rick, facing a lifetime of paralysis, could be concerned about her mother. "I'm going to make some coffee and then call Chuck." She turned back to Dave. "You can stick around if you like."

"Sure, I'm off today. And like I said, if I can do anything to help, I'd like to."

Brinna continued into the kitchen. She heard Maggie excuse herself, and soon her friend was at her shoulder.

"He's really a nice guy," she whispered as Brinna picked up the phone and punched in Chuck's number.

Brinna turned toward Maggie. "He's all yours. I kind of indicated I might have coffee with him, but romance is the last thing on my mind right now."

"And you want Jack, right?" Maggie gave a mischievous grin as Brinna was certain her face registered shock. But there was no time to address the issue of how Maggie knew what she had not yet voiced; Chuck's phone began to ring.

"You two mind if I take the dog out to the yard and toss the ball around?" David stuck his head in the kitchen, interrupting.

"Oh, thanks," Brinna said. "That would be awesome. Poor guy hasn't gotten much exercise lately."

"My pleasure."

Brinna watched Maggie watch Dave as he took Hero out the back door. "You were saying?"

Maggie turned back to Brinna. "It's obvious how you feel about Jack and how he feels about you."

"Seriously?"

Maggie shrugged and nodded toward the back door Dave just went out. "He really is cute, and I feel like a creep even thinking this way at a time like this, but . . ."

Brinna waved a hand dismissively. "Don't worry about it." *I'm not ready to discuss my feelings for Jack.* She felt her face flush and hoped Maggie didn't notice. Biting her bottom lip, she forced her thoughts back to where they should be: the current situation.

"A time like this." Brinna considered the words and the

surreal feeling of the afternoon. *Maybe all of this is just a bad dream, and I'll wake up soon.*

But as the ringing of Chuck's phone gave way to voice mail, Brinna knew she wasn't going to wake up from this nightmare anytime soon. The fear she felt for her mother seemed to have coalesced into a dull ache at the base of her skull. She rubbed her neck.

"Call me," she said to Chuck's voice mail.

Maggie made the coffee. Brinna sat at the counter to wait for the brew to finish.

"Look at the bright side," Maggie said. "Maybe no news is good news."

"No news means she's still out there somewhere with some crazed foreign dirtbag." Brinna rested her elbows on the counter and held her head in her hands. "Gosh, Mags, for the first time in my life I wish I could pray like my mom. Then at least I'd know how to plead with God for her to be okay." She pressed her fingertips into her forehead as tears threatened.

Maggie stepped behind Brinna and hugged her shoulders. "I don't have the right words to help you. I do know that the whole department is working hard on this."

"You're helping by being here," Brinna rasped in a ragged voice. "I really missed you when you weren't returning my calls."

"Yeah, well, I needed to figure things out."

"And what did you figure out?" Brinna looked up.

"That I was being too hard on you. Blaming you for Rick." She folded her arms and leaned against the refrigerator.

"We're cops, so stuff like this is bound to happen in our line of work. Look at all the officers who get killed every year. I guess I never thought bad stuff would happen to my friends." Her eyes filled. "I don't want to lose my partner, but it looks like that's what's going to happen. He told me himself that I'll need to move on."

Brinna stood. "I wish there was something I could say."

The coffee beeped.

"That's okay." Maggie ran a palm across her eyes. "Time to practice what I preach and be a glass-is-half-full person."

54

MAGDA WAS GLAD Anton had suggested they go straight to the police station because she wasn't sure how to go about contacting the police. She knew time was of the essence, but she'd had so little contact with American police, she didn't know who would take her seriously. She'd thought about dialing 911, but the first time she'd called 911 was the day she'd come home to find Anton beaten and tied up. The only other time she'd hit the three digits, she'd tried to report a traffic accident and been put on hold for twenty minutes. That wait just wouldn't work right now, especially given Simon's odd phone call. And Magda wanted to be certain that the police understood she was not overreacting or imagining danger. She didn't think she could get her point across to a faceless operator on a phone line without sounding hysterical.

Without further delay she and Anton jumped into his car. While he drove, Magda dug through her purse for the cards the two detectives who'd visited her shop had given her.

They arrived at the station in ten minutes, and together

she and Anton walked into the downtown lobby. Preceding them into the station was a uniformed police officer escorting a handcuffed prisoner, presumably to jail. Magda watched them pass through a door marked Authorized Personnel Only, and her courage faltered. Would that be her after she told the detectives what she knew?

She squeezed Anton's hand and drew strength from his presence. Stepping up to the counter, thick bulletproof glass separating her from the uniformed individual seated on the other side, Magda cleared her throat.

"Can I help you?" a young Asian man wearing the uniform of a police service assistant asked. His name tag identified him as G. Wang, and his voice sounded tinny through the speaker in the glass.

"I must speak to either Detective Jack O'Reilly or Detective Ben Carney. It's urgent." Magda leaned forward for emphasis.

The young man's expression never changed. "And what is this regarding?"

"They'll know when you tell them it is Magda Boteva asking for them."

G. Wang looked bored but picked up the phone and called for the detectives. After a moment he hung up. "Sorry, neither one of those detectives are in today."

Magda hadn't considered this possibility. She had no idea who else to talk to, which detectives she could trust. G. Wang looked around her, his expression saying clearly that she'd been dismissed and he had other people to help.

"Wait." Anton spoke up from her right. "Is Detective Darryl Welty available?"

Magda remembered the name as that of the detective who had handled the break-in of their house. The time Demitri had sent his message by beating and humiliating Anton.

Wang frowned and picked the phone up again. This time when he hung up, he actually smiled. "He'll be right down. Please have a seat."

Magda couldn't sit. She paced until Darryl Welty stepped into the lobby. A tall man with thick brown hair and brown eyes, he smiled, and Magda knew they were doing the right thing.

"What can I do for you two?" Welty asked.

"Detective Welty." Magda took a deep breath, wringing her hands. "The two women on the news—the officer's mother and the girl, the ones who were kidnapped—I know who took them."

55

A COUPLE MUGS of coffee helped Brinna shake the groggy feeling she'd awakened with.

Chuck phoned a few minutes after she'd left her message. While he'd had nothing to report about her mother, he did say that things were moving forward in the investigation—a good sign as far as Brinna was concerned. When things stalled out and leads dried up was when there was cause to worry.

The man who'd killed himself when they entered the house was as yet unidentified. The girls knew him only as Sergei. And besides Demitri, the girls could only give them two other first names: Simon and Gavin. Chuck promised composites and BOLOs within the hour. The house itself might eventually lead somewhere, Chuck said, if they could trace a buyer or broker.

"The house is owned by a corporation," he'd told her. "It's most likely a cover, a dummy business, but we've found three other properties owned by the same company, in three other counties. Judges are signing search warrants as we speak. We'll find your mother, Brin; I promise."

Brinna sighed, wanting to believe that her mother would be found soon and fervently hoping she was still alive.

After tiring Hero out, Dave shared a cup of coffee with Brinna and Maggie. He and Maggie chatted quite amicably. Brinna stayed out of the conversation using the excuse of being preoccupied by the situation with her mom.

"Here's my number," Dave said to Brinna as he stood to leave. "Call me if you need anything, anything at all."

"Thanks, Dave. I appreciate all that you've done." Brinna walked him to the door, truly grateful he was so helpful, but for her own peace of mind, and Maggie's chances, she needed to be clear with him. "I guess I should probably tell you that I'm kind of seeing someone right now."

"I think I got that." He smiled and held out his hand. "Still never hurts to have another friend."

"No, it never does." Brinna returned his smile and shook his hand. When she closed the door and turned to Maggie, her friend was holding her thumb up.

"That was nice, gentle."

"He is a nice guy."

"That he is. But he's not Jack O'Reilly."

Brinna nodded. "I know you don't care for Jack, but I think he's proven he's not the nutcase that you used to think he was. And he and I connect. He's told me he's ready to move beyond his wife. But I don't want to have this discussion right now. It's Mom I'm worried about, not my love life." She looked away as her eyes filled. "With every missing kid, I always trust my instincts. But now that it's my mom, my instincts aren't telling me anything." She wiped her eyes with her palms and stood.

"A lot of good people are on the case."

"I know, but I have to do something," she said, moving to the living room to pace. "I hate sitting and waiting. It's not raining today." She flung an arm toward the front window. "I could use Hero to search."

Hero sat up expectantly, watching Brinna's every movement.

"I'm open to suggestions," Maggie offered. She'd followed Brinna into the living room and stood leaning in the archway that separated the two rooms. "But just what do you want to search?"

Blowing out her breath, Brinna threw her hands up. "I don't know! This is so frustrating." She faced Maggie with her hands on her hips, a frown creasing her features. Just then there was a knock at the door.

"What now?" Maggie asked.

Brinna went to the door. She opened it, and there was Jack with a young girl. Brinna gaped. It was Gracie Kaplan, the girl with the case of hero worship.

"Hi." Jack smiled. "I don't know if I'm glad to see you up, 'cause it sure looks as though you didn't get the sleep you needed." He rubbed his chin. "Anyway, I'd planned to stop by and see if you wanted to go to the station with me. I figured you'd need to be doing something instead of sitting around." He looked down at Gracie. "When I got here, I found this young lady loitering in your driveway."

Gracie shot Brinna a pained expression. "I wasn't loitering," she protested. "I came by because I want to help. I heard about your mother and the lost girl. I wasn't sure if I should knock or not." Her blue eyes were earnest, and Brinna understood her desire. But she had no idea how to nurture it.

Brinna brought a hand to her mouth and studied Gracie out of the corner of her eye. *How do I encourage the girl without letting her see how helpless I feel?* she wondered.

"I'd love your help if I had something for you to do," she said after a minute. "For starters, you both can come inside. Maybe all of us together can think up a game plan." She stepped aside and Jack and Gracie walked in.

"Is it true your mother was kidnapped by gangsters?" Gracie asked.

"Uh . . ." Brinna thought carefully before she spoke. She remembered being that age and hating it when adults talked down to her, so she decided Gracie would be treated like a grown-up. "That's the best theory we have right now."

Gracie regarded her with a solemn expression. "I know how I would feel if someone took my mom. Even if you just want me to make you lunch, I will do that."

The girl was so serious, so committed, Brinna couldn't help but smile. "I appreciate that; I really do. Right now we're good, and I think this situation might be a bit too dangerous for you to get involved in."

"Could you use some moral support?"

"Yeah, I can always use that. But do your parents know that you are here?"

"I told them I wanted to help you."

"That's not a whole answer."

Gracie looked away. "Maybe I could have been more specific."

"The best support you can give me is to call your parents and let them know where you are and make certain it's okay for you to be here; got it?"

"I guess."

Maggie stepped up. "Why don't you introduce me to your friend and then we'll call her parents."

"Thanks, Mags," Brinna said. "This is Gracie Kaplan. She's the girl who took photos of Henry Corliss. Gracie, this is Maggie Sloan."

"Oh," Maggie exclaimed, "the little hero. How nice to meet you."

"I'm not a hero. Brinna is the hero," Gracie gushed. At the sound of his name, Hero got up to sniff the smallest new arrival. "Are you an officer too?" she asked Maggie as she scratched Hero's head.

"You kidding? I taught Brinna everything she knows." Maggie winked at Brinna, then directed Gracie to the couch and the phone on the table next to it.

Brinna turned her attention to Jack. "What were you going to do at the station?"

Jack sat in her recliner and shrugged. "I don't know— answer the phones, look through reports. I just hate waiting."

"You sound like an echo," Maggie said. "Brinna said the same thing a few minutes ago."

Gracie was punching in a phone number.

Brinna looked at Jack and nodded toward the kitchen. He followed her there.

"Did Chuck tell you what they found out about the house in Hawaiian Gardens?" she asked.

"Actually, Ben called me. He'd been out there with them all morning and was on his way home to get some sleep. The entire operation has been taken over by the Feds."

"Something has to come of the search warrants." Brinna pulled out a kitchen chair and sat, wishing she could hit something, but one broken wrist was enough. She did feel somewhat calmer now that Jack was here. He always seemed to stand on even ground, no matter what was swirling around him. She wanted to ask if he was praying and if he thought God was listening. She certainly hoped that he was.

Just then her cell phone rang. When she said hello, the voice she heard on the other end nearly made her drop the phone. She felt her face blanch and stood up from the chair so fast it fell over backward with a loud crash.

"Mom?"

"Yes, Brinna, it's me. I don't have much time. You have to listen carefully."

"Wh-where are you?" Brinna stared at Jack and pointed at the phone. He moved next to her, leaning with his ear toward the phone.

"I can't tell you that."

Jack held one hand up as he pulled out his cell phone and stepped away. "Stall."

In the background Brinna heard a man with a heavily

accented voice declare, "She's got a gun to her head. That's all you need to know."

"I need you to tell me . . ." Rose spoke again, pausing briefly, and Brinna could hear the man telling her what to say. "There was a man at the house the police found, where the girls were. Where is the man now, and what has he told the police?"

Brinna frowned, covered the receiver with her palm, and mouthed to Jack, "What should I say?"

He motioned for her to keep talking.

"Mom, I don't understand. Are you okay? Is Ivana okay?"

"Just answer the question, please, Brinna Marie. It's important."

Brinna sucked in a breath. Her mother had used her middle name. She hadn't heard that in years, and then she'd only done it when Brinna was in big trouble. "He's dead, Mom. The man in the house shot himself before we got inside."

Her mother repeated the message, and the connection ended.

"Mom? Mom?" Brinna looked at Jack and held the phone up. "She's gone."

Jack shot her a look, listening carefully to whomever he was talking to on his cell phone.

In the archway Maggie and Gracie stood watching Brinna. "That was your mom?" Maggie asked.

"Yeah. She didn't say much." Brinna righted the chair and sat, fearing her weak knees would not hold her up much longer. "At least I know she's alive."

Jack shut his cell phone, and everyone turned to face him.

"I just spoke to Darryl Welty. Remember the shopkeeper? Magda?"

When Brinna nodded, he continued. "She's in his office. She says she knows who has your mother and where she might be."

56

A STRING OF CURSES erupted from Simon when he heard Brinna's words about Sergei. He ripped the phone away from Mrs. Caruso and threw it across the room. Ivana cringed, certain this was the end for her and Mrs. Caruso.

"I don't believe them! They killed Sergei. Lying police. Lies, lies, lies," he ranted.

Ivana stood, rooted to the spot with fear, wringing her hands.

Finally he shoved the gun in Mrs. Caruso's face and pointed to Ivana. "Get back over there. I must think."

Mrs. Caruso moved to where Ivana stood, and the pair held hands. The other man began speaking in Bulgarian, and Ivana listened and watched, transfixed.

"We must call for help now," he insisted. "If they killed Sergei, we are next." He waved a hand in Ivana's direction. "Just kill them and let's go, now!"

"No!" Simon screamed. "I will not run. Animals run."

"You are a fool. They will slow us down." The man pulled

a cell phone out of his pocket. He turned away from Simon and headed for the door.

"Gavin," Simon called, "don't. I'm warning you."

Gavin ignored him. He reached the door, and Simon raised the gun, yelling one more warning.

"Stop now!"

Ivana gasped and cowered against Mrs. Caruso.

Gavin opened the door. Simon fired. Ivana screamed. The gun's report was deafening.

Gavin slumped against the doorframe and dropped the phone. His eyes were wide with shock. He tried to pull something from his pocket.

Simon fired again.

Ivana buried her face in Mrs. Caruso's shoulder, not wanting to look at the dead man or the gun in Simon's hand . . . now pointed at her and Mrs. Caruso.

57

CHAOS ERUPTED when Jack told Brinna, Maggie, and Gracie about Magda Boteva.

"I know that shop," Gracie exclaimed. "My neighbor Laura works there. Her boss is a kidnapper?"

"No, no, that's not what I said." Jack raised his hands to calm everyone down. "She has information about the kidnapping."

At first Brinna was speechless; then a seething anger began to boil up inside. "And just how long has she known this?" she demanded. "My mother has been gone for hours."

"Darryl didn't give me the whole story. You and I have to get down to the station, talk to the woman, and let everyone know about the phone call you just got."

"Should I go interview Laura?" Gracie bounced on her toes with anticipation. "Maybe she'll know something about all this."

"No," Brinna and Jack exclaimed at the same time. They exchanged glances, and Brinna shook her head, gesturing to

Jack, wanting him to explain to Gracie why that was a bad idea.

"Gracie, we appreciate that you want to help, but you have to leave this to the police, okay?"

"But, Detective O'Reilly! Maybe there's something I can do that the police can't."

Maggie stepped in. "Hey, Gracie, it's great you want to help, but the most important thing now is to get Brinna's mom and Ivana home safe. You don't want to jeopardize that, do you?"

The girl looked crestfallen. "No, but—"

"Mags." Brinna took a deep breath. "Jack and I have to get going. What did Gracie's mother say?"

"She was happy to know Gracie was here with us and said she'd come to pick her up if we want."

"She also said that I can stay if I'm helping. I want to help."

"You and Gracie can help me most by walking Hero and then feeding him. Then you should probably go home, okay?" She looked from Maggie to Gracie.

"Sure," Maggie said. "How does that sound, Gracie? After we take care of Hero, I'll give you a ride home."

"Okay, I guess." She was deflated but Brinna barely noticed. She was halfway out the door, fanny pack in hand, waving for Jack to catch up.

Maggie hollered from the porch, "Good luck!" Then she crossed her fingers.

Brinna held that image in her mind, knowing exactly what her mother would have said had she seen it. *"No use crossing your fingers. It's not fate or luck that controls our lives; it's a loving God in heaven."*

I don't really know how to pray, Brinna thought, *but oh, Lord, if you're there and you're real, please bring my mom home safe.*

Brinna realized how much she wanted to have another conversation about God with her mom. *Will I ever have the chance?*

Jack drove to the station. Brinna, in the passenger seat, had a white-knuckle grip on her seat belt.

"Darryl said this woman had a lot of information about Ivana and the trafficking?" she asked Jack.

"Apparently she knows a lot."

Welty's news that this woman, this shop owner, was in his office ready to come completely clean with what she knew about Ivana and her mother was shocking and enraging at the same time. Brinna seethed, wondering just how long the woman had had this important information.

"Did Welty tell you anything else?" she asked Jack through gritted teeth.

"That she knew who was responsible for enslaving the girls and where Ivana and Rose were likely being held."

"This makes me furious. If she'd spoken up sooner, she might have prevented everything!"

"We don't know that. And we don't know her involvement; maybe she is as much a victim as the girls."

"She runs a successful business and dresses in expensive clothes. She's not a victim."

"Just hang on until we know the whole story." Jack

reached across the car and gripped Brinna's hand. Brinna squeezed back and took a deep breath. Jack's touch and presence calmed her, but the anger was there, just beneath the surface.

The station was six minutes from Brinna's house if you made all the traffic lights. Jack got there in five. SWAT was mobilizing in the parking lot when they arrived. Jack and Brinna jogged to the station and took the stairs up to the burglary floor.

Brinna's heart was in her throat when she stepped into the office and came face-to-face with Magda Boteva. The woman sat in front of Darryl's desk, wiping her eyes with Kleenex. Holding her hand was a blond-haired man with one leg. Darryl had said that the woman came in with her husband.

"You guys sure got here quick." Darryl leaned back in his chair. "I'd like to introduce Magda and Anton. They've given us quite a bit of information."

There was only one bit of information, one question Brinna wanted answered. "Where is my mother?"

58

"MY LIFE IS OVER," Simon said, standing over the body of his coconspirator. For the moment he seemed to forget about Ivana and Mrs. Caruso, but Ivana could not forget about the gun in his hand.

Her entire body shook with fear. She had never seen someone die, much less be shot to death before her eyes, and now she couldn't force her gaze from the gruesome scene just played out in front of her. Mrs. Caruso held Ivana close and tried to calm her fears, but Ivana could tell the shooting had cracked Mrs. Caruso's calm reserve. The older woman shook along with Ivana, and Ivana wondered if they both were taking their final breaths.

Simon rubbed his chin and mumbled something Ivana couldn't make out. Her ears were still ringing from the two thunderous gunshots. When he turned and faced the two women, Ivana held her breath.

"There is no escape. Demitri will find me, or your police will kill me." He pointed the gun at Rose Caruso, and Ivana felt the older woman's body grow taut. "How did it come to this bleak place?"

Ivana's hand tightened on Mrs. Caruso's, and suddenly the room felt frigid. She stared at Simon, never having seen such dark, hopeless eyes. He had always been the cheerful, friendly captor, the only one she'd trusted. Now, watching him, and fearing the gun, she felt certain she and Mrs. Caruso were dead.

"As long as you have breath in your body, there's hope," Mrs. Caruso said, her calm voice eerie in the dimly lit room.

Ivana did not take her eyes off Simon to look at her friend. But she hoped with all her heart that Mrs. Caruso had the words to stop the madman, because Ivana couldn't find it in herself to even speak.

Simon grunted something Ivana didn't understand.

"It's not too late to end this." Mrs. Caruso continued speaking, her voice soothing. "American justice says you get a lawyer and a fair trial. Let us go; you haven't hurt us. I'll make sure the authorities know that you are not a bad man."

"You are wrong," Simon shouted, pointing the gun directly at Rose Caruso. "I am a very bad man!" A sob escaped him. "But I am not as bad as Demitri." He threw his head back, banging it against the door. "I do not fear your authorities." A strangled laugh bubbled forth. "I fear Demitri. Only death will provide me with escape from him."

Ivana agreed with Simon even as the name Demitri caused anger to build inside her. He was the devil behind all of this. The only thing she understood in this entire crazy situation was the fear Simon had for that man.

"I refuse to believe that." Mrs. Caruso continued to plead with Simon, interrupting Ivana's train of thought and desire for revenge. "If Demitri is behind all this, then he should pay. You can help the police here arrest him, and he will be held responsible. Any help you give will just make things better for you."

Mrs. Caruso extricated herself from Ivana and stood. "Please, I know how the police work in this country. Let us go. I'll talk to them, explain what you're afraid of. Explain that you felt threatened by this man you shot. Give yourself up, and tell them what you know. There is still hope for you."

"You know nothing!" Simon screamed and Ivana jumped. But Mrs. Caruso stayed still even as Simon released a stream of angry Bulgarian.

"I know that you are afraid," Mrs. Caruso said when he took a breath. "So am I, and so is Ivana. But there doesn't have to be any more bloodshed or brutality." She held her hands out. "You think you have no power, but you're wrong. You have the power to end this now and save three lives. Give me the gun; let us go. You won't regret it."

Ivana held her breath. Simon's face contorted, and his eyes seemed to grow darker. She remembered earlier, when Mrs. Caruso had sought to calm her fears by talking about God and the Savior Jesus. Mrs. Caruso had told her that when you had fear, if you prayed to God and believed that he was real and that he'd heard you, he would give you strength. Ivana wasn't certain about Mrs. Caruso's God, but she knew right now she needed strength.

With all of her heart she prayed, begging this God to

protect them both and to make Simon drop the gun. But the look in Simon's eyes caused her hope to flee. He was not a man who would pay any attention to reason now.

Her heart seemed to stop beating. She knew that, in seconds, both she and Mrs. Caruso could be dead. Praying harder, she begged for a God she barely knew to intervene.

59

"IF I KNEW EXACTLY where she was, I would tell you." Magda held Brinna's simmering gaze.

"But you know who took her and who killed Ivana's sister? You know that?" Brinna leaned into the woman's face.

Jack gripped Brinna's shoulders and pulled her back. "Let's hear what she has to say."

"She's already given us names." Welty held out a file of mug shots.

Brinna jerked herself from Jack's grasp and took the folder from Welty. They were in the burglary offices huddled around Welty's desk while in the back of the room a SWAT team was prepping for action. It was after 6 p.m. now and dark out.

"The head bad guy is Demitri Dinev," Welty continued. "He's got no record in the States but an extensive one in Europe. Interpol gave us the picture." Welty then went through all the information they had gleaned from Magda about the man who had exploited so many. Interpol provided a rap sheet from Europe. Most of the arrests were minor, and most had never been prosecuted, but the information gave the investigation a boost. It also gave them known associates.

"Simon Greuv, another petty criminal, is the one we believe has your mother and the Bulgarian girl."

Brinna pulled the picture of Simon from the file and studied it.

"A photo of him has been distributed to all the major news outlets," Welty continued. "Chuck and ICE decided a full-court press will be the only way to shake something loose."

"You're not afraid of scaring these guys into doing something rash?" Jack asked.

Welty shook his head. "According to Magda, Demitri is not in the country right now; he's possibly back in Bulgaria. It's just Simon we have to deal with."

"Going public might spook Demitri. He could stay in Bulgaria or another European country and never be arrested for his crimes in the US." Jack took the words from Brinna's mouth.

She sat back, leaning against a window. She didn't trust herself to speak with this woman in the room. They had yet to learn the entire story behind the human trafficking, but they did know one important fact: Magda Boteva had known what was going on for years. The girls were promised jobs at her shop. The thought of that deception was like a match to gasoline on Brinna's already-seething emotions.

Welty rubbed his chin and gave a half shrug. "There is a chance of that, but the priority at the moment is getting Rose and Ivana home safely. We want to put pressure on Simon. Magda gave us a great lead." He deferred to her.

"There is a piece of property near the harbor," Magda explained. "It's not owned by Demitri or anyone Bulgarian. It's owned by a Canadian associate of Demitri's. It's mostly vacant except for a large warehouse. Demitri takes all the girls there when he first brings them into the country. If Simon is not at the house where the girls were kept, he will be at the warehouse. I know of no other place he would hide."

"Is this warehouse normally empty?" Jack asked.

"Yes, he may store his car there and maybe some merchandise. But my guess is that it will be empty until he returns from Bulgaria." Magda cast her gaze to the ground.

At least she has the decency to be embarrassed about what she's allowed to continue, Brinna thought.

Detective Welty laid a map of the harbor on his desk, and Magda pointed out the location of the warehouse. The SWAT sergeant stepped close to listen in.

"He'll see us coming from a mile away," Brinna said as she studied the route through the harbor. "Talk about being hidden in plain sight. This warehouse was right under our noses; how is it that no one noticed something illegal was going on?"

"It wasn't where he was running his business, so he probably stayed off the radar," Jack observed.

"We have a signed warrant; everything is a green light. It won't be a problem for an armed team to approach on foot under cover of darkness." SWAT Sergeant Hall pointed to a path south of the warehouse that would provide reasonable cover for a team on foot. "I've got my teams ready to go—one for the ground assault and one assigned to vehicles." He stood ready, arms crossed over his black uniform, a wad of tobacco visible in his left cheek.

"Wait a second," Brinna protested. "If there are innocent hostages in the warehouse, you can't storm it."

"Relax, Caruso." The tobacco wad moved from Hall's left cheek to his right as he regarded Brinna with an unreadable expression. "The foot team will determine if a ground assault is warranted. After they determine if the targets are even there."

"If they're there, we'll need a negotiator," Brinna said.

"Got one—downstairs in MOC-1. It's Gomez."

Brinna sighed, happy with that information at least. She was on unfamiliar turf here and had to concede that the SWAT sergeant knew what he was doing. The team also had proficient negotiators—calm, professional, and trustworthy. If she'd been able to pick, Gomez would have been her choice.

"I'd like to hang out in MOC-1 and watch the progress of the team on the monitors," Brinna said. MOC-1, the Mobile Operations Center, was a large recreational vehicle outfitted with radios, satellite systems, phones—everything needed to be a rolling police command post.

Hall looked at the watch commander, Lieutenant Harvey. Harvey was probably the only weak link as far as Brinna was concerned, and she hated the fact that they had a history. He was new and so by the book, she feared he would not be able to make critical decisions quickly. Luckily Jack spoke up before Harvey could object.

"Okay, Brinna, let's get downstairs and into the RV so

we've got a good seat when this show hits the road." He grabbed her arm, and they left the office with no objections from Harvey or Hall.

Brinna shoved her hands in her pockets, not wanting to think about what would happen if Magda's information was incorrect. The warehouse in the harbor was the last best hope of finding her mother quickly. She hoped with all her heart that Rose was in the warehouse and that she was still alive.

* * *

FOX, the police helicopter, circled in the sky above the harbor. Brinna sat in MOC-1 viewing the video feed from the chopper. The warehouse sat by itself on an old pier. There was no activity of any kind around the pier, no ships docked close by and no vehicles on the dock.

"It looks deserted," Brinna observed. She chewed on an index finger since both of her thumbnails had already been gnawed painfully short.

"Don't let that fool you," the SWAT sergeant said. "The warehouse is large enough to hold several vehicles. It's possible our suspect pulled the car inside to make us believe the place was deserted. Our first team will reach the place in a few minutes."

He pointed over Brinna's shoulder to the screen at the six-man team that approached the warehouse on foot. A ground approach was the only way to make a stealth attack. The black-clad SWAT team moved efficiently across the space between the warehouse and the command post. Their only cover was scrub brush, but Brinna had to admire their skill.

She detected them because she knew what to look for. She doubted anyone in the warehouse would be able to see them coming.

"They'll get an eye inside the warehouse with a remote camera and microphone that will pick up any sound," he continued. "Then we'll have a better idea of what we're facing."

The sergeant left to confer with his negotiator. Brinna blew out a frustrated breath and searched for Jack. He was in another part of the command center on the phone. Brinna knew he was trying to figure out which vehicle the man holding Ivana and Rose might be in. Since the van had been impounded at the house in Hawaiian Gardens, they had no idea what mode of transportation they should be on the lookout for.

Jack hung up the phone as Brinna reached his side.

"Any news?" she asked.

"The van was a rental, a long-term rental to BVD Enterprises."

"BVD? Is that some kind of joke?"

Jack shrugged. "Not sure. But the other three houses that have been searched all had vehicles leased to the same company."

Brinna considered this information. She knew that the three search warrants Chuck had told her about had been served. ICE freed more women and several young men who were being held against their will. All were from Eastern European countries, and most of the women had been forced into prostitution, though a few were used as house cleaners. The men were used for various types of manual labor. As for the men holding the captives, six had been arrested, and two had died in gunfights with federal agents. The story was big news, and media coverage was exploding. Already two news helicopters had been warned away from the harbor.

But none of the arrests had gotten them any closer to Rose and Ivana, nor had any of the men arrested been forthcoming with information. They clearly understood the importance of American Miranda rights and were asking for lawyers. Equally frustrating was the lack of a paper trail. None of the houses turned up anything important—no computer records and, other than the documents belonging to the women, no paperwork.

"How are you holding up?" Jack asked, his full attention on Brinna. "Sorry I had to pull you back."

Brinna looked up at him, stepped close so their hands touched. "I don't blame you; I was out of control."

Jack stroked her forearm with an index finger. "No one here faults you for that."

"I need to keep control, so thanks for the brush back. You know me. I hate to be on the sidelines. I want to be in the game. Right now caution is the wise course, but I sure wish we could rush the place and find out what . . ." She looked away as she considered that they might enter the warehouse and find only bodies.

"Hang on." Jack took her hand and held it in both of his. "There is encouraging news. One vehicle rented by BVD is still outstanding. It's a four-door Chevy sedan. Could be that car will lead us to your mom."

"We have a visual on the inside of the warehouse." Hall's voice cut across the command post like a crack of lightning.

Brinna and Jack turned to look at him.

"No vehicles, no movement or sound." His brows furrowed as he concentrated on what he was hearing in his earpiece. "The place appears to be deserted. I'm sending in the vehicles; we're going in the front door."

60

Brinna stood with her arms folded, an uncomfortable position with the cast on her left, and surveyed the small room within which her mother had been held captive. She knew her mom had been there because of the slippers. Near the door, next to the dead man, they'd found two pairs of slippers. One belonged to her mother. They'd been a Christmas gift from Brinna last year. The second pair was new and smaller, and Brinna could only surmise that they belonged to Ivana. The fact that the slippers were there could indicate one of two things. Either Ivana and Rose left the building so quickly the slippers came off, or they weren't ambulatory and didn't need the slippers.

Brinna refused to consider the second possibility. And the scene didn't support it. There was no other blood than that of the dead man. He'd been shot twice, and they'd recovered two casings. No, she decided that Simon had panicked and rushed the two women out of the warehouse. Everyone was gone before SWAT arrived. But what spooked him?

The coroner had not yet removed the dead body, and they hadn't learned much from him. He had no ID and who or what he was in this mess was a mystery. Brinna didn't think he'd been dead long; she'd seen enough dead bodies to feel comfortable with her assessment. The coroner could pinpoint the time of death, but knowing that to the minute wasn't going to get her any closer to finding her mother.

Jaw set, she watched the lab tech work, clenching and unclenching her good fist beneath her elbow. Brinna felt frustrated by the fact that they had no more leads to follow. A federal forensic team would arrive shortly to go over the warehouse with a fine-tooth comb. Long Beach PD was bowing out; SWAT was demobilizing; everyone was going home. The last place Brinna wanted to go was home.

They had to do something, or she was certain she'd climb right out of her skin.

"Brin." She turned as Jack approached with a cup of coffee. He and Ben would be the department's liaisons with the Feds.

"Thanks." She took the offered cup in her good hand and gulped, nearly choking on the bitterness. "Has she come up with any other ideas?" Brinna rasped and nodded toward MOC-1, referring to Magda Boteva. The woman seemed shocked when they'd discovered the warehouse was empty. Brinna had avoided talking to her, still simmering with the knowledge that Magda had known about the exploitation of dozens of young women for years and done nothing.

Jack shook his head. "This is the only location belonging to Demitri that she was privy to. At least we know your mom and Ivana were here." He pointed to the slippers that had been marked but not bagged yet. The lab tech's camera flash went off every few seconds. "We were just late."

"I've been thinking about when kids are abducted." Brinna took a deep breath, blew it out, collecting her thoughts. "What do the bad guys do when they are on the run with a victim? In my experience, they either give up and throw themselves on the mercy of the judicial system, or they kill their victim, get rid of the evidence, and run. When they're cornered, they go with the option they think will benefit them most."

"This guy's got to know we're on his trail. His picture went out on every local and cable news station available. He's more or less cornered," Jack said. "Any insight on what you think he'll do?"

"I need to know more about him. When I chased Corliss, I knew the creep. I knew how his mind worked and what he was most likely to try. I refuse to believe catching him was pure luck. I was in his mind." She took another swallow of coffee, realizing that the only way she could gain any insight into the man who held her mother was to talk to Magda. She had to get past the anger that made her want to throttle the woman and instead pick her brain about this abductor.

"Chuck has everyone on alert at the other locations. It's possible this guy might flee to one of those houses."

Brinna drained the coffee cup, then crushed it. "Maybe." She faced Jack. "I need to talk to—" She jerked her head toward MOC-1. Tossing the cup in the trash, Brinna walked past Jack toward the command center, hoping she could keep all the frustration and anger she felt from bubbling over while she tried to get what she needed from Magda.

Magda and her husband had their heads together and were speaking in low tones when Brinna entered MOC-1. Welty was drinking coffee and munching on a doughnut.

"You mind if I talk to her?" Brinna asked.

Welty shrugged, his mouth full. His expression said, *Go ahead.*

"Excuse me." Brinna stepped toward the couple.

The woman looked up, her eyes red and puffy.

"I want you to tell me all you can about this guy, this Simon." Brinna leaned against a counter.

Magda cleared her throat. "I've told Detective Welty everything."

"Everything about where he might be. That's not what I'm asking. I want to know about the man. What's his position in this organization? What is his role with the girls? What kind of guy is he? Anything you can tell me about him will be helpful."

The woman took a deep breath. "I . . . I'm not certain. He's not Demitri's right-hand man—that would be Emil, and Emil is with Demitri." She glanced at her husband, whose expression seemed to encourage her to go on. "I think Simon was simply responsible for watching the girls. Demitri told me once or twice that Simon had a calming influence on them. He was not responsible for discipline or for recruiting. He lived at the home with the girls and saw to their needs."

"Their needs?"

"Yes—food, clothing, that sort of thing."

"A civilized jailer, you mean?" Brinna blew out a breath, right hand absentmindedly moving to scratch an itch on her left hand she couldn't get to. "And you never went to any of the houses where the girls were kept?"

"No. I was not part of that. I only—"

"You only lured the poor girls here by promising them jobs." Brinna's anger would stay bottled up no longer.

Magda's husband started to speak, but Magda waved him quiet.

"I never! That was Demitri." She stood and faced Brinna. "Demitri is behind all of this."

"Yeah, yeah, you're just as bad as he is. You knew what was happening, and you never lifted a finger to help those girls."

"What could I do? Demitri would have killed me, killed my family. He is a vicious animal."

"You were afraid," Brinna mocked the woman. "Then why come forward now? Couldn't he still find a way to kill you?"

"Yes, he could." When Magda met her angry glare, Brinna recognized something in the woman's eyes. Something she'd seen before . . . in the eyes of victims who'd been abused over and over until they finally decided to stand up to the abuser. There was a spark of fight in those eyes along with a glint of fear.

Brinna took a step back as the edges of her opinion of the woman softened.

"I can't stand by and let another girl be hurt, no matter what happens to me," Magda continued. "Whether you believe me or not, that is the truth. I must be my sister's keeper."

That statement took Brinna by surprise. "Your sister's keeper?"

"Yes. It is a story from the Bible. About a brother who murders a brother, and God—"

Brinna waved her quiet and cast a pained glance at Jack, who looked surprised. Rubbing her brow, Brinna grimaced. "I remember hearing that story in Sunday school. Let's get back on topic." She exhaled. "How do you know Simon if you never went to the house? How do you know what he did?"

"From time to time I would see him here. Every so often Demitri would bring me here when new girls arrived. He would help coordinate things for the girls." Her voice broke, and she seemed to pull strength from somewhere to keep from crying. "I didn't interact with the girls. Demitri brought me here to be sure that I knew he was in control." She blew her nose. "And Simon has also been to my shop."

"Your shop?"

"Yes, he had been there once or twice with Demitri, but most recently he came there when the girl ran away."

Brinna frowned. "Why did he come to you?"

"He thought I would help him. He knows I fear Demitri— we all do. He thought I would help him get the girl back."

"But you didn't," Brinna said, half to herself. "Does he know you went to the police?"

"I don't know. He may now if he sees his picture on television. But Demitri must never know. Do you understand that if you find Simon, we can stop this madness before Demitri returns?" She held her hands out, pleading with

Brinna. "If we stop Simon, perhaps we can stop Demitri and save many, many more girls."

Brinna stared at her, wanting to believe the intensity in her voice. But the anger simmering inside clouded her thoughts and threatened to boil over.

"How long ago did he call you?"

"Just before we went to the police station." Magda looked at Anton. "About seven or eight hours ago now, I think."

A glimmer of hope formed in Brinna's heart. "Maybe he'll call again."

61

A LONG LINE of federal vehicles wound down the road to the warehouse, passing MOC-1 as the RV transported Magda, Anton, and LBPD personnel back to the station. Once there, they set up camp in the detective bureau conference room. Brinna tamped down her smoldering anger with Magda and confronted the woman.

"You must know more than you are saying—you must! These people call you; they visit your store. How many years have you been party to their brutality?"

Magda seemed to melt into Anton. But when he started to say something, Magda stopped him.

"No, I will answer." She pushed away from him. "How long, you ask? Too long. I have lived in fear too long. But I was never a part of their brutality, and I'm trying hard to make up for it."

"What are you hiding? Are you protecting yourself from something incriminating? There must be—"

Jack stepped forward and placed his hand on Brinna's arm. "Brin, she's been helping. I think your anger is misplaced."

She turned on him, ready to hit him with both barrels, but the love and concern in his eyes stopped her.

"I have told you everything. If there were something else, I'd—" Magda's voice broke and she held both hands out, palms up, tears streaming down her cheeks.

Brinna blew out a breath as what Jack said cut through her angry haze. He was right—she wanted Demitri and Simon and was lashing out at Magda. She stomped away from the group to sit by the window.

Jack and Welty brought Ben up to speed. He'd come to the station after finishing up with Hawaiian Gardens and wanted to know what happened at the warehouse.

Magda and Anton settled in on the other end of the room and called the neighbor who was watching their children, asking whether it was okay that they stay the night. Though Jack had said they could leave Magda's phone in case Simon called and go home, Magda wanted very much to stay and see everything turn out for the best.

By now it was close to ten o'clock. Everyone was exhausted, but hope burned in Brinna that Simon would call Magda one more time and give them something to go on. The store owner's phone lay plugged into a charger on Jack's desk.

Brinna positioned her chair closer to the window. She sat as still as she could, fighting restlessness, and stared out into the dark night. That she was tired was an understatement.

She felt worn out, and her wrist continued to throb. It was difficult to keep her thoughts clear and not dwell on the discomfort she felt, emotional and physical.

Why did Simon move the women? she wondered again. *He panicked, left in a hurry. What spooked him?*

"Magda." Jack's voice cut into Brinna's musings. She looked to where Jack had pulled a chair up and sat close to Magda and her husband. "Tell me about you being your sister's keeper."

Brinna tuned in to hear the woman's response. Most of the anger she'd felt toward Magda Boteva had dissipated. She'd dealt with too many victims like her whose lives had been twisted and dictated by fear. Brinna realized that Jack was right; Magda was just as much a victim as Ivana. Demitri had reached out and brutalized her family, thereby brutalizing the woman. Now the anger Brinna felt was directed solely at Demitri Dinev.

"I came to realize one night, after hearing my husband tell our children a Bible story about Cain and Abel, that we are responsible for each other." Magda answered Jack as she smiled and squeezed Anton's hand. "I mean 'we' as human beings. I have been ashamed at myself for letting these girls suffer for so long. I had to step forward, no matter what the cost, to save myself as well as those girls. Please forgive me for being a coward."

"In Bulgaria," Anton spoke up, "Magda would have been murdered quickly for saying anything about this situation. She needed to be certain she could trust you American police."

"I understand your fear. It can be a paralyzing emotion. I've dealt with a lot of reluctant witnesses. I'm glad you came forward now. And Cain and Abel opened your eyes?"

"To me, the story showed a God who was giving Cain an opportunity to confess his wrong and be saved in some way." Magda squared her shoulders. "I'd felt dirty for so long. I desperately wanted to confess, to save those girls, and perhaps be saved myself in the process. Does that make sense, Detective O'Reilly?"

"Yes, it does." He glanced at Brinna, and she held his gaze, understanding more about Magda but still worried sick about her mother.

"I am ready to accept the consequences," Magda continued. "Will I be charged with a crime?"

Jack shrugged. "That'll all be up to the DA. He'll consider everything—what you hid, how you helped—all of it. That you were afraid to say anything will also figure in."

"That is what I have been telling her," Anton said. "My wife has been in fear for her life for years."

"I'm sorry I was so angry with you," Brinna said. "It's just that I—" Suddenly she couldn't finish the sentence.

"I understand," Magda said, eyes moist. "You fear for your mother as I feared for my family."

Brinna nodded and tuned the rest of the conversation out, considering Magda's reasons for deciding to be her sister's keeper. She knew the story of Cain and Abel and had always considered it simply in the context of mankind's first recorded murder. That it taught the broader implications Magda had voiced had never occurred to her.

My sister's keeper. That phrase kept repeating in Brinna's mind. As she thought about the story, she remembered the dodge Cain voiced when God fronted him off about where his brother, Abel, was. "Am I my brother's keeper?"

It was a typical criminal maneuver, trying to deflect guilt. A kind of early-man "Hey, you talking to me?" evasion. Of course, it had been perfected over the centuries; Cain didn't have anything on modern-day criminals.

That the story she'd always thought of as a folktale could be taken the way Magda took it surprised her. The discussions she'd had with her mother and Jack replayed in her mind. Evil, good, pain, death, God—the concepts she'd struggled with—seemed wrapped up in this simple story. Abel was good, Cain evil. Cain committed the most heinous crime when he murdered his brother. God knew, but he gave Cain the chance to confess. He gave Cain the chance for redemption, the opportunity for something good to come out of the evil and the pain. But Cain refused.

Am I like Cain? Brinna wondered. *Jack and my mom keep saying that what God offers is free. Is he offering me something I should take that will save me?*

She closed her eyes, thinking that her mom was in the hands of a Cain. What would this one choose?

* * *

A phone finally did ring, but it wasn't Magda's; it was Brinna's. She grabbed it and walked into the hallway to answer. It was Maggie.

"What's up?"

"Where are you now?" Maggie's voice sounded strange, like she was whispering.

"At the station. Where are you?"

"I'm in College Park. I took Gracie home but not before I got the address of her neighbor—you know, the one who works at the collectible shop?"

"I remember her mentioning that neighbor." Brinna perked up, wondering where Maggie was going with this. She hooked the free thumb of her casted arm in a belt loop and leaned against the hallway wall.

"I had to wait a bit for this Laura to come home, and I don't want to go into it over the phone. Can you get over here?" Maggie rattled off an address.

"Maggie, this is crazy. I'm not sure I want to leave right now."

"Come on, Brin, how many times have you talked me into crazy things with less information than I've just given you? Come here and—oh, stop and get Hero and a piece of your mom's clothing."

"Maggie, what are you saying?"

"If I'm on the right track, we'll call Chuck. If I'm wrong . . . well, I might be in trouble, and I for sure will owe you big-time. But I think I've found your mom."

62

When Brinna stepped back into the office, something was happening. Jack was involved in a serious conversation on the phone, and Anton and Magda were chattering in a foreign language. Welty was furiously pounding on the computer.

"What's going on?"

"Magda remembered something," Welty informed her. "Simon Greuv has a relative here. He owns a business in San Pedro. I'm trying to find an address, and Jack is on the phone with the Feds."

Brinna's throat felt tight as she considered her options: go chase down Maggie and her cryptic message, or stay here and follow this new promising lead. She decided quickly. She knew what Jack and Darryl were looking for. She needed to know what Maggie had found. She grabbed her fanny pack and leaned toward Welty.

"Darryl, I'm going home. I'm beat, and I'm no help here. But call me if you guys hear anything, okay?"

"Sure, you know we will." He never looked up from the computer.

Brinna raced downstairs and out to the back steps before she remembered Jack had driven her here in his homicide vehicle. She checked her key chain. Luckily all the Chevys were keyed alike, and she had a Chevy key. As she started the car, she hoped Jack wouldn't need it anytime soon.

College Park. Maggie had said she was in College Park. Why was she there? College Park was the name of a section of tract homes on the farthest east side of Long Beach, near the state college. Gracie didn't live there—Brinna knew that from the interview. Laura was Gracie's neighbor, so she didn't live in College Park either. With every question she asked, another popped up, but there were no answers.

Once home, Brinna quickly leashed Hero and loaded him into her black-and-white Explorer, leaving Jack's car parked on the street. There was no need to go to her mother's house for a piece of clothing. Rose had wrapped herself in a fleece throw the last time she'd been at Brinna's, and that would be enough scent for Hero. The night was dark and cloudy but dry, so if Hero was needed for a search, the weather wouldn't be a problem.

She'd just pulled out of her driveway when her phone rang again. Checking the screen, she saw it was Maggie.

"I hope you have more to tell me," she said when she opened the phone.

"Where are you?"

"Pulling away from my house. I'll be in College Park in a minute." She slowed, finding it awkward to hold the phone with her cast while she drove.

"Do you have Hero?"

"Yes," Brinna snapped. "Mags, what the heck is going on?" She slammed on the brakes when she almost ran a stop sign.

"Meet me at the 7-Eleven at Studebaker and Anaheim, and I'll tell you everything." The line went dead.

* * *

Since they'd left the warehouse, Ivana had gone from fearful to hopeful and back again. Simon gave them no explanation as to why he wanted to leave the warehouse. He'd just rushed her and Mrs. Caruso out and into the car. They'd had to step over Gavin's corpse. At first he'd planned to tie them up and force them into the trunk, but Mrs. Caruso talked him out of it, promising that she and Ivana would behave if they sat in the car. He drove around until it was dark and then brought them to this house.

When Mrs. Caruso asked him if the house was his, he said nothing. Once inside, he gave them street clothes to wear— again, there was no explanation for who the clothes belonged to. He would only say that he didn't want them "running around in nightclothes." Though the clothes were too large for her and Mrs. Caruso, they were a lot warmer than their thin nightgowns, and Ivana was happy to feel warmth return to her extremities. She found herself hoping, now that they were away from the warehouse, that Simon would relent and release them.

Then he turned on the television and saw a picture of himself on a wanted poster. Ivana was sure she and Mrs. Caruso were dead. Simon had smashed the television, then turned off all the lights and herded them into a back bedroom. He had his phone in one hand, the gun in his other. He'd forced them to the floor, where they were still seated, their backs to the wall, while he sat on the edge of the bed. He'd open his phone, close it, then repeat the process a few minutes later.

Mrs. Caruso tried to speak to him, but he'd ordered them both quiet. From time to time he'd curse in Bulgarian. Ivana could barely keep her eyes open, but every time she'd nod off, Simon would erupt in curses. He no longer held the gun in his hand, but Ivana knew that the dark lump on the bed next to him was the weapon, close enough to still be a threat.

"You're exhausted," Mrs. Caruso said and Ivana jumped. The room's only illumination was the glow from a backyard light. It was impossible to see Simon's features, but his head did turn in Mrs. Caruso's direction.

"What do you care?" Simon's voice was flat, hollow. He slid off the bed and sat on the floor, back against the bed.

"I care, whether you believe me or not. It's clear that you're lost, confused." She leaned forward. "End this. No one else has to get hurt."

Ivana held her breath. Her eyes went from Simon to the gun on the bed and back again. He made no move toward the gun.

"I'm a dead man walking; that's what I am. The one friend I thought I had has betrayed me." He emitted a mirthless chuckle. "Demitri will be back in two days. I either wait for him to kill me or let your police do it now."

"American police won't kill you. Can't you believe that?" Mrs. Caruso pleaded. "If you let us go now, no one has to die."

"Believe her, Simon, please." For the first time in hours Ivana found her vocal cords. Her throat was dry, and her voice sounded rough. "I've met these American police. They were kind to me. They weren't the demons Demitri told me they were."

"You weren't the one holding the gun." With that he stood and picked up the gun. "Stand. We're going for a ride."

63

Brinna saw Maggie as soon as she pulled into the lot. She stood outside her car and jogged toward Brinna.

"I think I found your mother."

The positive, confident declaration gave her a jolt. "You said that already." Brinna threw her arms out. "What is going on?"

"It was Laura, the neighbor, who cleared everything up," Maggie explained. "I went to talk to her, to ask her some simple questions. Turns out she saw who we think is Simon at the shop."

"You think?" Brinna stood, arms akimbo.

"He was a scary guy, according to Laura. She heard him talk and could tell by his accent he was Bulgarian like Magda." Maggie paused, and Brinna gestured for her to continue.

"Anyway, Laura had seen this guy someplace else before, but the day he visited Magda, she couldn't remember where. When we were talking, Laura remembered that she'd been in College Park at a friend's house when she saw him. He was at a house across the street. Brin, at her house, she had the news on the TV and the bulletin about Simon Greuv came on. Laura blurted out, 'That's him!'"

Brinna sucked in a breath and thought for a moment. "Why call me to come out here? This information should go to the Feds." Even as she said the words, she knew what she was going to do.

"Laura is kind of an airhead," Maggie continued. "I didn't think at the time she was reliable, so I drove out here to look things over for myself. I found the house with no trouble. There are several cars parked in front. Face it, this is thin, but I thought if Hero walked by and gave a sniff or two, you'd know if your mom were there or not."

"If there is a chance my mom is there, argh—Maggie, we can't go off half-cocked like this."

"Look who's talking. The queen of going off half-cocked." Maggie faced Brinna, an amused expression on her face. "Look, if we notify Chuck, ICE will mobilize, and that could take hours. If your mom is in that house, do you really want to wait hours? Plus, this is an off-the-wall hunch. If your mom isn't in that house, do you want the federal resources tied up for hours chasing geese?"

Folding her arms, Brinna looked at Maggie, knowing that if the situation were different, if it were someone else's mother, she would be making the same arguments. "What did you have in mind?"

"Like I said, stroll by with Hero. This Simon doesn't know who you are. And with me and Hero, it will just look like we're walking our dog."

"A walk at midnight?"

"If the dog needs to go, he doesn't look at the clock. If Hero hits on something, we call in the troops, okay?"

Brinna sighed and looked away from Maggie as she considered this. She looked back and said, "Maggie, what if we put my mom at risk?"

"All we'll do is walk by. This is a low-key thing to do."

Brinna tugged on her earlobe and paced, thinking. There was no one else around, though the lot was bright with light from the open convenience store. Her mother's life was on the line.

Silently, before she answered Maggie, she prayed for her mother's safety. *I don't know how to do this, Lord, but everyone says you hear and understand, so here goes. Please, please keep my mom safe.* Briefly she felt better, stronger, and thought to herself, *I'm finally getting the hang of this.*

She hesitated about calling Jack, knowing he'd insist on mobilizing the federal machine.

Looking up at the dark, patchy sky, Brinna made her decision and muttered to herself, "I hope it's the right one."

* * *

Jack tried not to worry about Brinna. She'd left while he was on the phone telling Chuck about this relative of Simon Greuv. She'd said she was going home, and the only thing that kept him from calling was the hope that she'd left to get some rest. He knew she needed it. He needed it too. He felt dead on his feet. But he wanted to see what came of this tattoo shop lead. Apparently the cousin, a Walter Arnaut, had a thriving shop in San Pedro.

ICE had descended on the shop, interviewing the cousin in the hopes he might have heard from Simon. But like a lot of situations in law enforcement that started out promising, this had turned into a hurry-up-and-wait scenario. All Jack could do was drink coffee to stay awake so he could pray.

* * *

"Now that you're in," Maggie said to Brinna, "how do you want to do this?"

"I don't want to walk. Even with the dog, it's too odd for two women to be out at this time of night."

"You want to take the Explorer? Won't that be more conspicuous?"

"No. What would be unusual about a single patrol car driving through the neighborhood at night?"

"I guess you're right. The gangsters do call us 'One Time' because they think we only drive by one time."

"Yep. We'll drive by at patrol speed, you'll run any vehicle plates, and then we'll drive out of sight to see what we get."

"All right, I guess that makes more sense than walking. Let's go."

They hopped into the Explorer. Hero stood in the back panting as if expecting something. Brinna drove at a slow speed.

"Okay, you said there were three cars in the driveway. I want all three plates in one pass. Can you handle that?"

"That's a big 10-4." Maggie had paper and a pen in her hand. She clicked on Brinna's under-the-dash light and got ready.

The house came into view. All three cars were sedans. One was a Chevy; two were Toyotas. Two were in the driveway, and one was half on the front lawn. Brinna kept her speed steady, resisting the urge to slow further, and recited one plate, then another, while Maggie scribbled. As they passed the house and turned the corner to another street, she looked at Maggie.

"Did you get them?"

"Yep, all of them." She positioned Brinna's computer keyboard toward her and began to type. Brinna made a U-turn and pulled up to the corner, parking where she could see a portion of the house in question. She switched off her headlights but left the car running. From where they were, the driveway was visible.

The computer began to beep with returns on the license plates. "Well?" Brinna said to Maggie.

"Two of the cars are registered to Walter Arnaut." Maggie frowned and glanced at Brinna. "That name familiar?"

Brinna shook her head. "What's the third?"

"That's the Chevy. It's a rental, to a BVD Enterprises. An underwear company owns the car?"

Brinna's heart flew to her throat. That was the car. Her mother was in that house.

64

"CALL JACK. He should still be in the detective office," Brinna told Maggie. "Tell him everything. Let him know that we'll stay here and keep an eye on the car and the house."

"Will do." Maggie opened her phone.

Brinna stared in the semidarkness at the house and drummed on the steering wheel with her good hand. The street was well lit, but the house was dark. She hoped that the rental car in the driveway would be enough for a warrant.

"No answer at the station," Maggie said. "Do you have Jack's cell number?"

"Yeah, I think it's on my phone." She pointed to her fanny pack, and Maggie bent to retrieve the phone.

"They might have left to check out the relative Magda remembered." Brinna regretted her hasty departure from the station. "I sure wish I'd stayed to find out a name."

Maggie got Jack's voice mail and left a message. "He might have gone home to sleep, if he was as tired as you look," she said as she closed the phone.

Brinna glanced at the house. "We'd better call dispatch—"

Just then a dome light went on in the Chevy as a dark figure opened the rear car door. Two people got into the backseat, and the light went out. They were too far away for Brinna to distinguish if the people were male or female. Next a driver got behind the wheel. Taillights glowed red, and Brinna knew the Chevy was leaving.

In tandem Brinna and Maggie leaned forward and looked to the right.

"That's the rental, the one registered to BVD Enterprises," Maggie said.

Brinna switched on her police radio. "Notify dispatch. They'll be able to get ahold of everyone who needs to know what's happening." She watched, fear gripping her like a too-tight handcuff as the sedan backed out of the driveway and started down the street.

* * *

Maggie phoned dispatch. It would have been too confusing to take up airtime on the radio when neither one of them were logged on or officially on duty at the moment. But on the phone Maggie could explain the situation and they could be given a designator and logged on by the dispatcher. Once they had a designator, speaking on the air was appropriate. Maggie would operate the radio, something Brinna couldn't do with her cast while she also tried to drive. As Maggie outlined the situation to dispatch, she sounded frustrated.

Brinna's stomach lurched. "What are they saying, Maggie?"

"They got snitty because neither one of us is supposed to

be working. They told me to stand by while they contact the watch commander."

"They told you to stand by?" Brinna glanced at Maggie and then at the sedan in front of her. "Did you tell them what's going on?"

"Yes, you heard me," she hissed. "Now they're trying to raise the watch commander."

"Don't tell me it's Harvey."

"I won't tell you, but that won't change the fact."

Just then the nasal voice of Lieutenant Harvey came over the radio using Brinna's designator. "King-44, your location?"

Maggie keyed the mike and relayed their location and direction of travel. Brinna held her breath while she waited for the lieutenant's reply. The sedan ahead of them wasn't moving fast. There'd been no indication the driver suspected he was being tailed. They were following a path that would take them into downtown Long Beach. There was minimal to no traffic.

"King-44," the radio crackled with Harvey's voice once again, "I've been in contact with the federal agent in charge of this operation. Apparently a team of agents is en route to Long Beach from San Pedro."

"En route?" Brinna frowned. "Ask him why, Mags. Why are they coming here?"

Maggie keyed the mike and asked the question.

"It's too complicated to explain over the air. Keep transmitting the location of the sedan. The federal agents are monitoring our frequency."

"Where's Jack?" Brinna wondered out loud. "He'd have a radio if he was with the Feds. We could talk to him."

"You want me to ask?"

"No, just keep giving them our location." She tapped on the steering wheel with her cast, frowning. "If the Feds are on their way to Long Beach, I wonder what they found in San Pedro. And Harvey wants us to stay with it." Her face flushed as she realized this had to be the car—that she and Maggie were quite possibly following her mother or at least following someone who had something to do with the situation. The vehicle continued at a steady, almost leisurely pace, and that put her on edge.

"Maybe they're trying to fool us," Maggie suggested. "Make us think they're innocent and decide to turn away."

Brinna said nothing. They were about to cross into downtown proper when the sedan made a left turn on Shoreline Drive. Shoreline Village! They were going to Shoreline Village; she was certain.

She looked at Maggie as the radio burst to life. Federal agents had entered the city limits. They would be traveling south on Shoreline Drive as Brinna and the sedan traveled north.

"Tell them I think they're heading to Shoreline Village."

"We might meet them at the entrance," Maggie observed as the turnoff for the Village approached. Several pairs of headlights were visible in the distance, about half a mile away in the opposite lanes.

The sedan made the turn into the Village, and Brinna allowed herself to relax. There was no way out now. Shoreline Village was built along the marina—one way in and one way out. If this was Simon, he had nowhere to run now. Was that better for her mom . . . or worse?

* * *

"They have found us," Simon said flatly. He kept glancing in the rearview mirror. Rose Caruso and Ivana sat close together in the backseat, holding hands. Though he made no move to flee from the car he insisted was behind them, Ivana could tell Simon was at the end, beyond desperate, beyond hopeless. He and the car stank of cigarettes. He'd been through three packs since dusk and had cursed when he'd finished the last one.

"Please, give yourself up," Mrs. Caruso pleaded. She'd been talking to Simon nonstop since they left the house. He hadn't told her to shut up, but he hadn't given any indication he was listening, either. "If they are following you, and you stop and surrender, no one will get hurt and you'll see what I've been telling you is true."

Ivana had no idea where they were as they traveled over dark streets. Gradually, the lighting and size of the buildings increased, and she could tell they were approaching the city center. They made one turn and then another.

Finally Simon spoke. "I have no wish to hurt you. I will give you one chance and one chance only. When I stop at Magda's shop, you will get out of the car, and you will get out quickly or I will kill you."

"What are you going to do?" Mrs. Caruso asked.

"That is not your concern!" Simon bellowed. "You will get out of the car, or you will die."

65

"KING-44—" Lieutenant Harvey's voice came over the car speaker—"hold position at the entrance to the parking lot. Agents will be there shortly to contain the situation. They'll block the exit and proceed as needed."

Brinna was about to say that sounded like a good idea when the sedan lurched away, tires squealing, smoke belching from burning rubber.

"Where is he going?" Brinna gaped, incredulous. "Does he plan on driving into the water?" Reflex set her foot down on the accelerator, and the Explorer leaped after the sedan. If he did drive into the water, could her mother get out in time?

The sedan roared right into the parking lot, very nearly on two wheels. It then cut over the empty lot in a diagonal line across the parking spaces. Brinna kept after it, slowing just a bit, mindful of the fact she was not alone in the car and this could get dangerous.

The sedan jumped the curb and roared along the walkway,

getting ever closer to the water line, then suddenly came screeching to a halt.

Brinna sucked in a breath and hit the brakes. The last thing she wanted was an armed confrontation. She watched from about two hundred feet away. The back door of the sedan flew open and two figures stumbled out. They'd barely hit the pavement when the sedan shuddered and squealed away.

Forgetting the vehicle, Brinna punched it toward the two figures picking themselves up from the ground. Her headlights illuminated them, and before she could think about it, the words "Thank God" burst from her lips.

She positioned the Explorer between the pair and the fleeing sedan, then jammed it into park and threw herself out the door. She was certain that her mother was surprised by the intensity of the hug, but Brinna just didn't care.

* * *

Jack met them at the hospital after Rose and Ivana were taken to exam rooms. Brinna was almost as happy to see him as she had been to see her mother. When he stepped forward and gave her a hug, she willingly hugged him back, not caring who was watching.

"I'm so glad we're celebrating this ending," he whispered to her as he stroked her head.

"Oh, you and me both." Brinna held tight, enjoying the feeling of his muscled back beneath her hands.

It was Maggie clearing her throat that got them to part. "The Feds want to talk to your mom and Ivana."

Brinna turned to see Chuck and a couple other agents walking into the emergency room. "Not sure if the doctor will let them." She yawned. "In any event, I'm out of this for now." She sat down in the waiting room, and Jack sat next to her, holding her good hand tightly in both of his.

"You're just going to sit there?" Maggie asked.

"I might sleep as well."

Chuck laughed. "You've earned a rest. We'll talk to your mom and fill you in later."

Maggie threw her hands up and sat on the other side of Brinna.

Jack told them that the house Maggie had been led to by Laura was actually the home of Simon's cousin, Walter Arnaut. Walter and his wife were on vacation and would not be home for another week.

"We got the address from a tattoo artist in San Pedro. We would have been there, but you two beat us to it," he told them.

He and Maggie started a spirited banter about who was the better detective, but Brinna decided she must have dozed off because it seemed like only minutes later that her mother, not Jack, was talking to her.

The sun was up when Rose and Ivana were released from Memorial's emergency room. Other than being emotionally drained, tired, hungry, and dehydrated, Rose and Ivana were given a clean bill of health. They'd been debriefed by federal agents and were more than ready to go home. Because of all the other girls ICE had jurisdiction over and the extreme shortage of shelter beds, Chuck said Ivana was free to stay with Rose.

Brinna watched Rose hug Ivana with the news and real-ized the ordeal had brought the two very close. She doubted Chuck would have gotten Ivana away if he tried.

"I'll call you," Jack told Brinna as he and Maggie said their good-byes.

"Sorry about that backseat," Brinna said to Ivana as they climbed into the Explorer, "but it's set up for my dog."

"That's fine. Anywhere is fine right now considering where I have been," Ivana said as she slid into the back.

"Boy, do I need a shower," Rose exclaimed.

"I wasn't going to say anything, but . . ." Brinna grinned at her mother.

"I'll probably sleep for two days," Rose said, ignoring Brinna's gibe.

"Well, before you go into hibernation—" Brinna looked across the car at her mom—"I'm curious about something."

"Oh?" Rose's eyebrow arched.

"Yeah. I was a basket case, all nerves, certain we were going to find you dead." She sucked in a breath as strong emotion she wasn't expecting threatened. "How were you doing? I mean—"

"Was I a basket case?" Rose asked.

Brinna nodded.

"I was frightened." Rose glanced back at Ivana. "But I was also certain that God was in control of everything, including the gun in Simon's hand."

Brinna wiped her eyes. "I wondered. I wondered if you'd still believe, if your faith would hold while your life was in danger."

"When my life was in danger," Rose repeated. "Oh,

Brinna, that was when my faith was the strongest. God is strongest when we are weakest."

"I don't understand that, not completely. But I'm trying. Jack and I even made a date to go to church. And it may have been lame, but I even tried praying for you a couple of times."

Rose beamed and gave Brinna another tight hug.

As they drove home, she told her mother and Ivana about Magda and being her sister's keeper.

"I never thought a story from the Bible could touch anyone like that," she admitted to her mom. "Turns out, it touched me as well. I may lose Hero and my right to be called a Kid Crusader, but I can still be my sister's keeper. I'm that every time I help someone, whether it be a kid or not."

"Wonderful," Rose said simply.

66

Two DAYS LATER, Brinna, Jack, Magda, and about twenty federal agents were stationed in various places at LAX. They awaited the arrival of a plane from Eastern Europe—Bulgaria, to be exact. Demitri, Emil, and Anka were due to disembark. Magda explained that for his trips to recruit girls he always flew, acting like a legitimate businessman. He only utilized ships when he was actually bringing captives with him. Magda was with them because she wanted to see Demitri humbled. She'd decided that only by knowing he'd lost everything, and that he had no reach to touch her, could she move on with her life, unafraid.

At the same moment the plane touched down on the runway in California, Canadian agents raided a container ship set to sail to America in a few days from Vancouver. Ten young women were discovered secreted in a container on one of the upper decks.

Though ICE had already decided to board the plane and take Demitri into custody before all the passengers were let off, Brinna and every other law enforcement agent had with them a photo of Demitri Dinev in case there were any glitches. He was tall, six feet four, about two hundred and forty pounds with dark hair graying at the temples. His eyes were mean and cold. Brinna wished she could be the one applying the handcuffs, but this was a federal op now, and she and Jack were simply observers.

It was a miracle that Dinev had not heard of the entire breakdown of his organization in the States, since it had been big news. He'd called Magda and asked her if everything was okay. Magda happened to be with federal authorities—at Simon's hospital bed—when the call came in to Simon's cell phone. He'd wondered why she was answering Simon's phone, and she made up a story about having asked Simon to come help her move some heavy items at the shop. It was not anything Magda had ever done before, but Demitri had bought it. She'd assured him that, yes, everything was running smoothly. He then wanted to talk to Simon. He didn't know that Simon had turned state's evidence and was being interviewed extensively about all he knew of the human-trafficking operation.

Without missing a beat, Magda handed Simon the phone. He spoke to Demitri from his hospital bed at the jail ward of Los Angeles County–USC Medical Center. Yes, everything was fine, he assured his boss. The girls and his business were thriving. He recited the time of arrival and flight number of Demitri's plane while an ICE agent wrote it down.

Miracle, yes, Brinna thought as she watched the airline employees prepare the gate for the arrival of passengers, *but not the only miracle.* She'd been considering the miracle of her mother and Ivana emerging from their ordeal unscathed after Simon ordered them from the car.

Simon had driven his vehicle to the end of the marina roadway, through a barrier, and into the ocean, hoping to end his life and escape the wrath of Demitri and the police. It was touch and go for a short period of time as the heavy sedan sank rapidly. But Simon was eventually rescued by an army of agents and local officers who had arrived at Shoreline Village about the same time he kicked Ivana and Rose out of his car. They had followed him, diving in to pull him from the cold water. Though he would be charged with murder, Rose insisted that since the police had rescued Simon, this had a part to play in his decision to cooperate with the authorities.

"Answered prayer" was what her mother and Jack called all of these fortuitous events. Brinna agreed. The idea of answered prayer was growing on her.

The door to the gate opened, and four agents disappeared into the tunnel. Four more stayed at the entrance of the gate. Demitri and Emil would be arrested, and after being thoroughly interviewed, Anka would be allowed to leave with Magda. Magda had been granted full immunity from prosecution in exchange for her cooperation and testimony.

A few minutes later, yelling and cursing could be heard from the gate. Passengers waiting at the gate stopped what they were doing, and all heads turned toward the open door. Brinna felt Magda stiffen next to her.

"That sound like Demitri?" she asked.

Magda nodded, and Brinna watched the color drain from her face. That she still feared him was obvious.

"Don't worry," Brinna offered. "He won't look so scary in handcuffs." She thought about how satisfied she felt when a child predator was apprehended and cuffed up.

Just then the agents appeared, Demitri between two of them. He looked outraged as he struggled, but the cuffs were on, and his hands were firmly behind his back. In addition, each agent had a tight grip on an arm. None of Demitri's protests or gyrations could do anything to loosen the holds the agents had on him. He looked very small and very impotent. The second man, Emil, came next, but he was quiet and walked meekly beside the agent. Behind him, the fourth agent escorted a bewildered-looking Anka.

Brinna heard an exhalation of breath from Magda.

"You're right," she said with a smile. "He is nothing but a man. Not someone to fear any longer."

67

"I HAVEN'T BEEN on the Matterhorn in years!" Brinna giggled, her heart soaring. Jack's hand was tight in hers, and they were walking through Disneyland, enjoying sights, sounds, and smells neither had experienced in a while. She had grown used to the cast, and it barely bothered her anymore.

"I think the last time I was here was as a teenager." Jack's shoulder bumped hers as the crowd jostled them. They were part of a group that included Magda and her family, Brinna's mother, Ivana, and Maggie with Rick's kids.

Jack and Brinna had purposely lost the group somewhere in Fantasyland, wanting to spend time alone, so to speak.

"This is an interesting place for a date, Mr. O'Reilly," Brinna teased as they found the end of the line for the Matterhorn ride.

"I thought it was lighthearted enough to get everyone's mind off the drama a couple of weeks ago." His gray eyes danced and held hers.

"Definitely. Ivana looked like a five-year-old when she saw Mickey Mouse on Main Street. The bruises have faded, and my mom says there haven't been any more nightmares."

They inched forward and Jack pulled her close. "So now that emergencies and dramas are behind us for the time being, I thought maybe we could just concentrate on us for a while."

"Great plan." Brinna leaned into him, living in the moment but also loving the promise of the future.

*   *   *

Brinna's forearm felt tight and tired as she polished the intricate basket weave of her Sam Browne belt for the third time. She'd only had the cast off for a day—it had been removed a week early—and her left arm was weak. She'd finished her shoes earlier, spit-shined to a high gloss, and they sat next to her locker, waiting for her. She just couldn't get a satisfactory shine on her belt because of the fatigued arm.

"Hey, we have to get going. That's shiny enough," Maggie said. She was already dressed in her class A uniform—belt and shoes shined to her satisfaction. Brinna knew this was because Maggie had paid someone else to polish the equipment for her. Cheater.

"All right, let me just wipe it down, and I'll be ready." Brinna felt restricted in the long-sleeved, stiff wool uniform. Her normal working uniform was a nonrestrictive cotton jumpsuit, the uniform of a dog handler. But the wool dress uniform was required for the annual police awards banquet.

"I know you're nervous because you and Jack will be center stage, getting a meritorious award for heroism. But they won't change their mind about the award because your belt is dull," Maggie teased.

"Oh, stop it," Brinna huffed. "It's not the award. Janet's at the budget meeting today."

"Oh." Maggie slapped her forehead. "I forgot about that. You find out about Hero."

"I'm the one who has to walk up on stage and shake the chief's hand," Brinna mumbled as she hooked her belt on, "not knowing if I have a partner or not."

"Look at the bright side. No matter what, you still have a job—and your best friend." Maggie grinned.

Brinna snapped her belt keepers, grabbed her tie, and went to the mirror to clip it on. "Now if I could only teach you to run an agility course."

"Ha-ha." Maggie folded her arms. "Just enjoy your moment of accolade and deal with what happens to Hero later."

Her tie and tie clip on straight, Brinna shoved her cover under her arm and looked at Maggie. "I'll do my best. Let's go."

Together they left the locker room. Jack O'Reilly stood outside, brushing lint off his uniform. Brinna smiled at him. The memory of the blast they'd had at Disneyland still played in Brinna's mind. They'd been together a lot lately, including a standing invitation to attend church together every Sunday. Brinna had never looked forward to Sunday mornings as much in her life, and it was not just because of Jack's company. The messages were sinking in, and she loved the feeling of family there. She and Jack were set for a formal date after the awards banquet, and she'd asked him to surprise her.

"Hey, you didn't even have to wear this monkey suit," Brinna said when she saw him. "You're a detective. You could have gotten away with a suit and tie."

"I was a patrol officer when we stopped the robbery, so I thought I'd dig my class A out of mothballs." He smiled and pulled Brinna close for a kiss, and the warmth from his lips jolted Brinna to her toes.

"Okay already, save that for later." Maggie snorted with fake annoyance.

They parted and Maggie looked Jack up and down. "Not bad—for a rookie."

"Very funny, Sloan. At least I shine my own leather," Jack teased. "By the way, have they decided who's going to be sentenced as your permanent partner yet?"

In the weeks since Rick's accident, while he was home learning to adapt to life in a wheelchair, Maggie had bounced around from partner to partner. Brinna wondered if she was deliberately being picky.

"Nope. No one has measured up to my exacting standards yet."

Brinna strolled between her two friends and listened to the banter. It helped keep her mind off what was bothering her. As they walked the two blocks to the convention center hall where the awards banquet would be held, they were joined by several other officers and civilian employees all going to the banquet.

Rose Caruso was already waiting at the hall when Brinna arrived. She stood talking to Gracie's parents, with Ivana nearby. Ivana had blossomed under Rose's care. She'd been granted a student visa and planned to enroll in a few college courses. Right now she was taking a driver's training course and would soon be a licensed driver. She'd also become a part-time nanny for Rick and Molly, helping with their three boys while Rick went through rehab. Ivana loved kids and had a knack for dealing with the boys. She bore practically no resemblance to the battered waif who'd been pulled from the flood control. Magda and her husband, Anton, were also in attendance.

Magda had offered Ivana a job at her shop, but the girl declined. Anka had been deported back to Bulgaria. She would not believe that her father was the criminal the American police said he was. To her credit, Magda was trying to help the women rescued from Demitri who wanted to stay in the country. A number of the women freed from Demitri's horror houses had opted to go home; the rest were still in ICE custody until it was determined what was best for them. Magda was working hard to be an advocate for them. Brinna had forgiven the woman and reached out to her. They'd formed a friendship because they both wanted to help those who were exploited.

Gracie saw Brinna, and her face brightened. "Officer Caruso!"

Brinna hadn't seen the girl since the day she'd shown up at her house. Her lead had led them to Rose in a night that everyone was calling the "smackdown at Shoreline." Cops could turn anything into a joke, and a situation that had Brinna in a cast, driving, with Maggie in the passenger seat and Hero in the backseat, turned into an endless source of jokes and pranks. But she couldn't believe she'd received high praise from Lieutenant

Harvey for showing restraint and protecting her mother and Ivana.

"How are you doing, Gracie?" Brinna shook Mr. and Mrs. Kaplan's hands and accepted a kiss on the cheek from her mother.

"I got an A on my school report about helping you find your mother," Gracie gushed. "My teacher thought it sounded like a news story and said I'd make a great reporter someday."

"Reporter?" Brinna arched her eyebrows.

"Well, yeah. Then I can be a part of the action and tell everyone about it later." Gracie's eyes wandered the hall foyer. "Oh, excuse me. There's Tracy Michaels. I have to go talk to her."

Brinna watched the girl jog away toward the reporter and wondered why she felt let down. She hadn't been ready for the burden of being someone's hero; shouldn't this take a weight off?

"Tossed over for a reporter. Will wonders never cease?" Maggie teased.

Jack put an arm on her shoulder. "Kids are fickle. Don't let it get to you."

"Officer Caruso, you'll always be my hero." Ivana grinned at Brinna.

"And mine." Rose stepped forward and gave Brinna a hug. "Now let's go inside so I can snap a lot of pictures, be excruciatingly proud, and make you uncomfortable."

Brinna laughed and shook her head. "At least some things will never change."

With that they joined the line filing into the convention hall.

68

BRINNA SIGHED and tried not to get emotional again. While Hero was now officially her dog—she'd written the check two days ago—he was no longer an LBPD search-and-rescue dog. The city had declined to pick up his contract, and tonight was her first night back to work, cleared for full duty, with no partner. She'd already turned in her take-home car and now had an armful of uniforms, plus the kit that held all of her law enforcement forms and books to put in her locker. No more dressing at home and driving into the station with Hero panting behind her.

She had joined a civilian search-and-rescue outfit and looked forward to training with them, but their first meeting was not for a month. Hero would have to adjust to being a civilian dog.

"See you later, buddy." She hugged the dog one more time, then grabbed her gear and lugged it out to her truck. Once at the station, it took two trips to transfer all her equipment from the car to her locker. Notes had been stuffed inside the locker, condolences for her loss of Hero but welcoming her back to patrol. Jack sent her a text to be safe and to go easy on her new partner.

"Hey, Officer Caruso, sorry to hear about your dog," another afternoon officer said, patting Brinna's back as she walked past to her locker. "Know who you're working with?"

"Nope, not yet," Brinna answered. "I think I'm a Robert car for a couple nights at least." She worked hard to be upbeat about the current situation. As a Robert car, she'd be stuck taking reports on low-priority calls like burglaries with no suspects, and that usually meant a boring night, certainly not what she was used to with Hero.

No use whining about something that can't be, she scolded herself.

Banter died down as everyone finished dressing and, one by one, headed for the squad room.

Maggie wasn't in yet, which was normal—she usually breezed in at the last minute, so why would tonight be any different? Brinna had met Maggie's new partner the other day. His name was Mark, and he'd just transferred to the afternoon shift from days to help deal with child-care issues at home. He seemed nice enough.

Brinna dressed in a short-sleeved shirt for the night, hating the scratchy feel of the long-sleeved wool shirts. If she got cold, she had her jacket. Once dressed and ready to go, she still had ten minutes before the start of squad meeting. She grabbed her kit and flashlight and strolled out to the lot to find a car. She found a clean black-and-white unclaimed, stowed her kit, and made her way to the shift meeting.

In her mailbox were more welcome-back-to-patrol notes. She grabbed them, found a seat in the squad room, and read through them.

"Officer Caruso."

Looking up, Brinna saw Lieutenant Harvey at the doorway to the sergeants' office. He motioned her back to the office.

"Gosh, you haven't even been back for a day, and you're already in trouble," Maggie whispered in her ear, voice laced with amusement.

Brinna jumped; she hadn't seen Maggie come in.

"When did you get here?" Brinna asked as she stood.

"I'll tell you later. Don't keep the LT waiting." She nodded in Harvey's direction.

Janet Rodriguez sat at a desk in the office, and Harvey leaned against the file cabinet.

"I have a letter of reprimand here for you to sign," Janet said, sliding the document from internal affairs across the desk. "It has to do with the pursuit in the rain."

Brinna nodded, surprised she'd gotten off so light. She read the letter and signed it. There was a section at the bottom where she could protest if she thought the discipline excessive, but she had no problem with the reprimand. She slid the paper back to Rodriguez.

"Thank you, Officer Caruso," Harvey said, moving away from the cabinet and toward the door. "I'm glad to see you can admit when you're wrong." He left the office.

Brinna stood to leave, but Rodriguez waved her back. "One more thing. You want to know who your new partner is?"

"I thought I was odd man out, a Robert car for a while."

"Things change quickly around here; you know that. I can't guarantee you'll get along with your new partner as well as you got along with Hero, but maybe this one will speak up and keep you out of trouble." Rodriguez smiled and handed Brinna a slip of paper with her new call sign and the name of her new partner. Her jaw dropped when she read it, and Rodriguez laughed.

"Get back to the squad room and sit. We're late."

Brinna found herself giggling, truly feeling upbeat, not having to fake it. She hurried back to her desk. Maggie had appropriated the seat next to her and grinned.

Sliding into her seat, Brinna whispered to Maggie, "How long have you known?"

"Just since yesterday. Afternoons weren't working for Mark's family, so he had to go back to days. I wanted you to be surprised."

"I was." She couldn't keep the grin off her face. "We're working beat 2."

"Yep."

"You don't have any problem with looking into missing kid cases or keeping tabs on sex offenders, do you?"

Maggie shook her head, then leaned close to Brinna's ear. "Just remember. I don't sit and stay on command, so you better get used to sharing the driving."

A NOTE FROM THE AUTHOR

It seems as though every day there is a new article about someone being arrested for human trafficking. According to HumanTrafficking.org, an estimated 14,500 to 17,500 people—mostly women and children—are trafficked to the US each year.

When I was still working in law enforcement, I saw a training video that told the story of an apartment complex turned into a virtual prison by traffickers. They brought laborers to the US illegally and then kept them in apartments, only letting them out to work, and even then they were closely monitored. They even set up a company store in the apartment complex for the captives to shop at, but they charged exorbitant prices, basically taking back the little money they paid the captives for their day labor. The apartment complex was not out in the boonies; it was right in the middle of a normal neighborhood.

Traffickers often prey upon the poor and the struggling. They promise high-paying jobs in countries like the US, Italy, France, and Germany. The victims often leave their home countries willingly with the trafficker, but once they get to the desired country, the trafficker will confiscate the victim's ID and papers and keep him or her confined, unable to do anything but what the trafficker wants. Traffickers tell their victims that the police can't be trusted, that they are in the country illegally, so if they complain to anyone, they will go to jail.

I got this from the FBI website in May 2013 (http://www.fbi.gov/news/stories/2013/january/targeting-human-traffickers-helping-victims): "Last month, a Kentucky cardiologist and his ex-wife pled guilty to recruiting a Bolivian woman to work as their domestic servant and holding her unlawfully for nearly 15 years. The couple took her passport, threatened her with deportation, and falsely promised that her wages were being put in a bank account."

Traffickers are not always shadowy men who look like drug dealers.

Also on the FBI website are resources if you have information or suspicions about a situation near you: "If you believe you are the victim of a trafficking situation or may have information about a potential trafficking situation, call the National Human Trafficking Resource Center (NHTRC) at 1-888-373-7888. NHTRC is a national, toll-free hotline, with specialists available to answer calls from anywhere in the country, 24 hours a day, seven days a week, every day of the year related to potential trafficking victims, suspicious behaviors, and/or locations where trafficking is suspected to occur. You can also submit a tip to the NHTRC online" at http://www.polarisproject.org/what-we-do/national-human-trafficking-hotline/report-a-tip.

1

"I SWEAR IT'S AS IF my life is caught in a riptide, Joe." Carly hated the whine in her voice, but the frustration in her life that started six months ago had lately built to a fever pitch. "I feel like there's a current pulling me under, and every time I try to raise my head, I get buried by a wave." Her angry strides pounded an uneven path across the damp beach.

"Don't raise your head, then; you'll just get water up your nose," Joe responded. He walked alongside, dodging the sand Carly's feet kicked up.

She shot him a glare. He laughed, and in spite of her mood she managed a half smile. "What would I do without you? You always try to cheer me up even when I bet you think I'm just whining."

Matching her stride, Joe placed a calloused hand on her shoulder and said, "Hey, I know this isn't you. Being wrongly accused sucks—doubly so when you can't even defend yourself. I'm not sure I'd have handled the last six months as well as you have if I were in your shoes. If you need to vent, vent."

Carly stopped a few feet from the surf and blew out a breath as tears threatened. Emotions a jumble, she was touched by Joe's unwavering support. He'd been her partner on the force for three years—until the incident six months ago—and they'd been through car chases, foot pursuits, and fights together, developing a partnership that was as comfortable as her favorite pair of sweats. She knew, no matter what, she could count on Joe. She was lucky to have him, and he deserved better than her current bad attitude.

For a minute they were both silent, standing side by side watching the waves churn the salt water. The crash of the surf—a little rougher than she had expected—and the smell of the sea relaxed her a bit as the tableau soothed raw nerves.

Joe broke the silence. "Anyway, nothing will happen until all the facts are in and the litigation ends. Request your transfer back to patrol then. For right now, relax and be patient."

Carly swallowed the tears and dropped her beach bag. "I'm a horrible bench sitter. You know me; when they handed out patience, I stood in the ice cream line."

At that, Joe laughed and Carly was glad to hear it. One of the things that made them a good pair was the divergent way they looked at problems, Carly ready to kick the door in and Joe willing to wait hours if need be. Other officers teased them, labeling them Crash and Control. Carly would jump into things with both feet, while Joe would test the waters first with his big toe.

"I shouldn't dump on you. I'm just frustrated." Carly met his eyes and forced a smile.

"I don't mind listening." He shrugged. "That's what partners are for. You've listened to me enough over the years. We'll work together again." Joe tossed his bag next to Carly's.

Nodding, she bent to pull a towel out of her bag, biting down on her bottom lip, trying to swallow the frustration she felt and embrace the encouragement her partner gave.

"You sure you need to celebrate your birthday with a swim in this kind of weather?" Joe asked, hugging his arms to his chest. "Can't I just buy you a milk shake?"

Glad for the subject change, she followed his gaze to the water. The Pacific was a stormy deep-green color, pinched by small but choppy swells, melding to a gray and overcast horizon. Far to the left, several surfers bobbed on their boards, riding the swells while waiting for a good wave. Though late February, Southern California's mild water temperature made surfing and swimming possible. Dark, cloudy weather didn't bother Carly; it simply mirrored her mood. And for her, water normally made things better—even when it was forbidding and cold.

"It's good training." She looked down her nose at Joe. "You're not going to chicken out, are you? And you can also buy me a milk shake."

"No chicken here. Just giving you a chance to back out

gracefully." He peeled off his sweatshirt and rolled his shoulders. "I mean, it could be embarrassing for you, the ocean star, to get an old-fashioned thrashing on your turf by a pool swimmer."

"Ha. I plan to *give* an old-fashioned thrashing. You haven't been training." She pointed to his slightly paunchy stomach before she pulled off her own sweats. The cold air brought on a shiver.

Joe proudly patted his bit of paunch. "This will only make me more buoyant."

Casting Joe an upraised eyebrow, a cop glance reserved for obviously guilty crooks who protested innocence, Carly laid down the swim's ground rules. "Okay, it's a mile and a half to the buoy. Last one back to the beach buys lunch, milk shakes included."

Joe nodded, and they both pulled on their goggles and shook out their arms. She counted, and on three they ran together into the surf and dove into a wave. The cold winter water took her breath away, but Carly wasn't worried, even when Joe pulled ahead. Joe was taller—five-ten to Carly's five-seven—and took longer strokes, but he also carried a good sixty pounds more than she did. In spite of her teasing, it was mostly muscle, which made him denser in the water, not more buoyant. All she needed to do was settle into her stroke. This race would go to the one with stamina.

Carly warmed up fast and swam hard, determined to leave her frustration on the beach. Joe was right; this wasn't her. She rarely indulged in pity parties. But today, as she woke up to her thirty-third birthday, everything in her life seemed to converge in a perfect storm of failure.

The divorce had started her funk; the final papers had arrived two days ago, and reading them abraded Carly's still-raw heart. Now was the time she always imagined she would be starting a family, not filing away the proof that one had disintegrated. Nick had taken so much of her with him that she felt hollow. As good a partner and friend as Joe was, he didn't understand.

And Carly felt like a failure when she faced her mother. No one in the family had ever divorced, until now. Mom's solution was church, as though that would somehow fix a busted marriage. Her roommate Andrea's response was more realistic but even less doable: "Forget about him and find a new man."

Work used to be her respite, a place of security, support, and camaraderie, but lately her assignment in juvenile was more a black hole of boredom, sucking her life away. Compared to LA, a neighbor to the north, Las Playas was a small city, but it had its share of big crime. Carly wanted to be back on patrol, crushing her portion of it. Joe hadn't talked about it, but she knew the entire force was on edge over Mayor Teresa Burke. The popular and high-profile mayor had been missing for four days. Carly wanted to be out in a black-and-white, chasing clues and leads, not stuck inside babysitting juvenile delinquents. She kicked the water with a vengeance.

Carly caught and passed Joe just before the buoy. Ignoring his presence, she made the turn and sliced through the swells with her best training stroke. Her shoulders heavy with fatigue, she pushed harder. She conjured up an image of Joe as a shark bearing down on her heels, his fin parting the water in hot pursuit, a mind game to keep her from slowing.

A local celebrity in rough-water swims, Carly laid claim to a perfect record: undefeated in eighteen races. "Whenever life closes in, retreat to your strength" was an adage she lived by. Lately the ocean was a second home.

The shoreline loomed before she was ready to stop punishing the water. But the ache in her shoulders and lungs forced surrender, and as she eased up in the waves, pushing her goggles off to look back for Joe, she realized she did feel better. The ocean was magic. She'd beaten an imaginary shark in Joe, and even though there were still real ones on land threatening to drag her down, she felt energized by the swim.

Carly glided to where she could float and relished a peace she hadn't felt in a while. She willed it to last. Joe was right on his second point as well—there was no reason to be impatient. Between the buffeting swells and the pounding of her heart, she wondered if she should just take a few days off, get away from her current assignment in juvenile, with all the reminders of what she couldn't be doing, and relax somewhere far away. She breathed ocean air and tasted salt while floating, the water a rolling cocoon, protecting her from life's demands and drains.

Joe soon joined her, and together they treaded water, facing one another.

"Boy," Joe gasped, "you swam possessed. Bet that would have been a record."

Carly splashed her friend, the smile now not forced. "Thanks for the swim. I feel better."

He splashed her back. "My pleasure. Just call me Doctor Joe."

She laughed and it felt good. "Anytime you want a swimming lesson . . ." Carly turned with another splash and kicked for the shore.

"Ha," Joe called after her. "You missed your calling. Instead of a cop, you should be a sadistic swim coach somewhere, yelling, 'One more lap, one more lap.'"

Carly headed straight for her towel as the cool air turned her skin to gooseflesh. Joe followed.

"You need to get back into competition again," Joe said as he reached for his towel. "Admit it, you're half fish."

"I'd like to, but working an afternoon shift makes it difficult." She quickly slid into the comfort of dry sweats and wrapped her thick auburn hair in the towel. "But you're right; the water helps my mood as much as good ole Doctor Joe does."

The shrill chirp of a work BlackBerry cut off Joe's rejoinder. He looked toward his bag. "Yours or mine?"

"Mine." Carly dug the offending device out of her pocket, eyebrows knit in annoyance. The BlackBerry, or "TrackerBerry" as most officers who were issued the phones called them, rarely brought good news. The text message flashing across the small screen read, CALL THE WATCH COMMANDER ASAP, 911, 911. Her pulse quickened with a jolt. *What kind of emergency?*

"Look at this." She showed Joe the message.

"Whoa, I wonder what's up."

Carly shrugged and hit the speed dial for the watch commander's phone.

"Tucker."

The name took her by surprise. Sergeant Tucker was the head of homicide. Why was he answering the watch commander line?

"Uh, Sergeant Tucker, it's Edwards. Did you page me by accident?"

"Nope, you're the one I wanted. We found the mayor and . . . uh, hang on."

Carly could hear muffled voices in the background. Shock brought on by the sergeant's comment about the mayor left her slack jawed. *We found the mayor* coming from the *homicide* sergeant was not a good thing. She'd just been thinking about the woman! Speculation about Mayor Burke's fate had run the gamut among department personnel during the past four days. Now Carly's stomach turned as she guessed at the reality. She repeated the sergeant's words to Joe, who whistled low in surprise.

"You still there?" Sergeant Tucker came back on the line.

"Yes, sir." More questions clouded her mind. *Why is Sergeant Tucker calling me about the mayor's case?*

"I can't tell you much right now. The area is crawling with press. The mayor was murdered. We need you at the command post ASAP."

"What?" Carly's hand went numb with the confirmation

of her suspicions. "Uh, sure, where?" *Mayor Teresa Burke was murdered.* This news would devastate the city she worked for. Carly listened as the sergeant told her where to report and broke the connection.

"Earth to Carly, you still with me?" Joe tapped the phone. "What happened?"

"Mayor Burke was murdered, and they want me at the crime scene now."

"Wow." His face registered the shock Carly felt. "What do they want you to handle?"

"Tucker didn't say." She held Joe's gaze. "Why me? I work juvenile invest, not homicide."

"My guess would be there's a minor involved somewhere. But why ask why? Go for it; this will be an important investigation. The fact that they want you says something."

"After six months of telling me to pound sand, suddenly they need me?"

Joe laughed. "You know what they say about gift horses? If you look them in the mouth, they bite! Just go and be the outstanding investigator I know you are." He gripped her arm. "Stop thinking less of yourself because they've stuck you in juvie. You're a good cop."

"Thanks. You're right, I guess, about doing my best with whatever they've got for me." She shrugged. "At least I've got nothing to lose. Thanks for the swim."

He applauded as she left him at the water's edge and jogged across the mostly empty beach toward home, a block and a half away.

After a quick shower to wash away the salt, Carly took a minute to shuffle through her wardrobe. Juvenile was a non-uniform assignment, the dress code business casual, which for her afternoon shift usually meant jeans and a department polo shirt. But this was a big case. Deciding that she wanted her appearance to scream competent and prepared, she chose a pair of black slacks, a dark-green sweater, and hard-soled shoes rather than the running shoes she normally wore.

A quick glance in the mirror left her satisfied. She double-checked the gun and badge in her backpack on the way to the car, the familiar ritual helping to calm her jumping nerves. But the adrenaline rush was intense.

I'm going to be a cop again. I'm going to do police work, sang in her thoughts. She locked the seat belt across her chest and started the car. A question popped in her mind and zinged her pumped-up nerves like tinfoil on silver fillings.

Why would anyone want to kill Mayor Teresa Burke?

ABOUT THE AUTHOR

A FORMER LONG BEACH, California, police officer of twenty-two years, Janice Cantore worked a variety of assignments, including patrol, administration, juvenile investigations, and training. She's always enjoyed writing and published two short articles on faith at work for *Cop and Christ* and *Today's Christian Woman* before tackling novels. She now lives in a small town in southern Oregon, where she enjoys exploring the forests, rivers, and lakes with her three Labrador retrievers—Jake, Maggie, and Abbie.

Janice writes suspense novels designed to keep readers engrossed and leave them inspired. *Visible Threat* is the sequel to *Critical Pursuit*, featuring Brinna Caruso. Janice also authored the Pacific Coast Justice series, which includes *Accused*, *Abducted*, and *Avenged*.

Visit Janice's website at www.janicecantore.com and connect with her on Facebook at www.facebook.com/JaniceCantore.

DISCUSSION QUESTIONS

1. As *Visible Threat* begins, Brinna ignores direct orders and continues to pursue a suspected kidnapper. What do you think of her actions? Is she being reckless? Or does the end justify the means in this situation?

2. Magda Boteva feels trapped between wanting to do what is right and facing the wrath of her cousin Demitri. Are her fears justified? What does it take to finally prompt her into action? What would you do in her shoes?

3. Brinna soon learns what it feels like to be considered a hero, and she wonders if she can live up to a young girl's expectations. How do you think she does as a mentor, someone to admire? Have you ever felt you were in a position to be a mentor to someone else? If so, how did the experience affect you?

4. In chapter 28, Brinna asks Jack what he would have done during the Henry Corliss chase, and he responds, "I would have prayed that someone else stopped him." Have you ever faced a situation where you weren't sure

how to proceed? How can you know when to take action and when to step back and let God work?

5. What do you think of Jack's statement "If he is a good God, why would he stop something in your life that will make you stronger, make you a better person?" Do all difficulties result in personal growth? What are some times in your life you can point to that support this idea? Can you think of any exceptions?

6. What makes Rick and Molly so willing to accept his diagnosis? Do you think it's possible to be upbeat and positive in the face of a life-altering tragedy?

7. Rose Caruso opens her home to Ivana even before she has met the girl. How do Rose's actions measure up to Jesus' directives in Matthew 25:31-46? What tangible things can you do to help people in need?

8. In chapter 42, Jack contemplates Brinna's desire for perfection—"perfect justice and a perfect world." Is it naive to pursue perfection? What are the benefits of striving for excellence? What are the costs? What does Psalm 37 have to say about God's justice?

9. Also in chapter 42, Jack thinks about and understands Brinna's desire for justice but notes that he has "been grounded in the belief that God was real and directing his steps, guiding his life." Why does Jack's foundation make such a difference in his life? How is that reflected in this story? Where can you see a solid foundation and belief in a sovereign God playing a role in your life?

10. Jack tells Brinna in chapter 49, "Just because bad things happen doesn't mean God isn't good." Can you think of a time in your life when something bad happened, and in the end God worked everything out for good?

11. Magda reveals startling secrets to her husband in chapter 50. Read Ephesians 5:25-28. In what ways does Anton act out these instructions? What other passages of Scripture illustrate his response?

12. At one point in the story, Simon admits he's done wrong but claims that he's not as bad a man as Demitri. Would you agree with him? Does his statement seem to suggest that there are degrees of sin? What's wrong with that idea?

13. In chapter 61, Magda explains what being her sister's keeper means to her. How would you define that term? What does it mean to you personally?

14. Were you surprised to learn that human trafficking is a growing problem worldwide and even in your own backyard? Check out the US State Department's list of twenty things you can do to help combat human trafficking (http://www.state.gov/j/tip/id/help/). Which of these tips can you put into practice in the next month?

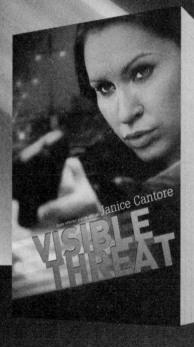